STAR STORY BOOK ONE: ANCHORED

Jameson Owens

Lost Child LLC

Thank you so much for picking up Star Story Book One: Anchored. This project is the culmination of my medical career, and my passion for science fiction. I dedicate it to my friends and family; your love and support gave me the courage to follow my dream.

PROLOGUE

The child's story began when his mother's ended.

The woman labored for no more than an hour before the newborn parted from her. His eyes peeled open to stare at the Pazish Nun who delivered him, then collapsed again as he wailed a healthy cry from a healthy child.

The mother peered down at her son. She had changed since arriving at the birthing home three months earlier, and looked anything but healthy. Her eyes, once green and lively, now appeared a stormy grey. Muscle had melted from her body, and the roots of her colorful hair glowed ghostly white in the dim lighting. No doctors in the city had been able to diagnose her unusual deterioration, and now the young, beautiful woman named Tanshanine looked an unnatural thing. Her mismatched eyes lost their focus as her head fell onto the pillow below.

Dead, before she could even hold him, thought the Pazish Nun. The child's crying ceased as suddenly and the tiny creature seemed content in her arms. He, like all the children born to Uncut street urchins, would be raised in relative comfort at the orphanage for the next seven years. The Pazish Order would feed and educate him, while the city's Inquisitors tested his aptitude. If he excelled at his studies, he could be sold to an apprenticeship. If he did not, he'd serve out his remaining decade of life in the city's slums.

A death sentence, the Pazish Nun knew. The destitute conditions in lower levels of the city saw to the demise of many orphans, yet it was not exposure, violence, nor starvation that killed most of them. The biggest threat to the children in this city, and around the planet, was a disease called the first rot.

The Pazish Nun turned the child's right arm over in her hands. His teslac organ glowed faintly underneath his skin. A network of veins extended from his forearm, reaching down to the tips of his fingers, and upwards to his shoulder, where the tangle of lines dove into his torso and disappeared. The organ would speed his growth and mental development, help him fight illness, and make him proliferant, but in 16 years' time, it would also wilt and poison him. Only surgically, and methodically, cutting out the organ would keep this boy from a dark fate.

The Pazish Nun looked at the mother's unscarred forearm; she was Uncut. While the rot spared women until they reached their twenties, Tanshanine would only have been able to spend a few years with her son before the disease took her. *If she even wanted to,* the Pazish Nun thought, aware that only half the mothers giving birth that day would choose to stay at the Deep Home. The fleeting lives for the Uncut meant fast lifestyles. Their gravitation towards carnal pleasure resulted in hundreds of Uncut women giving birth to litters newborns every day. More often the parents would return to the slums, while their children would remain to fuel the city's economy. The cycle of abuse sickened the Pazish Nun, she regretted her part in it.

She looked again at the boy cradled in her arms. He shared his mother's ghostly appearance, and the sight of him turned her stomach. Fear rose in her as she wondered what the Inquisitors would do with such an anomalous child. Yet, as she stared at him, his white hair and grey eyes slowly filled with colors suiting a child born in the city of Ehtlentin. He had an abnormal birth, and the Pazish Nun suspected, seemed destined for an abnormal life. A feeling of hope stirred in her.

"You will be different," she whispered.

CHAPTER 1
Glade Jadamara

16 Years later

Glade Jadamara stood looking at the most incompetent dock technician she had ever seen. *A real bumbling idiot*, she thought. He had not stopped talking to himself since he started fumbling at the hangar console fifteen minutes earlier – blurting out excuses, apologies, and mumbling curses under his breath. Her silent contempt unsettled him, she had given up on feigned courtesy years ago. *So will this boy whenever he becomes a man*, she thought.

His superior's voice buzzed over the comlink and the boy's babbling was replaced by "uh-huhs" and "yes sirs." He shot her a sheepish look, then set down the comlink, laid on his back and reached his arm under the console as far as he could manage. He cursed and grunted until the monitors on it went dark. Ten seconds later, they came back to life and he climbed back up, smiling nervously as he fervently went back to work documenting her vessel.

She left the dock with a fierce urge to punch something – anything that would crack without breaking her knuckles. *Wood would work, also a cheek bone*, she thought. She pondered how she would expel her frustration until she walked under the grand archway of the spaceport and into the salty breeze and warm sun that reminded her she was in a paradise zone, on what would come closest to a vacation in three years since becoming captain of the *Spear Throw*. The sound of grinding metal and ships departing was at odds with the view before her. The port where the *Spear Throw* docked, the only port she had been permitted to land at, was built on its own island 130 klicks out from the city of Ehtlentin. She studied the sight of the metropolis in awe.

The massive, ancient city was built upon a mountain surrounded by blue sea. The mess of disorganized docks around the circumference of the island gave way to white writ-stone buildings permeated by green overgrowth and golden towers. Bridges spanned over canyons on the mountainside, and within those chasms, more structures carved into the cliffs. Great walls striated the city, zig zagging their way up the hillside. The peak of the mountain was no peak at all but a flat ring where waterfalls plummeted from reservoirs around the rim and into cavernous holes thousands of meters below.

Jadamara began mouthing the word "wow" when a girl darted past her leg screaming hysterically, followed by three boys who tumbled into and around her. She scowled scathingly as she remembered her loath for children, hissed when she saw their absent parents staring open mouthed at the view, and sighed when she realized she had been doing the same moments earlier. She slung her pack over her shoulder, touched her pistol to make sure it was easily reachable from its concealed compartment, and ran her hands over her father's blue Ehtlentin blade secured on her belt. She spared one more look at the city, then left for the shuttle that would take her to it.

Her ride over the blue ocean went smoothly and quickly. She stepped off the shuttle in Ehtlentin with one eyebrow raised. The 320 kph ride to the city in the elegant open-top shuttle felt like luxury, *but that didn't feel like 320 kph,* she knew. She brushed back the two shades of her red hair, slightly tossed from the journey, frowned and began walking. She knew where she needed to go. The city map was stored in the ingevein device integrated into her left arm. An audio vein leading from the device to her cochlear nerve told her where to go. The ingevein did not speak to Jadamara but she heard it all the same, as if recalling a memory of being instructed where to go, one street at a time. The sensation disoriented her at first, but she had learned to do much with the utility tool she inherited from her mother.

Once out of the shuttle port and into the courtyard a new world filled her senses. Cyan cloth hung over a white arch ahead of her. A design embroidered in the center with two circles, one encasing the other, represented the insignia of Ehtlentin. Five-story buildings surrounded her other sides, all made from the white unweatherable writ-stone that had done so well to give the city a clean appearance from 130 kilometers away. Children exploded from alleyways with adults on their heels. Sounds of haggling and laughter filled the air, occasionally drowned out by the sound of cargo entering or leaving on shuttles. The smell of the salt ocean was gone, yet the smell of fish lingered heavily amongst many other unpleasant odors. Jadamara clutched her bag close and began her journey out of the heart of the market and the madness. She looked suspiciously at the taxi craft who caught notice of her gaze and rose to pitch his service. She turned her head quickly and moved on to the next street.

Fifteen minutes later she closed in on her destination but regretted her decision to bypass the taxi craft. She pushed her way into an area of the market flooded by hundreds of children with no less than ten at a time yelling, Uncut arms stretched outwards, for anything she might have. They begged and cried, cursed her with words she did not know or simply crumpled to the ground in front of her. *These are not kids*, she thought. Looking around it became clear that the children did the selling in this part of the market. Their stolen goods, rotting fruits, and bodies on display, being picked over by Cut men of varying age and cleanliness. In the shaded alleys between buildings, older boys with painted faces stood sentinel outside basement stairwells.

"Defend yourself!" called a voice through the scrum. Jadamara knew the advice was for her. She chose the boy clutched onto her arm, trying fruitlessly to remove her ingevein, and commanded the device to send a jolt of electricity through him. He shrieked and flew backwards but the others did not seem to notice. She yanked back on the hair of another boy prying at her belt. He screamed as she twisted him in her grip until his back was to her and his sobbing face displayed for the others. She released him and he spilled onto the floor. She saw looks of fear fresh on some of the younger children's faces, but the older ones stared at her hatefully. She met their gazes one at a time, her hand resting on the blade at her waist. She had been warned about the Uncut in Ehtlentin. The pack around her were lean and strong, like most Uncut, and their wild eyes confirmed their feral reputation.

She walked cautiously to the voice that called out to her and found the man it belonged to. Jakvujine, who everyone referred to as JV, was an Ehtlentin and looked every bit of it: dark skin with dark hair - now greying - interrupted by streaks of iridescent navy color. His matching blue eyes hinted that both of his parents were Ehtlentin. Cyan paint embedded in his skin told the story of his life from the marking of "exceptional" tattooed at the orphanage, to the marking of "First Mate" he received when he took the position serving her father aboard the *Spear Throw* decades ago. Jadamara remembered his deep booming voice and massive build from her childhood, neither of which had diminished over time. His smile failed for a moment when he saw her ingevein but returned when he met her eyes. They embraced. For the first time since her mother's death, she received a hug that made her feel better.

"Welcome to my city sweet girl!" he shouted. "Take it in, because it will never be as beautiful as it is today!"

Jadamara looked around and knew it to be true. The city had been in a state of decay for a century, a fact that was most evident in the lowest levels of the city. The riches sequestered at the peak of the mountain, hoarded by the Twice-Cuts and wealthy elite, barely trickled down to the lowest levels. A failed rebellion led by the Pazish Nuns years ago to liberate the youths had left swaths of the city scorched with no plans to rebuild. Jadamara could feel the desperation of the children pressing in on her, she eagerly followed JV out of the rabble and to his home.

They talked in JV's modest home until the sun set. They

sat at the table around a vegetable stew that tasted sweet and spicy to Jadamara.

"Rest and repairs, eh? So why not rest?" teased JV. Jadamara knew what he was hinting. She was Once-Cut, and 22 years old. If she wanted to have a child, and be alive to raise it, she needed to have one soon. The second rot would kill for her in twenty years, just as it had her mother, just as she suspected it was beginning to kill JV.

I'll rest when I'm dead, she thought, but said cordially, "Thank you for having me, I'm glad to see you. I can tell even now, you have my father's best interests in mind." She had come more for repairs than to rest. A week ago, she received a promising offer from Ehtlentin's foremost shield engineer, a friend of JV's, to upgrade the *Spear Throw* with prototype shielding. *Tomorrow we go to the wire district to meet your man, and see if he is a real engineer or a Twice-Cut you want me to marry,* she thought.

They both laughed but neither of them needed to say any more. Jadamara could pass on her parents' gift, have a child and pay for its first cut. But she would die before she could ever pay for a second cut to extend her own life. In certain cities, such as the Alliance capital of Omphala, first cuts were guaranteed to all citizens. Jadamara was not a citizen of any of those cities, her parents gave her a future at the expense of their own.

The two continued talking about what each had seen since their last parting: Jadamara's mother's passing to the second rot, about the city and its many orphans, the Pazish nuns who cared for them and their failed rebellion to free them. They mostly talked about Jadamara's father, however, and the trouble he and JV got into during their childhood in the city. Eventually, she rolled into JVs guest bed and closed her eyes. She found the sounds of the city a soothing change from the emptiness of her ship's cabin. Soon she drifted off.

They spent most of the next day sight-seeing. JV seemed to know the history of every building in the city. They walked through caverns, over waterfalls on grand bridges, and along the ramparts of the great walls. Their route took them up massive elevators and down waterways that spiraled from the rim of the mountain to their destinations. Despite multiple detours, they steadily progressed up the city slope. About a kilometer below the rim of the mountain, at the base of the last lift, sat a giant structure Jadamara knew to be an Ehtlentin shield generator. The structures were relics from the golden age of the city. They hadn't been used since the barbaric Mongrelai invaders sacked the city almost 200 years ago. JV remarked, "No one is even sure if they still work." The technology fascinated Jadamara, as no other city had come close to creating a shield network that rivaled what the ancient engineers had constructed. That knowledge had been lost though, as the Mongrelai had eradicated the structural schematics from the city's databases upon conquering it.

The pair of them ascended to the Rim, the most affluent level of the city. Jadamara held her breath. *There should be a hole three kilometers wide leading to the labyrinth,* she knew. She remembered the stories her father used to bring back from his adventures charting the great network of tunnels below the city. He gave the best descriptions of the places they visited, but JV always told the best stories. However, when they took the *Spear Throw* through the passage fifteen ago, JV returned with the ship, but not her father.

Finally, the lift cleared the last of the buildings revealing a lake, three kilometers wide, surrounded by city. The lake was empty save for a few lonely buoys and luxury yachts.

".. the hell?" Jadamara mumbled.

"It's there," laughed JV reading her mind. "They sealed this entrance to the labyrinth a decade ago. Traffic goes through the auxiliary tunnels now. The reservoir is much prettier I think, though I've never seen it this empty." Jadamara wondered if JV ever went into the labyrinth after her father's death. She guessed not.

Her ingevein told her the *Spear Throw* had successfully docked at Hangar 42.

"Your engineer is not far," said JV, noting her distraction.

"He's your man," she corrected.

JV looked puzzled. "He got a hold of me *after* you said you were coming. He said you were meeting at his home." Jadamara had thought it odd they weren't meeting at her ship, she had assumed it was a guise by JV to set her up. "A trap?" JV asked. She studied the streets around her with a new perspective. There was a palpable urgency buzzing through the Rim, but no one paying much attention to their passing through.

She shrugged and patted the knife at her hip. "I guess we will find out," she said.

JV paused, then resumed pace alongside her. "You haven't changed," he sighed. They continued towards their destination, the towering white and silver spire clinging to the edge of the Rim.

The engineer's apartment truly exemplified his quality and price. An automated door recognized them and opened to a large but elegant home, filled with imported amenities and wired with an impressive network of electronics. A home for a genius to be certain, but the man it belonged to did not turn out to be as impressive. The engineer was a short soft looking man with an annoying mustache and on an equally annoying face. Jadamara imagined it wiggled when he spoke, at least when he was alive. They followed the foul stench of his passing to a bedroom closet where they found his dead body slumped on a shoe rack. He wasn't long deceased but the blackened crater where his chest should have been explained the pungent smell.

"We need to contact the city guard," JV said as he cautiously evaluated the room.

The apartment dissolved in front of Jadamara as she channeled her focus into her ingevein, searching for the data communication lines with which she could report the murder. Instead, she found her access to the city guard network cut off. *All public access is blocked from within the apartment,* she realized after trying to ping several other public networks. *Maybe a private transmission could work.* She accessed the *Spear Throw's* data stream, only to find herself locked out of it. Her stomach rose to her chest as the sequence of events aligned "I think my ship is being stolen," she said in disbelief. "What do we do?"

She dissociated from her ingevein to see JV hacking the door to the apartment.

"I'd say get out of here, but we're locked in," he answered. The screen on his ingevein flashed red as it detected a counter hack. He pulled himself away from the door and frantically began scouring his ingevein for the malware. The unsteady movement of his hands was not lost on Jadamara, who had seen the same symptoms in her mother as the second rot stole her coordination.

"Stand back!" Jadamara warned, as she pulled her father's blaster from her bag. She ran her ingevein over the door. *No weak points*, she sensed. Her arm continued its arc, sampling molecular and structural data from the room around her. A single window near the ceiling of the living room offered the best chance of escape. She turned her blaster towards it, the crystal encased within hummed as the energy siphoned from its many facets turned the weapon warm. "So much for a vacation," she said. She released the bolt of energy once it reached its full charge. The blast burst against the window, scorching the walls holding it. When the debris settled, a melted hole wide enough for them to climb through had appeared.

They managed to climb out of the smoldering window, survive the fall to the street, and hobble their way back to the lift. The scene outside had become frantic, and no one seemed to give the explosive blast, and their descent from the apartment, much mind. Once free of the apartment's network lockdown, Jadamara accessed her ingevein again.

The city guard network was abuzz with emergency protocols and Jadamara was queued behind hundreds of other citizens reporting danger. She reached out to the docking network next, which informed her the *Spear Throw* had been cleared to lift off from the market. "We have to get back to the market," she urged, and pulled JV back the way they came. As they approached the lift station, the streets became more crowded with citizens now clearly fleeing an unseen danger.

"What is happening?" asked Jadamara. She was ready to access her ingevein again when JV pointed towards the reservoir.

What had once been a calm lake now raged wildly. Geysers of steam shot into the sky and vortexes of water swirled into the voids left from their wake. The jets ceased firing and a second after the entire body of water seized upwards. The liquid held form for a moment before washing over the structure which penetrated through it; a massive gray pyramidal vessel larger than any Jadamara had ever seen. As it rose, the reservoir structure collapsed around it and the sea of water plummeted down the labyrinth, now restored to its former vast emptiness.

Bodies stopped moving around them, and the city seemed to hold its breath as the pyramid slowed its ascent. A collective scream followed as shimmering bubbles shot from the pyramid in all directions. The projectiles detonated against the streets and buildings, flooding the city in swathes of smoke. Amongst the bubbles, dozens of green bolts of light streaked towards the Ehtlentin military fortress that sat on the lip of the mountain, engulfing it in fire. Its shielded, writ-stone defenses defied the initial blasts, but green and yellow flames doused the stone where the energy bolts penetrated their shields. They arrived at the elevator terminal and JV yanked her away from the chaos in the distance to the chaos in front of them.

Inhabitants and visitors of the Rim clambered to find a spot on the full lifts. A wave of panic swept the mass, as onlookers of the battle pointed out dark shapes spilling from the pyramid. *Those are fighter craft, and larger frigates too*, Jadamara knew. Green bolts of light shot forth from the ships, lighting up the paths in front of them. Jadamara had seen war videos from the battles that united the Alliance against alien Mongrelai invaders during their occupation of the Capital Continent. *They are creating landing zones,* she guessed, watching the larger beetle shaped vessels descend to the ground. If there was an Ehtlentin military response, Jadamara did not see it.

JV was still for a moment staring ahead emptily with his hand on his own ingevein. "This way," he said, "there's more than one way out of here." They ran past the elevator and three more like it, through an inconspicuous door and down a long stairwell. "Beyond this door is where they store maintenance vehicles for the lift." Jadamara leapt ahead down the last flight of stairs. She couldn't do anything masterfully with her ingevein, yet hacking basic doors had been the first function she learned. The metallic door did not resist her. The screen next to it lit and it opened to them. The prospective vehicles resting in the hangar beyond were not ideal. None of the skiffs or loaders looked particularly capable of escaping the onslaught outside, but getting back to the lower levels on foot seemed even more unlikely. Then she noticed a young man, scrawny for an employed Uncut, sitting in a loader with his hands dug into his hair. He stared wide eyed at the controls in front of him until he caught sight of them and shrieked.

"We need to go to Hangar 42," she told him.

He didn't respond but looked at them and murmured, "it came from the labyrinth..."

"If you can fly this thing to Hangar 42, I can save your life," she lied.

He looked at her as if she meant to harm him. "There are too many," he responded shakily.

"The defenses are strongest here at the top levels," she assumed, "if we leave now, whoever is attacking the city will not follow." A lifetime of watching her mother and three years of captaining had endowed her with inspired half-truths. *If I'm wrong, we are dead,* she knew. *If I'm right, we still may be dead.* Without waiting any longer, she entered the passenger seat beside the shaking pilot. JV took a seat in the back. "We need to leave now," she said again, this time showing her father's knife holstered in her belt. The pilot gulped, activated the loader, and they lifted from the ground. He angled it towards the opening and they accelerated out of the hangar.

The scene outside had changed since their submergence

into the garage. The Ehtlentin military had formed a line along the great walls on the eastern side of the mountain. Gunboats and frigates attempted to use the walls to escape the volley of artillery hammering them from the floating pyramid that occupied the peak of the mountain. The walls of Ehtlentin were not designed to defend an assault from inside the city, but seemed to provide some defense. The battle raged at the peak of the mountain as the Rim's defenses awoke to meet the invaders.

A global writ-shield rose over the smoking Ehtlentin fortress on the far side of the crater. The iridescent dome of energy arced over the structure, halting the hail of green bolts raining down on it. Veins of light intermittently coursed from emitters to receivers as it strained under the burden. Vector shields also sprang to life, striking outwards to preemptively detonate barrages of missiles. The global shield peeled opened momentarily to let a battery of Ehtlentin artillery shells pass through. However, the blasts detonated against similar shields encasing the pyramid, and the two fortresses continued to hammer each other relentlessly.

The navigation computer locked onto Hangar 42, their route took them past the Ehtlentin defensive line away from the massive pyramid, now obscured by smoke and swarming ships.

"They will flag us as friendly, and whatever it is attacking may not bother with us. Stay low," Jadamara ordered. The loader jetted out of the garage and took a deep dive making for a chasm in the mountain. *This pilot is terrified, but has a good instinct,* she thought. Fire and stone erupted around them as foreign snub-fighters hoped to curb their descent to the Ehtlentin line. None of the blasts found their mark, but the loader shook violently nonetheless, and the three occupants could not help but fall on each other.

"They aren't pursuing," muttered JV who sat cross legged the back of the loader, eyes closed. He brushed a blue lock of dreaded hair out of his eyes as he opened them.

He's been scanning with his ingevein, Jadamara surmised. She exhaled an unsteady breath. Her hand had found its way to the comforting presence of the dagger at her side. "You can read them?" she asked.

JV shook his head. "Not exactly, but their ships run on iridinium, just like our vessels."

Their pilot shook from his rigid posture to shudder. "Then they are from the labyrinth," he said. The loader soared out of the canyon, over a wide span of street, and plummeted down the wall to the third level of the city. On a bridge ahead of them, Ehtlentin infantry lobbed glowing spears at a line of black and grey, armored war contrivances. The spears exploded, sending the machines and other black armored troopers flying. As the loader puttered below the bridge, more flashes of light lit the ceiling above and the bridge came down upon them. Jadamara looked up, eyeing the piece of bridge that would crush them, when the lifter attached to the front of the loader swiveled from its forward position to settle over their heads. A moment later a crushing force pushed them downwards. A siren howled from the loader's console but the lifter arm shifted backwards and they squeezed out from the debris as it crashed down behind them, sending stones tumbling over the metal mesh roof.

Jadamara stared wild eyed at their pilot, wanting to praise him but finding the words stuck in her throat. "Hangar 42," he squeaked. "Where are we setting down?"

Jadamara spotted the *Spear Throw* leaving the hangar in a wobbling, unskillful fashion. "There," she said, pointing at the open loading bay on top of the ship. It was just large enough for a personal skiff to land. The loader was quite a bit larger than that. Their pilot shook his head and began to protest. He released the wheel, eyes quivering as he searched for a solution that would save him. Jadamara thrust the sticks forward as she climbed on top of the pilot. Her elbow swept across his cheek in the process. She sent the loader in a downwards spiral, straightening as she rounded on the frigate, and thrusted the sticks forwards into one final dive.

CHAPTER 2
Glade Jadamara

Jadamara woke, though she wouldn't describe it as waking so much as coming to awareness of a great throbbing in her head. She willed her eyes open and shifted to her side. Pain racked her body. She had been placed on a cot in the cargo bay inside the *Spear Throw*, her head rested on a pillow that lay upon another's leg. A hand softly brushed her hair behind her ear.

"Easy child," said a familiar voice. She awkwardly struggled upwards till she was looking at JVs face. She expected worse. He didn't look in considerable pain, but a legion of bruises covered his forearms from where he had sheltered his head. Relief washed over her.

She let out a series of breaths, still coming to terms with her condition, too disoriented to access her ingevein. Her face twisted in pain, JV simply kept his eyes on her, smiling sympathetically. She scanned the room and stopped at her first officer, Gren, leaning against the wall. He looked up as he felt her gaze. Two dark welts surrounded each eye orbit and dried blood caked the better part of his face below a broken nose. Jadamara was relieved again.

She continued her look about, passing over the sisters Eva and Ava, her back-end team responsible for managing logistics, until her eyes found their thin pilot holding himself on the cot next to her on the adjacent wall. His eyes stared ahead, diverting for just a moment to meet Jadamara's, then continuing their thoughtful vigilance upon the wall. His only apparent site of trauma was the swollen scrape on his right cheek where Jadamara had clipped him. She found her face again twisting into an expression of disbelief that they had emerged alive.

She tasted blood in her mouth and felt it in her hair. It still had the semi-fresh gooiness which told her she had not been unconscious long. She turned back to Gren wondering what question to ask first. "What happened?" she decided. *That should cover it.*

Gren took time to organize his thoughts. "Polsh, Tank, and Perin left for the city. Paluck, the sisters, and I stayed behind. However, unbeknownst to us, we had taken on another crew mate." He coughed, working up blood and mucus from out his palate. "I…" he paused, "I'm not sure what I saw, but the fucking little shit who stole the ship also put a crater in Paluck's chest." He pointed at his face next, "I don't remember how this happened, but the sisters say I have him to thank for it."

Jadamara wondered if her lack of caring about Paluck's death was from her injuries, or from her indifference to him in the first place. Seven of the eight members of her crew had served under her mother, they were the brothers and sisters she grew up with. Paluck was the only one who didn't share that commonality. She leaned back against the wall and closed her eyes. "The engineer I went to visit also had a crater in his chest. You say a kid did it?"

Gren nodded. "A dock worker. He poked around the ship during inspection, he seemed a bit…" he paused again, searching for the words. "Skittish. *Uncut* skittish," he clarified.

Jadamara knew what he meant. She remembered the turbulence of her thoughts before she was cut; her insatiable hunger for excitement, and the impulsion that landed her in youth prison more than once. However, unlike many Uncut in Ehtlentin, she always knew her mother would pay for the procedure to have her teslac removed, and that her life would continue. She had the luxury of knowing her life would go on. Orphans in Ehtlentin, and many other cities, became desperate as they neared their rotting ages.

This kid would have been a skittish pile of smoldering ash if the fail-safes had worked, she thought, disgruntled.

Gren saw the contemplation in her eyes. "They managed to..." But he never got to finish. The door to the cargo hold opened, washing them in white light. It closed quickly afterwards, leaving behind a boxy metallic contrivance in the room. Its single red eye scanned over them.

The more complex a contrivance, the better natured they tended to be. Even the most powerful machines repetitively defied orders to harm; however, they would talk a person to death given the chance. Despite the ability to philosophize existentially, only a handful ever generated true creative thought and the vast majority led content lives serving the organic society that created them. The boxy automaton that entered did not seem overly intelligent, nor content.

"Booooop!" it let out a single low-pitched rumble and spun its treads, swiveling its rectangular body and working its stubby claw to point a blaster at each of them threateningly. It let out a low growl as it reversed backwards through the door, which opened again to allow its departure. Jadamara looked beyond the doorway into the main cabin for the moment it remained open. The roar of twenty Uncut children matched the site of them. She guessed the majority were as young as eight to as old as twenty, she could not tell if they were celebrating or panicking. An older girl covered in painted tattoos scowled in her direction. She met Jadamara's gaze and held it until the door shut between them.

Five minutes later they opened again to a young man with the painted girl in tow. He was just a bit taller than her, maybe around 5'11. His hair was a mess of gold and blue, his eyes were oceans of emeralds. He wore an ill-fitting dock technician outfit but had discarded the hat which had covered his hair the day before. Jadamara moaned in disbelief, *the bumbling idiot?*

The boy seemed just as surprised to see her again. "*Really?*" they both asked simultaneously.

Jadamara's fists clenched the cot below her and she lifted herself up. The painted girl stepped forward to display the blaster at her side. Jadamara recognized it. Eva, the weapon's rightful owner, stared at her blaster, then at the painted girl with rage burning in her eyes. She and Ava were the best tempered Uncut Jadamara had ever met, but she worried Eva's impulse would get the better of her. The painted girl met Eva's stare with a wink, then the corner of her mouth curled upwards into a smug smile.

Eva looked away, towards her sister, as she often did when she became uncomfortable. The tension in the room seemed to dissipate and Jadamara turned back to look at her captor. He evaluated her, scanning up and down, frowning the whole time. Finally, he laughed.

"You don't want to help us," he stated. "But you will. Come on."

Jadamara did not answer immediately. *The Spear Throw is moving,* she sensed. She held her gaze while a knot rose in her chest. She remembered Ehtlentin on fire, and the civilian ships gunned down as they fled over the ocean. *Yet, somehow, we are still alive.* She did not see any other option but to obey her captor. "I'll help my crew," she finally answered.

The boy and the painted girl escorted Jadamara to the bridge in silence. Her ship swarmed with Uncut and the hallways were thick with the stench of garbage and unwashed flesh. As they walked, children and young adults looked up, some with mischievous grins, others with expressions of curiosity. All of them were Ehtlentin, and most of them Uncut. Judging by the rags and the smell, they came from the slums of the city, though she spotted the inquisitor markings of "exceptional" on many wrists.

"Brought some friends along for your joyride?" she asked sarcastically, rubbing her head.

"I wanted to show them my new ship," the boy replied casually.

She stifled her anger as quickly as it came. Her tone turned cold. "You're going to get them all killed."

They paused just then, before entering the bridge, and

the boy searched her face. Jadamara stared back with practiced stoicness. He frowned for a fraction of a second, not seeming to find any answers, then crooked his head to the side and smiled the same bullshit smile he had given to her yesterday while checking in her ship. Finally, he replied, "I have faith you can save us all." He turned and proceeded to the bridge, Jadamara's escort prodded her to follow.

Once the door behind them slid closed, the bridge became the quietest, best smelling place on the ship, save for the cargo hold turned brig. The captain's chair sat empty in the middle of the deck, positioned forward to look at the window beyond. Below and around the top deck, four consoles faced outwards angled towards the front of the ship, allowing the captain to see past the technicians manning them and onto the screens in front of them. Red light bathed the room indicating the ship was in partial lockdown.

Jadamara once relished the feeling of walking onto her bridge, but the scene had changed since she had left it last, and so had that feeling. For one, the familiar sight of blue sky through the forward window had been replaced by the pressing darkness of the Labyrinth. For another, her trained Once-Cut crew had been replaced by children running through tutorials at the four stations.

The *Spear Throw* had been modified so many times over that it no longer resembled the Ehtlentin ship it originated as. Yet now, surrounded by the rainbow haired crew, she felt like she had gone back in time 100 years. The children looked up as the trio walked to the center of the room.

The boy motioned to the captain's chair. "We tripped a lockout mining your data stores, I need that deactivated first," he said.

Jadamara moved to the chair, touching the armrest as she walked along it. She sat down and sensed the boy anxiously hanging over her shoulder. The ship was, for the most part, in the condition she left it at the dock, excluding the partial lock-down. She decided to investigate. A contrivance, now melted to the floor in the server room, had tripped the lockdown. It had come close to breaking into the deeper data stores, but apparently could not outpace the *Spear Throw's* counterhack.

"If it will be quicker for me to hack my way through the lockdown, I will," said the boy with a touch of impatience.

The thought flashed through her head to activate the other intruder protocols. She visualized children's corpses piled on one another and decided against it. *And I wouldn't survive long.* She placed both hands on the console, spoke the deactivation sequence, and the console flashed to acknowledge the triple security clearance. The screen's background turned red to blue and the lights returned to the normal white lighting.

"What are you looking for?" Jadamara asked absently as she cleared access to the data vaults.

The boy looked pleased with the situation. "Your father's labyrinth maps," he replied, equally absent, his eyes fixed on the screen. His response pushed Jadamara's barely contained fury past her ability to control it. She spun around and her knuckles landed on his cheek with the satisfying crunch she desired. He stumbled backwards but the painted girl rushed forward, her fist cocked. Jadamara jumped out of her chair. She deflected the girl's right hook, brought her close, and sent her own elbow swinging towards her ear. The girl's head shot backwards, avoiding the bulk of the strike, but Jadamara's foot pushed into her chest, sending her toppling over onto one of the stations below. The painted girl pulled her stolen gun out. Jadamara reached forward with her ingevein.

She had hacked the weapon's power source when she first saw it on the girl's waist in the cargo hold. Now, the magnetism emanating from her ingevein neutralized it. A puff of red smoke spat out the barrel of the gun instead of a bolt, and the chamber which housed its energy crystal glowed red. The painted girl repeatedly pulled the unresponsive trigger until the heat from its overcharged core burned her hand.

The motley crew of children looked onwards but none moved to stop Jadamara. She had not planned this far. "Computer, activate protocol…" but she never got to finish – a tight grip on her shoulder swung her around. She used the momentum to fling a blind punch towards her aggressor that stopped in mid-air. Her fist slammed into her captor's open palm. His fingers slid to her wrist and pulled her across him. He jabbed his own arm into the side of her ribs.

A scream escaped her lips as she remembered her injuries, and her legs gave out beneath her. She crumpled to the ground in front of him clutching her torso and gave no more resistance. The boy's expression returned to a passive state, yet the beginnings of a bruise formed below his left eye. *Worth it*, she thought.

She used the captain's chair to steady her as she pulled herself up and shot him a venomous look. "Stealing my ship, murdering Paluck, leaving me to die at the Rim?" She took some quick breaths and continued. "Are you sorry that half my crew is abandoned and burning with the city? Are you sorry your master is a dead body in a closet?"

The boy nodded, slowly realizing the futility of responding. His tattooed guardian had climbed back to the top tier. She regarded Jadamara's ingevein wearily "Cass, take her to Culus. Have him put a block on her ingevein," he said. He turned to a boy who had appeared at the door after hearing the commotion. "Creline, round up Kill Bot and five painted boys to escort her compatriots to the medical hold."

Within a few steps, it became clear that Jadamara would not make it to whatever room he had deemed the "medical hold." The painted girl, Cass, grumbled when she saw this and slung Jadamara's arm around her neck to support her as they walked out of the bridge. What had once been a narrow locker lined storage compartment had been transformed into a now narrower locker lined storage compartment with a stained cot and an odd-looking man stuffed in the corner. His pale skin and plain gray hair indicated he was not Ehtlentin. The age of his face surprised her. *He must be in his mid-fifties. He is Twice-Cut,* she guessed. Jadamara couldn't help herself from being awed. His demeanor didn't have the air of superiority that she noted hung around many of the upper-class citizens she had met.

"Captain," he addressed her. He looked her up and down then approached, taking her other arm over his shoulder to help her towards the cot. It took twenty minutes for him to clean and suture the lesions scattered around her body and head. He rifled through one of his many first-aid kits until he pulled out a glass vial filled with chalky rocks. He ground one of them in a mortar and pestle, poured the powder into a cup of water and handed it to her. "For your head."

Jadamara hesitated but took the solution and gulped down the bitter concoction. In moments, she felt the pain in her head, and to some extent her ribs, dissipate.

Then the man hesitated, "I need access to your torso."

Jadamara looked back at Cass, who shook her head to indicate she was not leaving, but stepped further into the cramped space. She closed the door behind her to give some privacy from the busy hallway outside. Jadamara stripped off her woven tank, the doctor delicately oozed a clear gel around the bruised region on her lower chest. He ran his ingevein over her and stared at a screen on his lap, gently working his arm back and forth to shift the x-ray image.

"I have just the thing for this!" he said. He dug into a locker that once housed the cleaning supplies and pulled out a circular brace. As soon as she pulled down her tank he had it fastened around her stomach and lower chest. He touched his ingevein and instead of hugging her as she expected, the brassiere pulled her chest outwards. A moment of sharp pain was followed by a respite from its dull predecessor and Jadamara breathed normally again. The doctor nodded his head, a grin plastered on his face. "I designed it myself!" He took note of her unenthused expression. "Oh, well."

Gren and the scraggly loader pilot appeared in the door.

The doctor's eyes widened at the site of Gren's face. "I'll get around to your ingevein after I tend to your crew." Cass did not like this, but allowed it all the same after a brief quarrel with the doctor. It seemed to Jadamara they were olds friends. There was not going to be enough room for everyone in the cramped space so Jadamara shuffled past Gren and into the hall. Cass remained in the makeshift clinic but two Painted Boys stood guard in the hallway. They had standard issue Ehtlentin swords in hand, and light scale armor over their bodies.

These are no orphans, these are full-fledged soldiers, she realized. She wondered what madness had driven the warriors to defect, as the punishment for such an action was imprisonment until death by rot.

The skittish loader pilot stood in the shadow of the soldiers. When he caught sight of her, he became startled, and laughed a nearly noiseless, nervous laugh.

Jadamara looked around and became aware of JV's absence.

She fidgeted unproductively with the brace to force it lower, the pilot stood against the wall with hands in his pockets, and Gren moaned on the other side of the door. Soon he reappeared, his lesions sutured and face cleaned of blood. He managed a smile before the painted girl pushed him out the door.

"Get moving!" Cass said to him, with more annoyance than malevolence. "You're next," she said to the pilot.

The scrawny man had steadily been working up a panic-attack. Jadamara wondered if he was always so pitiful or if it was just a result of a day gone to hell. He marched silently into the clinic, the dirty orange door shut behind him. Jadamara felt tired of standing and slouched carefully down the wall across from the door. Despite herself, her thoughts began to drift.

The clanking of footsteps walking swiftly down the corridor interrupted her daze; footsteps that belonged to her captor, who did not look well. *He's rotting,* she guessed. He clutched his right forearm as he walked towards her. The webbed matrix of his poisoned teslac crawled up his neck, yet, it looked profoundly blue, unlike the typical black that signaled one's descent into death. Even more startling was the brilliant white hair which had replaced his gold and blue lochs, and the stormy grey irises which had overtaken his green eyes. Without his dock worker uniform, she may not have recognized him.

The Painted Boys made room for him to pass, though they looked uneasy. *They fear him,* she realized. The boy ignored them, but his eyebrows raised with his gaze as it made its way up Jadamara from girdle to face. He stared wide eyed at her for a moment then opened the orange door beside him. He passed into the med bay, and Jadamara was again surprised by what she saw within it. The pilot sat on the cot almost entirely naked. Symmetrical scars marred his entire torso down to his legs. He attempted to cover himself as the door shut behind the boy.

He is Twice-Cut, she thought, shocked. His frail stature, thin hair and boyish, gaunt face made placing his age difficult. *Cut too young at any rate. His Teslac didn't have enough time to develop his body.*

The door opened and the pilot walked out, shamefully. Painted Boys escorted him away, and soon the doctor came out into the hall and silently deactivated Jadamara's ingevein. Cass appeared as he finished.

"Move!" she ordered.

Their walk toward the cargo hold was like their departure: kids lying in strung up hammocks, kids playing games on the main cabin's consoles, kids slumped over with bottles of her crew's liquor. A few shot her sideways glances, but overall, they seemed less interested in her now.

They rounded the corner almost into collision with two Painted Boys carrying JV in between them on an improvised stretcher. It took a moment for the gravity of what she was seeing to set in. She maneuvered around the stretcher and to his side. The soldiers looked at Cass, who nodded. They set him down and JV offered up his left hand.

"How bad is it?" she asked.

JV drew an unsteady line diagonally from his right shoulder to his left hip and squeezed her hand. *He managed a shield with his ingevein, but not enough,* she assumed.

"That is it. I can't feel or move a thing otherwise," he replied, somewhat annoyed.

She shook her head and smiled down at him. Tears welled in her eyes but she told him, "You'll be alright! This is my fault, I'll figure this out," she promised futilely. He smiled back but they both knew nothing would be alright, nothing could be alright. Paralysis was bad enough, but JV was 45 years old, and the injuries his body took from their crash had sped the rate the second rot spread through the remaining teslac network in his body. A fresh web of black veins crept forward from his hairline. Jadamara saw the same patterns envelop her mother's head before her descent into madness. *He will lose his mind soon as well. First, he'll be paranoid, then angry, then unintelligible, then dead.* Already he seemed confused, ready to blame her for his plight, ready to hold her to her impossible promise.

The Painted Boys lifted him up and continued towards the med bay. Something in her broke as they parted, she felt empty; alone. She stood in a daze, her tears already melting into nothing on her cheeks. She wiped what remained of them off her.

"C'mon," said Cass, somewhat softly.

Jadamara and her crew talked freely in their metal cell. She filled Gren in on her time in Ehtlentin, their escape from the battle leading to their descent into the *Spear Throw*. She learned from the Twice-Cut pilot, who called himself Weg, that an hour before the invasion Ehtlentin lost contact with the labyrinth mining city of Retine. Eva elaborated on what she saw through her bedroom door while locked behind it the day earlier: a bright flash of light and Paluck's smoking body hitting the floor. Despite the distraction of conversation, the weight of JV's absence felt heavy. However, she had been assured by Creline, the Painted Boy who brought them food and escorted them to the bathroom, that their captor, Sincret, was taking care of him in her old quarters.

The ship moved all night, and judging by how cold it had become, they had traveled quite a distance into the labyrinth. The crew huddled together in the unheated cargo hold and waited. Jadamara regretted not wearing a powered jumpsuit to Ehtlentin like she did on every other mission. *What a god-damn vacation,* she ruminated. Upon the next morning, the door opened to the green-eyed boy, Sincret, who entered alone. He did not look as sick as Jadamara expected, and his ghostly white hair and eyes had returned to their normal hues.

"Good morning. We need to talk," he said. "I stole your home. I killed your friend." He looked at Jadamara. "I left you to die." The beginning of his speech elicited a middle finger from Gren. Jadamara's face remained expressionless. "I'm sorry for that?" he asked rhetorically.

Juvenile little shit, she thought.

"You little shit!" growled Gren.

The boy put his hands in the air. "Do you think anyone wants you here? You're visitors to our city! Your kind takes what they want. I did what I did because I could, and I had to." He crossed his arms. "We are alive because of those decisions, and so are you." Arguing seemed pointless, they let him continue. "Last night the city was taken, we lost touch with the surface broadcasts once we descended past their range. We won't be able to leave but that's never really been an option. Our first stop is a lake two days' flight."

"And then?" Jadamara asked.

The boy gave a look as if the answer was obvious. "We are going to get fresh air and deservedly drunk." The twins' faces lit up. He shrugged, "we'll take on water…"

"That sounds like a bulletproof plan," Jadamara interrupted. Despite her sarcasm, she didn't have a better one. She laid back on her cot and grunted, the injuries from the day before sore, like new friends she got to know better with each movement. She couldn't help herself, "What's your story?"

The boy shrugged again, "My name is Sincret," he said, then stopped as if that was the entirety of his life.

"What's with your eyes?" piped one of the twins, Jadamara didn't see which.

Sincret replied, "I'm not sure."

"What's with his eyes?" Gren asked Ava.

"They turn white. And his hair too," she answered.

"It's new to me, it happens when I fight. Culus' best guess is it has something to do with my teslac rotting," he explained, though he didn't seem confident in his answer.

Jadamara found another question. "Did you know what was going to happen?" she asked.

He took a moment to think, "No, I didn't know the city would be attacked." Then before anyone could ask, "I planned to steal your ship weeks ago. The shield engineer I was apprenticed to discovered something in the labyrinth that could be important enough to buy our cuts. The *Spear Throw* has comprehensive maps, and the technical components to navigate these tunnels; stealing it seemed like our best hope. And judging by how many ships were shot down trying to flee over the surface, the labyrinth seems like the safest place to escape to anyways. I feel like I don't have any real answers for you."

You have one. "Where is JV?" she asked.

"He's in your old quarters," he answered. "You may see him; the ship is open to you."

CHAPTER 3
Getaeight

The *Omedegon* hovered above a city ablaze, spitting out energy bolts, artillery salvos, and toxin filled bubbles. A flotilla of Psyperial warships spilled from it and charged the smoking landing zones to cement its hold over the cratered peak of the mountain. Encased in the shielded writ-steel pyramid stood Aemon the Proven, surrounded by his loyal retinue: obsidiron armored Storm Marines, Shadowed warriors, a loyal spy.

A son.

"Sir?" the boy asked.

Aemon turned to walk down the long runway towards the bridge's exit. The 16-year-old, white-haired boy named Getaeight matched pace beside him. He looked quizzically at his commander through stormy grey eyes. "Lieutenant, coordinate the artillery emplacements. Once they are settled, report to me," Aemon ordered. Getaeight nodded and did not linger. He belonged on the ship to execute his master's plan. His master belonged in the thick of battle to execute his enemies.

By night the city was all but captured. The battle in the skies had been won, but a final cavernous fortress at the Rim resisted. Getaeight followed behind the front, making his way towards the Battlelord, eager to learn as much as he could from the man he had the honor of precepting under. Cleaved cindering bodies with iridescent hair surrounded Aemon when Getaeight reached him. A green ribbon of fire and lightning crackled above his master and came down on the soldier in front of him. The lash split the boy's torso from shoulder to stomach and he fell forward smoking. Aemon continued his march forward, his writ-whip loudly intercepting bolts of blue light jetting towards him. A green glow coursed through his body to his left hand and turned yellow at his fingertips. A ball of light hovered in between three digits which he cast forward, sending a torrent of dust blasting from the writ-stone barriers. Three bloodied and burnt bodies scrambled out of the debris.

Aemon paused. Metallic contrivances ran past him, spraying bubbles filled with thick yellow gas into the dust. The drusen bubbles exploded against the Ehtlentin scaled armor and covered the ground in a sickly fog. Amongst the stalactites of the dark cavernous ceiling above them, two black Shadowed warriors dropped upon the armored Ehtlentins. Plumes of fire erupted downwards from their outstretched arms as they landed. The blasts sent rings of flame outwards towards the panicked soldiers around them. The two masked figures rose from the epicenter of the crater. Fiery writ-blades of purple and red sprang from crystals in their hands, and with uncanny speed they swept towards the line of surprised defenders. Like Aemon's, their crackling blades found exposed flesh between plates of scaled armor, dismembering the Ehtlentin's effortlessly.

The last few native warriors threw down their weapons and raised their hands, pleading in a rhythmic language that, even in their frantic state, sounded elegant to Getaeight. He signaled to a squad who surrounded the captives and escorted them out of the chamber. *They are beautiful*, he thought as they passed by him. The opalescent colors of their hair matched the vivacity of the city, and the cyan tattoos painted over their bodies seemed to tell stories. He sighed. His eyes lowered to the lines of torched bodies scattered throughout the chamber and he felt conflict rise. He did not relish battle, in fact he hated it. Like most Psyperial students, his military internship had been reserved for last in his school rotations, yet he felt no amount of time could have prepared him for this day.

The smoking whip dragging by Aemon's side extinguished with a final crack and he motioned for explosives at the door. Soldiers began placing charges when the doors opened willingly to them. The two masked figures flanked Aemon while silver soldiers and black storm marines rushed into the elaborately designed room. Five jeweled individuals, three men and two women, sat at the end of the room in a line. They were the fattest and oldest citizens Getaeight had seen in the city yet. Aemon bowed.

The gesture seemed to please the fattest and oldest amongst them. As he stood, the others rose. His hands stretched out and he yelled a greeting in the same melodic tongue. When he finished, they clambered down to their knees, heads bowed to the ground in a gesture, Getaeight assumed, of submission. This pleased Aemon.

Twenty minutes after meeting the leaders of the city, four of their corpses lay on the ground. One by one, Aemon took their heads into his hands, using his shadowed training to body-bend their minds and seize their thoughts. Finally, he approached the youngest and thinnest of them, a man with simple black greying hair who seemed a different make than his colorful counterparts. He sat on his feet yet made no move to beg for his life like the others. Aemon clutched his head and stepped into his consciousness.

He spent much more time interrogating the final man. After several minutes, his host began to grow uncomfortable and reached up in a weak, uncoordinated effort to pry Aemon off him. Aemon gripped harder then released him. The thin man gasped, fell to the ground and picked himself back up. Aemon eyed him. The room had been silent since he began, but even the air seemed to hold still as the host that had gathered waited for his judgement.

"This man deserves neither pain or death," he announced. "He will receive both."

Aemon latched back onto the thin man. *He has found something, something that surprised him,* Getaeight surmised. He had never seen a Shadowed writ-bend, nor body-bend, nor been present for a Shadowed court; to witness all three used so cruelly was almost more than he could take, but discipline kept him quiet. After minutes of screaming, the man collapsed before Aemon, dead. Aemon's eyes remained closed as he announced a proclamation. "Gather anyone without colored hair and detain them aboard the *Omedegon*. They are visitors to this city and will have knowledge of this world. I name a burned Pazish Nun a desirable, she is to be brought straight to me, alive." He walked towards the golden thrones ahead of him and sat in the elevated seat at the center. Shadowed who had come to witness Aemon's mandates exited the room, save for the two who perpetually guarded their master. Getaeight approached.

Military command raised him to a temporary bridge lieutenant upon seeing his aptitude, but it seemed to Getaeight that Aemon had taken him as an apprentice. He learned his master's methods well in the months since being elevated to his position, but knew almost nothing about him. He found him quiet and unnaturally knowledgeable; the two worked in tandem to give him an unsettling presence. Yet until today, rumors of his competency as Shadowed warrior had just been words shared amongst other military officers. Getaeight stepped around the bodies at the base of the stairs and looked up into his master's eyes. His heart jumped when he saw their unordinary grey intensity, but they shifted back to the normal brown so quickly Getaeight assumed it was a trick from the light. He kept his expression composed, doing his best to move past what he had seen.

Aemon's expression softened. "Lieutenant Getaeight, how would you proceed?"

The wheels of occupation turned smoothly and two days later the city was shrouded in Psyperial influence. Shadowed interrogators took knowledge and property from the wealthy who dwelt at the peak of the mountain. They passed judgement during court for their own reason and purpose, so long as they had earned the right to do so. Desirables with information threads were identified and searched out. With every interrogation, the web of accounts recorded aboard the *Omedegon* grew to tell the story of the city.

The lower levels of the mountain did not need help conquering themselves: street urchins had taken them in the lawless chaos of battle. Rich or poor, the dead littered the streets. Grander homes were turned over and Uncut dispensed their own form of judgement to former masters. When the invading forces made no move to disturb them, their debauchery escalated.

Four days into their occupancy, the new masters of the city understood a great deal about the world they had arrived in. Information gathered by their instruments confirmed what knowledge they pulled from the population. They were on almost the same planet, orbiting around almost the same two suns, in an entirely different galaxy. As far as anyone could tell, they were in a completely different universe. Since they shared the same mineral resources, the native's technology resembled theirs in principle, though it seemed to the Psyperial engineers that over time this city's understanding of energy manipulation had regressed, save for an advanced understanding of anchor shielding, evident in several ancient installments. However, the location of the power source had been scourged by an enemy who were astonishingly familiar to the Psyperials: the Mongrelai. The spacefaring barbarians, who had eradicated Psyperial satellite cities several hundred years ago, appeared to have done the same to the cities of this world. Theories abounded to explain their existence in both universes, but the natives knew as little about the warriors as the Psyperials.

Besides a common enemy, the natives also shared a similar biology with the Psyperials, allowing Shadowed to body-bend the inhabitants' teslac networks and gain insight into the populace's hidden thoughts. However, the people of this world lived with the presence of death growing inside their teslacs – a disease they called the rot. It became apparent to the Psyperial military leadership that the people of the city never stood a chance against them, but they learned many other nations on the planet were not so weak, and a vast number of them were united under an alliance. The *Omedegon's* prisons swelled with the diverse peoples of those nations and soon discourse occurred through contrivances with newly acquired translation lexicons.

The mystery of the world disappeared and a plan formed in its place.

Aemon held daily court atop a section of great wall reinforcing the rim of the mountain. Cloaked Shadowed and uniformed Officers surrounded him in silent observation. Getaeight stood by a cohort of his peers who shifted uncomfortably. Traditionally, officers were only invited to these meetings for judgement. Otherwise, their interactions with the dark figures were limited to communicating orders or following in their wake during battle. *They are recalling the ways Shadowed killed the natives*, he assumed.

However, he could only guess why Aemon summoned the Officers. *It could be that he wants to instill fear in them, it could be there are not enough Shadowed to carry out his wishes, it could be he wants us unified.* Getaeight more often did not know the answers to his unpredictable Battlelord, nor how the Shadowed felt about the change in attendance. He had grown used to the figures that followed his master, but seeing the fifty who had come aboard the *Omedegon* gathered in one place intimidated him. Their brief experience stranded on this world had altered ages of tradition in a mere four days.

Getaeight agreed that such a radical change of environment garnered a change in their customs. He looked at his cloaked counterparts. Overheating did not concern them in Psyperia, but their black robes and masks looked out of place in the white city and blaring sun. *If we were home, we would be atop the pyramid citadel overlooking a larger city.* Similar fortresses would be perched across a range of mountains in all directions, the black beaches several klicks out. Now he only saw blue ocean. *Were this home, I would feel the whip of rain from a ruined atmosphere.* Instead, the setting sun's rays washed the clouds in orange and red and he felt its waning heat hanging in the air.

Though he was Shadowed himself, Aemon the Proven did not wear a mask. He had laid his face bare for the Psyperium to see, a change he made when he was elected Battlelord sixteen years ago, after the previous Battlelord's assassination. Just as he had for his ascension to Battlelord, he adapted to the new climate in Ehtlentin the first day, exchanging his reinforced black officer uniform and leathril robe for a thin wine colored tunic, grey vented pants and black boots. His new garb revealed dense muscles and a scar that ran over his shoulder and along his arm. The sun stained his pale skin tan and bleached his dark lochs. His vivacious appearance was a stark contrast to the ragged woman dragged before him: the Pazish Nun he had named desirable during his first court in the cavernous fortress.

A writ-glass mask, Psyperial made and painted to resemble a beautiful woman, covered her face. A series of blood splattered chips marred the left jawline from chin to cheek and a muffled hysteric laugh echoed from behind it. The officer who brought her forward explained his troopers found her in a cell with two dead Psyperial soldiers. Dried blood caked her hands and she looked starved, as well as feral. Black and purple veins covered her shoulders and the back of her head. *This is the second rot,* Getaeight thought with repulsion. Aemon nodded to the man's canteen which he then offered her. She did not seem to see it in front of her and laughed harder. She flung her arms around wildly, her feet kicked out and she toppled over. In an uncoordinated effort, she tried to prop herself back up yet failed. The uncomfortable officer presenting her stiffened as Aemon approached.

Aemon grabbed the woman by the head and the black tendrils of her rotting teslac began to glow green as his fingers probed forward, weaving through the black and sea-colored hair that remained on her head, anchoring his thumbs behind her mask. Her laughter took on a choking quality, but he did not hold her for long. She swayed from side to side when his hands withdrew, then she clutched her head and shrieked. It was not a scream of fear or pain, but a howl of anger, a war cry directed at

Aemon. She made no move towards him but the soldiers behind her kept her restrained.

Aemon regarded her then dismissed his court. "Thank you for your witness," he said. Masked figures bowed and turned. The officers disbanded silently as well, although Getaeight noticed questioning glances shared between them. Aemon had not made his intention with the woman known, he announced no judgement nor plan for her. Getaeight pushed his way through the waves of cloaks and pressed uniforms towards Aemon, Lieutenant Kyphothree appeared beside him.

Getaeight surmised that if he was Aemon's right hand, she was his left. She wore a similar officer's uniform to him, though with a few additional ranking designs to display her graduation from basic education and enlistment in Special Operations. She braided her hair tightly against her head to allow a hat to sit on top of it. She shot him a smile out of the corner of her mouth. Her presence deprived Getaeight of any feeling of uniqueness that came with Aemon's attention. His master even seemed to favor her more. She knew that he knew it and an air of smug condescendence varnished their interactions. He was glad she rarely occupied the same space as him or Aemon

"Kyphothree, bring her to my chamber," ordered Aemon as they approached. Kyphothree pulled the Pazish Nun up and moved along the wall towards the setting sun. The uncomfortable officer moved to follow but two Shadowed intercepted him. A grand staircase sunk in front of Kyphothree and she descended into the wall beneath them.

Aemon dismissed the officer and turned to his son. "Lieutenant Getaeight."

"Yes sir."

"Call upon the Remaker, bring his surgeons to my chambers, we will operate on the Nun today."

"Sir." Getaeight nodded. Their surgeons had only been successful half the time removing the teslac network from the natives' bodies – a procedure the natives referred to as the second cut.

Aemon sensed his hesitation. "Her madness brings a turbulence I cannot navigate when I body-bend her. I need her mind cleared of the rot or else she will die with her secrets. I will perform the procedure. You will watch."

"Yes, sir."

As he had days earlier, Getaeight found himself astonished by the brutality and skill of his master. With the help of him and Kyphothree, the surgeons splayed the Nun across a small stone table in the center of the wall's grand dining hall. They bound her feet and hands to newly drilled handles. Contrivances surrounded the woman, prodding her with syringes of local anesthetics which did nothing to abate her madness. When Aemon removed her mask, she appeared an inhuman creature. The soft angles of her half-melted face hinted at the beauty she lost from whatever fire had consumed her. Black veins stretched from her head downwards and disappeared under the layers of scarred flesh. Her eyes were the same sea-green as the streaks running through her hair; they darted about wildly. When Aemon slid his hands around her head, she spat and howled, defecated underneath herself then bit at him. The surgeons looked onwards anxiously and prepared a sedative.

"No, she needs to be awake, she needs to be aware," Aemon said. "Bind her head. Place a respirator tube."

They secured a band across her forehead, gagged her, and fastened both leathril straps to handles. One of the surgeons pulled a long tube and threaded it through her mouth while the other depressed her tongue. The tensing muscles of her neck betrayed her agony. Aemon touched her head again and closed his eyes. He traced his fingers along the black lines running across her face. Slowly, he drew his fingers down her head and the network glowed green. Suddenly, every muscle on her face sprang to life. Her body began convulsing so forcibly that her arms dislocated from her shoulders, giving room for her back to rise and slam against the stone table. When the surgeons moved to strap her down further Aemon spoke calmly, "No, Kyphothree will pin her. You remove her rags then strap her torso down."

Kyphothree jumped onto the table over the nun, planted her hands on her chest and pushed her weight downwards. The surgeons cut the top of the nun's ragged dress and tore it open. Kyphothree gave way for a moment to let the cloth fold past her then replanted her hands on the woman's gnarled skin. The burns covered only a quarter of her body and stopped just below the front of her shoulder and upper arm. Beneath tracings from her poisoned teslac snaked over her torso. Getaeight stared, she was the first woman he had ever seen naked. Despite her half-starved state, he found his eyes shamefully drawn to her. When the surgeons had the strap across her ribs, Kyphothree leapt from the table and landed next to Getaeight. She flashed a knowing smile before pivoting beside him.

With effort, he commanded his eyes to return to his master and not the tortured woman. A quiet gasp escaped Kyphothree's mouth. In front of them, bright white streaks arose in Aemon's hair and a glowing green ambience lifted from his skin, illuminating the tracings of his own teslac network. When he heard Kyphothree's exasperation, his eyes, now grey and cold, penetrated them. He wiped his hands with a cloth in front of him and looked back at the Nun.

"Now we begin," he said.

He dragged his glowing fingers along her arm, leaving an absence of black lines but a presence of bruises in their wake. He worked his way towards her torso, until the teslac network had been dragged from her arm and collected in a mound underneath her shoulder. He finished the other arm then gripped her leg and did the same. Sweat drenched his tunic, he took a moment to wipe it from his face while the surgeons finished cleaning the woman. Then he continued, pushing his hands up her thighs to her torso. Steadily, a black mound collected underneath the base of her neck. Aemon quickly removed the respirator tube but kept her jaw secured in the open mouth gag. The Nun choked in the absence of an open airway, spit flowed from her mouth followed by blood. Aemon reached into her mouth and slowly drew a glistening black form from her throat. The last of the teslac slipped past her tongue and her gurgling turned to a gasp. The dangling vine of gore appeared to Getaeight like a great weaving that had come undone, yet still a hint of its humanoid mold remained. Kyphothree approached wide eyed.

"Flip her over," Aemon said. "Once again."

CHAPTER 4

Getaeight

Getaeight descended the mountain with a translator, three military grade contrivances, and a retinue of armored soldiers. He donned lightly plated mesh armor for the expedition; he felt grateful for the coolness of the clouds and ocean breeze, yet cautious of the thick mist which swept in with it. The fog hovered in the lower levels of the city and when the sun peaked through the clouds it illuminated the area in a crystalline glow. It fascinated Getaeight to the point of distraction. The young officer had been acutely aware of the weather since he arrived in the city. Every day he learned of another way the sun could feel on his face. He woke to watch it rise and wandered from his work to see it fall. Most of all he loved the cool wind on his body at night and the salty smell it brought with it. Tasting the diversity of the city's climate became a mission to him. He reluctantly wrapped a scouting eyepiece around his head to insure he would not be taken by surprise in the mist.

Much had changed at the base of the mountain. The fighting had finished but cells of resistance remained, though their defiance to Psyperial control manifested only in the deletion of records and concealment of Shadowed's desired targets. The invasion, specifically the drusen gas used during it, had unintenionally eradicated the elderly population living in the upper half of the city and from the lower levels a new class of people rose. The cutting operations performed by Psyperial medical teams rejuvenated the slums. For the young Ehtlentins living in those areas, life had new meaning. The surgeries also quelled their tenacious instincts and conditions improved for all citizens of the city. They became a people united by the Psyperium.

When their squadron descended to the second level, boys and girls smiled at them, raised their arms to show newly acquired scars and offered them goods from their stalls. The soldiers pushed through the crowds, waving their hands in refusal of food and trinkets, nodding in their helmets to giddy girls. Getaeight remained focused ahead but aware of the disordered line behind him. He was not the only one being tested by the distractions of this world.

"Tighten up!" he barked. As with the other officers, as with his Battlelord, Getaeight's face remained bare of cover to display his courage as well as his wrath. The group tightened formation. The swell of people tapered and died as they moved on, soon they walked through empty streets. Their route took them well beyond the market to the burnt district where evidence of the Pazish uprising remained apparent in the blackened craters and crumbling stone buildings. Somewhere ahead amongst the debris, an underground orphanage held records pertaining to Aemon's new desirable, a boy named Sincret.

Two blocks out, signs of life reappeared: a fire glowed in the second story window of a half-collapsed building, and sounds of footsteps and whispers could be heard in the alleyways. Further along, brave young mothers ventured out of doorways to stand along their path. They looked at them hopefully, Getaeight motioned for soldiers to dispense rations to them. *So young, some are not even a decade old,* he thought. Their eyes conveyed fear, curiosity, excitement and desire; yet they always settled upon Getaeight. He shuffled along, avoiding their gazes and reflected on the failure of his training to prepare him for such a scenario. A young woman, older than the others, revealed her breasts to him and stared intensely as he passed. *This is how empires fall.*

The moment of bliss soured as memories of the naked Nun's scorched body flooded into his mind. The beauty in front of him disappeared, replaced by the vision of her melted face.

The memory of the woman's violent procedure broke to the surface of his mind at every opportunity. When he showered, he felt her skin. When he defecated, he smelt her feces. He slept restlessly and his appetite had left him. He found himself dwelling in self-loathing born from his perceived incompetence during the ordeal and exacerbated by his inability to move past it. Getaeight did not feel like himself.

The troop passed into a large open space. A massive blasted stone building stood in the middle of the courtyard. A young Ehtlentin woman with purple hair leaned against a cracked stone pillar by a crumbled corner of the building. She looked at them as they cleared the buildings around the courtyard. Getaeight walked towards her and signaled his squad to fan out to get a read of the area. He understood that the delicate dance between strength and mercy was necessary to remain in control of their new home.

"I'm told this is a place where one can come to seek help," he said. His voice sounded odd coming out in the rhymes of the native language after being processed by his translator. The woman's eyebrows raised and she nudged herself away from the pillar. The deep color of her lips captured him as they moved.

"What could a man with so many friends need of me?" she asked. Her eyes passed from soldier to soldier, they settled on one of the humanoid contrivances for a moment, then back to Getaeight. He sensed the unusual whiteness of his eyes startled her. As a youth, he resented them, but had learned to use them to an advantage. Now they practically spoke for him.

"I am hoping to make a friend of you. I am Lieutenant Getaeight. We mean you, nor your wards, no harm. I only want information." He paused, she said nothing. "So far, I know there is a substructure underneath this building known as Deep Home, your name is Quantine and you are its governor." He paused again, she seemed unfazed. "Somewhere in this place are records of its history. I need your help finding those records." Though he did not need her help exactly, but stunning her and quelling any resistance they encountered would be a mark against their occupation.

"I'd like nothing more than to be your friend. You are welcome inside." She gestured him to follow her. Getaeight inferred from her attitude that allowing a large influx of his men into the building would be unwise and motioned all but two soldiers and one contrivance to remain at the entrance. They wound through the ruin and upon an opening in the floor that appeared before them like the one atop Aemon's wall. The staircase led them deep underground. He guessed they were descending into a cavern between the second and first levels of the city. The air grew cooler, finally they walked through and opening into a busy room lined with at least fifty shanties and more people than they could support. Getaeight signaled his men to post at the inside of the door out of obvious view. Immediately after entering the room, Quantine took a sharp right turn into an adjacent area. As they walked through the arenas filled with shanty homes and stores, Getaeight noticed a large part of the population comprised of middle class members of their society; Once-Cut refugee's driven from their homes by the flames of revolution.

The low ceiling and strong smell of damp sheets pressed on him. They took another staircase down to a cooler room where a gentle breeze aired the hallway and freed him of the musk. The two of them walked down the dimly lit corridor until Quantine paused and took out a key to a dusty locked door. She opened it to an equally dusty square room lined with storage lockers and a lone blank console on the opposite wall.

"The answer to your problems, I hope," she said.

"I hope so too, thank you," he replied. The contrivance hummed softly as it passed between them and integrated with the console. A series of tones emanated from it and were translated by the device housed in Getaeight's inner ear. The search was running.

Quantine looked from the contrivance to Getaeight and said, "So, he's the hacker and your friends are the muscle. You must be the brains." Then she smiled and added, "or at least the pretty face."

"We are all just servants to our people," Getaeight replied, "in whatever capacity is needed."

"Then we are not so different; however, I am unsure how to serve my people best when we know so little about our new… neighbors," she said carefully.

"Allow me to help you then," he offered.

"So far, I know that you are not from the labyrinth, your cloaked warriors can take control of our minds amongst other impossible feats, and you, Lieutenant Getaeight, are close to the man who leads your campaign." Getaeight tried to keep his face stoic. "You won't tell me any secrets I can give to the Alliance but you can show me the face and mind of your people."

Getaeight slid his hand into a pouch on his belt and withdrew a folded paper. It was a card containing the information most relevant for the native people to understand. He handed it to her but she held it aside uninterested. She crossed her other arm across her chest, looking overall displeased.

"I've seen your propaganda. These are words, what I want is to understand you," she said.

"Words are the bridge to understanding," he quoted an old Pysperial motto.

"Words are the ferry between our people. Love is the bridge." She stepped towards him, making clear her intention. Getaeight again felt his command of the situation tested. Just in time, a song came from the direction of the contrivance indicating its task was complete. Getaeight motioned for it to follow him and he walked past Quantine. She hovered in the doorway. Getaeight's march was arrested by courtesy to not leave the situation so abruptly. Soon though, Quantine followed and then led ahead of him, back up to the top floor. They walked in silence until they entered the first arena they arrived at earlier. The boom of a hundred people speaking drowned out all sound but the ones within the immediate area. Getaeight turned to Quantine.

"Here is my contact link. It is integrated with your city's system so you can find me on the net. I am happy to answer your questions but words will have to suffice," he said.

He left the refuge feeling proud of himself and the manner he handled the mission. He took the data directly from the contrivance's memory hardware. Before entering a shuttle to return to his quarters aboard the *Omedegon*, he dropped by an abandoned mansion from which he had taken to watching the sun set. When he arrived, he poured himself iced water from the dispenser and walked to the balcony. Quantine was sitting on the railing when he emerged. The sunset behind her enveloped her figure and illuminated the purple in her hair. Getaeight was struck by the vision of her beauty. He stood still as she slid down and approached him. The soft sea breeze he loved so much tossed her thin violet dress and long dark hair carelessly. The salt and smell of her fragrant skin filled his nostrils when she was upon him.

"You are going to help me learn of your people, in whatever capacity is needed," she said. Getaeight knew it was so.

The next hours seemed a dream to him. All thoughts left his mind except for those focused on the woman pressed against him. His body twisted with hers to find the forms where pleasure took them farther from sentience. Even after Getaeight spent himself, he could not stop exploring her, and soon his flesh caught up with his spirit and they bound themselves together once more. Afterwards, they fell upon the grand bed and aired their bodies with the breeze passing through the open balcony door. Quantine put her head into the crook of his shoulder and traced her hands over his chest. He felt his body wash with comfort at the turn of her fingers. Her tactile lullaby brought him into a drunken trance and soon he rolled over to hold her and fell asleep.

He shook himself from his slumber as he remembered the curfew that limited his time at the mansion. He lifted himself on an arm and looked down at his muse. She smiled up at him and raised her eyebrows in the same curious nature she had when they first met. He felt a smile rise in the corners of his mouth and resigned any effort to control it. *This is the feeling life is born from,* he thought, *but not for me.*

Getaeight, like every Psyperial citizen, would remain sterile until he turned twenty-six years old. If he chose to have a child after that, the Psyperial system would distribute it to qualified guardians to raise for seventeen years. In that system, there was no room for love to lead to distraction or errors in upbringing. When Getaeight looked deeply into her purple eyes he felt passion stir inside him and for the first time in hours realized the magnitude of his decision. *She owns me,* he knew. He leaned down to kiss her, she grabbed his hair and locked her lips to his. When he finally pulled away he looked through the balcony opening and at the two pale moons shining down on them.

"You need to leave?" she asked, bringing him back to the moment.

"Yes," he replied as he stroked her cheek.

"I was learning so much about you." She grinned because it was true. In a matter of hours, she measured his excellent level of fitness, felt the presence of similar organs under his skin, deduced he was a virgin, and learned that beneath their trim uniforms and cold plating, a rebellious nature could be awoken in the Psyperials. It was more than she could have hoped for. Even better though, she liked him. There was a sweetness about his reserved personality, and though he had never had sex before, he seemed uncannily in touch with her body. His natural talent was not unlike the last lover she had taken – the same boy her new one was hunting - Sincret.

Getaeight laughed and replied, "I've learned much as well." A nagging thought urged him to discuss where they would go from here, but she shushed him as he opened his mouth to begin.

"I can be discrete, I can be yours." She brushed hair from his eyes and kissed him again.

Through tremendous willpower, Getaeight pulled himself away from her long enough to dress then commanded himself to say goodbye. As he walked out the door his head rang with alarm. Despite the potential of reprimand, he felt content. However, by the time he boarded a shuttle heading to the *Omedegon* his joy had turned into shame. He remembered Aemon's court, the Nun and her bloodied veil. The crafted mask her rapists styled to resemble a Psyperial woman. He resolved to not stray to the dark places some of his compatriots had. He took the data drive from his belt and clutched it in his hand. When he arrived at his room he went straight to his console to decipher the files.

The records did not tell much besides a few oddities. Sincret was the only child born from his mother, which was a rarity for an Uncut, as was the fact that she died giving birth to him. As a boy at the nunnery, Inquisitors recorded he showed potential in many fields of interest but most notably physics and circuit science. He was painted "remarkable" and adopted by an off-world shield engineer. Getaeight took what he needed to know about the engineer and ran a search on the *Omedegon's* server for the man. He was not logged in the ship's manifest, so was therefore not captive in the ship. Getaeight decided to sleep. *I'll visit the engineer's home in the morning, if it is still standing.*

Fortunately, the structure was undamaged when Getaeight arrived the next morning. He came with only one contrivance to gain entrance and download any data. The apartment door gave the floating black sphere resistance for a time but eventually yielded to it and let them pass. The smell of decay rolled onto Getaeight and threatened to make him choke. He pushed through and searched the apartment for clues about what happened. His journey took him to the master bedroom where he found the engineer's dead body slumped against the wall in his closet, a black desiccated hole blasted through his chest.

A voice came from behind him, "You really do stare anxiousl..."

Getaeight had his weapon out and pointed at Kyphothree before she could finish. She leaned against the bedroom doorway in an unperturbed manner and a spiderlike contrivance appeared above her. The machine was an artifact of a much older people whose technology remained largely undeciphered.

This particular artifact had been unlocked and given to her by Aemon as a gift. Iridescent colors flexed around her, evidence of the writ-shield encasing her. Getaeight traced the shimmering colors back to the artifact projecting it. Its single glowing eye trained on him.

"What am I looking at?" he asked, lowering his weapon towards the dead engineer.

"Someone wiped the surveillance data," she answered.

Getaeight waited, knowing that wouldn't have stopped her.

"He was killed by an immolation blast, so whoever did it can writ-bend. The boy Sincret, in all likelihood our culprit, covered his tracks but not entirely. A ship called the *Spear Throw* is implicated. It docked at Hangar 42 just before our assault. Footage from the battle place it flying into a labyrinth entrance at the base of the mountain. Our patrols lost it shortly thereafter."

Getaeight sighed, Kyphothree relished teaching moments. "I will set hunters to the task," he said automatically.

"And I'll be sure Director Anansi humors you with a response. There is more. We never spoke about the Nun." This surprised Getaeight, he and Kyphothree never spoke about anything. "Follow me," she said.

She led him to a lounge in the back of the apartment. A fogged writ-glass cylinder occupied the center of the room. She punched in a command on the console next to it. The cylinder peeled apart to reveal two simple wooden chairs. Kyphothree walked to one of them and motioned Getaeight to take the other. As he passed into the space, writ-glass rose around them and locked snug into place against the ceiling. A dull hum reverberated about the small room and Getaeight felt anchor energy pull him in every direction.

"This is a black box. No one can transmit data to or from it. Every type of recording device will malfunction. Save for your memory of it, this conversation never happened," she told him.

"This conversation should not happen," he retorted.

STAR STORY BOOK ONE: ANCHORED

Kyphothree proceeded anyways. "What Aemon did, the way he changed." She looked him up and down. "His eyes, his hair - he looked like you."

Getaeight pushed the memory away as quickly as it came. Serving his Battlelord had been the entirety of his purpose since meeting the man. He trusted Aemon's plan and felt honored to be trusted in turn. He said nothing, though she spoke the truth. He had long rationalized his white hair and grey eyes as an aberrant mutation he would identify when he turned 26, but looking at Aemon that night had been like looking into a mirror.

"I see, soldier," she said finally after no reply came. She opened the doors again. "We were put upon this task together. I've done my part, now do yours." Getaeight waited until she was out of the room before following. Her and her spidery contrivance were nowhere to be seen when he returned to the main room. He kicked around the debris from a shattered window above, thankful for the breeze that carried the scent of death out of the room. He spent some time browsing through the rest of the apartment.

It was an elegant space with an alien design. He had not seen architecture like it in the city, nor many of the amenities that he assumed had been imported. He had his contrivance hack the balcony door open. The sun met him as he walked out and seemed in no hurry to lift from the ocean horizon. Below him, the many levels of the city sloped outwards, its populace appearing as mere specs from his vantage.

A much better view than the mansion, Getaeight decided. He returned to the apartment, touching the dried and dying plants on either side of him. He searched the cupboards in the kitchen till he found a pitcher. He activated the sink to fill it and was pleased to see running water, as Aemon had made it a priority to keep the utilities functioning in the city.

After watering the plants, he inspected the assortment of imported devices. *Learning how to use these could be educational,* he thought, *or at least an interesting distraction.* He ordered a cleanup crew to the premises and decided he would submit a request for residence as soon as he returned to the *Omedegon*. By the time the crew arrived to remove the body, he had cleared Kyphothree's operation to track the *Spear Throw*. He had done his part, though he suspected his participation in finding Sincret was mostly for his own benefit.

He had other concerns for the day: an officer's meeting to prepare for the mounting Alliance counterattack. He hurried to his single seat transport, leaving the contrivance behind, and sped through the empty streets. *All department leads sharing what they've learned. We will hear reports from the garrison left at the gateway that brought us here, information obtained by spies and scouts, statistics about the physical and mental health of the crew.*

The meeting took place in the cavernous center of the *Omedegon*, the heart chamber. Aemon sat at the end of a black table flanked by Admiral Veric Visparion on his right and Chief Physics Officer Elian Alceta on his left: the leaders of his fleet and army respectively. Leaders from twenty other divisions were present as well.

Kyphothree sat beside Alceta while three officers filled the seats between Getaeight and Visparion. One hundred other officers of importance lined the table, its diverged looping shape distributed them evenly in front of Aemon and his council. Only Lazaeron the Remaker, the Chief Cybernetics Officer, was absent from the table. In his place, he sent his biologic daughter Anansi the Spider, who smiled seductively at Getaeight from across the table.

A thick composite report lay before each of them. As the officers spoke pages gently flipped to where their queries could be answered. After three hours of review regarding challenges, Admiral Visparion stood to summarize the leadership's assessment and plans for the direst of them: "An Alliance flotilla left their capital, Omphala, two days after we took the city New Psyperia, or as the locals refer to it, Ehtlentin. Stafford garrisons are joining them along their path, others have assembled in the city of Corala. Most of the forces are not anchor capable though, it will take them two weeks to reach the city." He took a breath and continued, "Trace anchor tether readings do indicate at least a dozen ships have space faring capability. We cannot gauge their potency but a moderate level of coordination and formation suggests some measure of competence." He paused for the words to settle in.

Aemon's gaze passed over them. "We did not choose this location to settle for nostalgia. New Psyperia sits in an ocean of food, on a defensible mountain, and two anchor jumps to the gateway. Our physicists will find a way to open the passage back home. We will hold here until they are successful or we are destroyed," he said.

The Officers nodded their heads in silence. Aemon sat down and Alceta rose.

"An array at the home side of the gateway works constantly to send tethers through detected manifestations. If our tethers here move through the same manifestation as one from the other side, it should hold the gateway open. The challenge we face is launching the anchor through the open doorway before it closes shut in a microsecond. The patterns have slowed before, hence how we came here. Until it does so again, we will study the anomaly and develop other methods to hold the gateway open." He sat down and this time doubtful murmurs from the officers bounced off the black gleaming table and up to the cavernous ceiling. They fell silent as their words returned to them.

Aemon rose again. "The obstacles to our survival are not only external. Chief Health Officer Phrenshon." He motioned to an older man in a white uniform with a whiter mustache. He stood and bowed to Aemon. "The points of your analysis, please."

"Anyone who has walked on the surface of this world has felt its intoxicating effect," said the peculiar man, his outlandish mustache bouncing as he spoke. "Desire has taken discipline for some people and they have been punished according to the laws of Old Psyperia. For others, the conditions have strengthened their will to do good." Getaeight always felt that

Officer Phrenshon was more eloquent than one would expect from a scientist. "For those communicating through our psych report system, their input has revealed an overwhelming desire to settle the city, especially amongst nest families living aboard. Conflicts about feelings of passion are the second largest sense of anxiety for the crew, next to the Alliance retaliation. Reports from the field indicate that while military personnel maintain an acceptable level of obedience, ninety percent of the crew find themselves distracted for a variety of reasons." He scanned his peers with an offsetting smile. He halted his survey when he met Aemon's stare. "Battlelord Aemon assembled a committee of psychoanalysts to address these concerns."

Aemon rose once more. "We designed legislature aimed to mediate the crew's gravitation towards exploration with a need to remain united. As Shadowed claimed domain with blood, you will claim yours through acumen. All requests for residence have been heard, responses are waiting on your personal consoles." Raised eyebrows and cheerful chatter abounded in Aemon's silence. Getaeight remained still and endured the excruciating seconds before officers farther down the table became aware Aemon was still standing. "However," he said darkly, "Shadowed do not sleep in the edifice they have taken, and neither will you. When this crisis has been averted we will address this issue again. Until then, a curfew remains in effect." The officers in the room nodded automatically as his words sank in. Getaeight had done the same the day earlier when he read the advanced copy of Aemon's mandates.

We are here to stay, he knew.

CHAPTER 5
Glade Jadamara

The old crew found no respite from the cold in the *Spear Throw's* hallway. Jadamara draped a thick sheet over herself and the others followed suit. They entered the main cabin and upon a blanketed mass of orphan children. *The youngest of the lot,* she guessed. Along the adjacent wall, four Painted Boys carrying medical equipment circumvented the shifting mound towards Jadamara. She scanned the room before moving out of their way. The Painted Boys passed with Culus behind them. The red-eyed jailor contrivance zipped around the doctor and stopped between him and Jadamara. It hummed violently while Culus smiled in a way of excited congratulations. *Obviously, he's happy to have anyone half his age on this ship.*

"Hey! You look better! Looks like it's riding up though," he said, nodding towards the brace, "come by sometime today." Jadamara gave him a reluctant smile. The contrivance slowly wheeled behind him, red eye fixed on her, until they were down the hallway.

She rubbed her arms for warmth. "Couldn't find the thermostat?" she asked Sincret who sat in the lounge staring at them.

"Found the thermostat but someone left the skiff bay door open. We will sort it out once we reach the lake tomorrow," he replied, then turned back to the game she had distracted him from.

She walked to her quarters without a response. The twins departed as she did, no doubt to see the state of their rooms.

They left Weg standing awkwardly. Jadamara reached her room, paused and knocked on the door. She heard a welcoming response from the other side and walked in, relieved to see JV sitting on her bed. He leaned against the wall, and overall, seemed in the same exhausted condition as when she saw him last. She closed the door behind her.

There wasn't much to talk about. He was completely immobile except for his left arm, neck, and head, which sporadically jerked during their conversation. He told her that last night he slept on her bed while Sincret slept on the kitchen's pull out cot. The black contrivance, Jadamara learned was named Kill Bot, or KB for short, had stood sentinel between them until morning. She had questions about the boy, and opinions to share.

"Our world is enormous and the labyrinth even larger. I have seen more than most of both and haven't even scraped the surface. Of the people I've met in those travels, Sincret is an anomaly to be sure," he took a moment to think. "Most people would have tossed me out of the ship by now."

Jadamara blew air out between pursed lips. "You know what I'm saying. I can't get my head around how convenient his timing was," she whispered.

He moved his head closer. "Fear fuels his madness and you are wise not to trust him," he attempted to lean closer, "but from what I can tell, he is not untrustworthy. If the arrival of that pyramid and Sincret's heist are related, I think the explanation is unknown even to him."

Jadamara considered pointing out that it wasn't JV's ship the boy had stolen but she thought against it. The *Spear Throw* had been JV's home for ten years while he served as first mate under her father. After her father was murdered outside the labyrinth city of Retine sixteen years ago, JV brought his vessel and body back to Jadamara and her mother. Her mother quickly retrofitted the *Spear Throw* to carry cargo on surface flights. JV stayed aboard for five years to train her how to captain the vessel. Jadamara remembered those years filled with laughter and joy and sadness. But also love.

"The murderer thief is trustworthy. That's a whole lot of comfort," she said sarcastically, then out of curiosity she asked, "What do you think my father would have done if this happened to him?"

"Your father..." JV smiled and pondered the question, then frowned. "Your father's curiosity made him a great charter. In the end, it killed him." His answer startled Jadamara. He saw the look on her face. "He did not care about property or position, just the story of his life. He would not have been able to resist the adventure ahead of you." Jadamara sighed and felt the slight sting of tears collect under her eyes. JV's response was unusually blunt, a product of the second rot robbing his social grace, but nonetheless honest. Her mother told her that her father always loved her, but given how often he was absent from their home in Corala, she never decided if she believed it. JV's account only affirmed that uncertainty. "There is no point in your question child. This is your story," he said, resigned.

Jadamara found the conversation entirely unhelpful. "You are all I have now."

"I'm not going anywhere." He smiled jokingly, referring to his disability. Jadamara forced a laugh and made herself not to look at the black veins peeking through his hairline. "You are smarter than your father and more courageous than your mother. I have a feeling your life's story will be very interesting."

"We'll see," said Jadamara, doubtfully. *Depends how long it lasts.*

A knock on the door was followed by the appearance of Sincret. "We could use your help on the bridge when you're ready," he said to her. He extended two dense bars of mashed nuts, meat, and leaves to them. Jadamara's nose curled at the smell of fish and grain. "Garvis' special recipe. He doesn't share what makes it so special though." He looked down at the bars. "Probably for the best." They took the bars and Sincret exited.

Jadamara forced the concoction down her throat, stifling the recurring urge to vomit until her stomach finally submitted to digesting the slum cuisine. After suffering through the last bite, she made her way to the *Spear Throw's* deck where she found Gren and the twins already hovering over the technicians at their stations. The painted girl, Cass, hovered over them. Sincret occupied the captain's chair, his hands a blur as he cycled through functions as fast as the computer could keep up. He looked up at her for a moment but his hands continued to find the points of light displayed below them. He stacked functions on top of one another until a map of a segment of labyrinth formed on the screen in front of him, and a route charted through it.

"No just let me do it!" shouted Gren as he moved into the pilot's seat, at the same time evicting its former occupant. Cass glowered down at him and the twins turned to look between Gren and her until it was clear she would allow it. The boy he displaced looked young and frightened at the interruption, but clung to the back of Gren's seat and peered down at the screen and controls as he flipped through them. Gren looked back at Jadamara and shook his head mouthing the words, "We are fucked," then he turned to Sincret who barely seemed to notice.

"What's happening?" Jadamara asked Sincret.

"We are being followed," he said in a monotone. "We've been moving through the routes that never made it into the Ehtlentin archives, but we exited into a charted tunnel an hour ago and something has picked us up." He motioned to the screen. "It could be another survivor, or one of the invaders. Either way, we will lose them in the maze here," he said, though not too confidently.

She eyed the route on his screen then looked out the window ahead of her. The maze had narrowed to a space so tight Jadamara questioned if the *Spear Throw* would be able to maneuver through it. None of this seemed to bother Gren as he pushed the ship forward and downwards. The ship's internal writ-field kept her feet anchored to the floor, but her gut felt the lurch of acceleration all the same. Gren kept his eyes focused on the screen ahead of him, occasionally calling out for reports. Jadamara made her way around the technicians, answering Gren's requests and hoping the children learned something in the process. *For better, but most likely for worse, our lives are in their hands,* she thought.

The new command crew was far from the team Jadamara had grown to know, but they were competent. Creline, a Painted Boy with a raspy voice and darting eyes, worked power delegation and shield operation, though only the former was needed for the time. Garvis doubled as the ships unofficial cook and communication officer. When he wasn't touching the console in front of him, he held his hands up at his shoulders as if the computer would crumble if he touched it without a clear intention. Isla was the youngest of the lot, only about ten years old by Jadamara's estimate, but impressed Jadamara with her constant chatter of helpful information she gathered from the instruments outside the ship: the radar, sonar, anchor field tracking, and gravity monitor. Without her updates, the *Spear Throw* could end up falling into a gravity well or disabled from anchor storms emanating around the rivers of lava that occasionally appeared along their path. Cass had the commanding hard-ass disposition of a first mate but none of the other qualities. Jadamara had no doubt that in time she could become a very capable officer, but she was older; about twenty years old and well into her first rot. By midday she looked ready to fall over.

"We haven't seen that other ship for a few hours, we ought to change shifts," Sincret suggested. He had been immersed in the ship's maps for hours and seemed exhausted as well. Jadamara looked him over. There was nothing sinister about him but she still felt like he could use a matching bruise on his right cheek. However, even she needed a break from the stress of the deck. The pain from her injuries had returned in force.

None of them replied to Sincret's suggestion but his crew punched in the idle function commands, rose from their seats, stretched, and moved for the door. The ship came to a complete stop, hovering in the narrow passage. Gren and the twins looked at Jadamara. "We need to keep moving," she said to Sincret.

"And we will," he answered. He walked down to Gren's station and jerked his thumb towards the door. Gren did not move and suddenly Jadamara became aware that Sincret was alone on the command deck. This thought also arrived in the boy's mind at the same time and made itself apparent in his expression. She saw the rot almost come to life underneath the skin on the right side of his exposed neck as he tensed. Though again, luminous blue etchings appeared under his skin in place of the expected black rot. *He is not as vulnerable as we would like to believe,* she knew.

"Gren, find Weg. You'll train him how to pilot the *Spear Throw*. Ava, I'll give you access to the database, I want you to mine it for information on the labyrinth empires. See if anything matches our invaders. Eva, tour the ship and report back to me. I'll be in the... medical bay." They moved to follow her orders. Jadamara gave one more sideways glance at Sincret as she walked to the captain's seat and punched in commands to clear Ava to access all the public and private records stored on the ship. She did not know what to expect when she logged on her profile, but felt some comfort when she saw she still had full access. Or at least so it seemed. "I'll be back," she said to Sincret. She couldn't tell if he looked relieved or nervous.

She exited the bridge, every step bringing new noises and smells to her attention. Several children in the hallway played a game with dice on the metal floor. They looked up at her and scooted themselves against the wall as she passed. The main cabin was heavy with smoke and the sweet smell of Ehtlentin rum. Always, the wet presence of body odor mingled with spoiled food pressed against her. The puddle of blanketed children in the center of the room had dissolved, and now Uncut of all ages pressed themselves against the walls, smoking and talking. Some fed crumbs of food into their mouths idly while others seemed to have tasks to accomplish. Jadamara found herself grateful she had a place to go to distract herself. Eva was in the far side of the room, engaged in conversation with a young man holding up a cigarette in his rotting hand. She looked embarrassed as she pushed it away smiling.

Jadamara arrived at the med bay to find Doctor Culus already overwhelmed with a battery of rotting young men and women. He looked up when she entered and motioned for her to take a seat. In twenty minutes, most of the Uncut had left the room, there didn't seem to be much the doctor could do for them but assess how far along they were in the process. Jadamara felt a chill run through her. She touched the scar on her arm and felt the old sense of privilege reinforced by years of witnessing such sights around the continent. Culus walked up to her. KB wheeled along at his hip, a syringe grasped in its claw. The doctor extended a barrier and removed her girdle. She felt short of breath immediately after it released her, as if the foundation had been suddenly taken from the base of a building.

He raised her soiled tank and ran his blue and red ingevein over her bruised torso. She felt a dull stinging sensation as it oscillated over her. The screen on his wrist morphed as he moved up and down. He worked the girdle for a time then announced, "It is still too soon to tell if your ribs are setting where they should be but I've readjusted the balance on the brace." She put it on and her breathing returned to normal. The doctor adjusted it a bit more then sat back looking pleased with himself.

"It feels good to do some good," he said. "My brother's saying."

"Is he a doctor as well?" she asked.

"He was, now he serves as a Councilman of Ehtlentin." He noticed her expression and added confidently, "A foreign invasion is a probably a nice respite for him from the usual cloak and dagger threats he deals with."

"Booooop!" said KB as it handed the doctor an instrument which he placed just under her right eye then into his ingevein.

"Yes, very good. Just do a round on the sick bays and make sure everyone is comfortable," he said to it. The contrivance reversed its treads and wheeled backwards. It swiveled its body around and disappeared past the barrier.

"Your little helper sure has a lot of attitude," she pointed out.

The doctor chuckled. "You'll have to excuse him, he's spent the last ten years keeping thieves and the like out of my clinic. He hasn't had proper maintenance in ages. A gift from my brother."

Jadamara found herself idly fidgeting with the brace again but stopped herself and leaned back on the cot. "How did you and it end up on this merry adventure?"

"Well, actually at the end of KB's blaster. Sincret hacked him remotely I suppose, and then several of the orphans I treated came and moved my clinic supplies to the dock."

"Did they expect you to cut them?" she asked.

"If I could I would. But only the clinics at the Rim have the equipment. There were some of us that... tried to help in that regard. Years ago. Our plans fell apart though, Ehtlentin hierarchy preferred the lower levels the way they were."

He's talking about the Pazish rebellion, she realized. Jadamara again reflected on his peculiar disposition. *He is the kindest Twice-Cut I've met,* she realized. Ehtlentin and Corala both existed in the Alliance but were far from the power seat of the government. In Corala there were slums, crime, and power perpetuated amongst the Twice-Cut, but no inquisitors or droves of orphans, and almost everyone found a way to afford first cuts for their children. Twice-Cuts had long controlled the destinies of those below them, rarely for those people's benefit.

"You are a curious man, Culus," she said.

He laughed. "I still haven't decided how I feel about being here, but I am glad to have you with us. I can tell the children are too. The closest thing many of them ever had to parents were the Pazish nuns. They need us, and we need them."

Jadamara snorted, "I'm not interested in adopting any children, let alone a hundred of them. And as far as needing them, we were doing just fine before."

The doctor laughed again. "There are 134 people on your ship and most of them above the age of seven were designated as exceptional by the inquisitors. This is a ship of engineers, linguists, warriors, mathematicians, artists, and inventors. There is a reason we are having this conversation and are not just smoking corpses in a twisted pile of melted metal."

"By the looks of it, half of these geniuses will be dead within the year anyways, including your fearless leader," she whispered darkly.

For a few seconds the doctor stared at his ingevein and said nothing, then replied, "Perhaps. He seems determined to live, as do they all."

Jadamara leaned forward again, "Well, when we arrive at the cut bargain sale you just let me know." The doctor looked finished with her so she jumped off the cot. "Thank you, Doc. It feels much more comfortable now. I'll be on the bridge if you need me."

The next day Jadamara checked her ingevein. Had they been on the surface, the sun would just be peaking above the horizon. *I can't remember the last night I got a good sleep,* she thought drearily. She saw the weariness in the crew's eyes as well. They had piloted the *Spear Throw* through the night and made considerable progress to the body of water they intended to rest at. They landed the vessel in a rock outcropping, and when they cut the forward lights the view outside went pitch black.

Since entering the tight maze that Sincret routed, there had been no sign of their pursuer, but Jadamara still felt uneasy about leaving the bridge for her quarters. The twins shared Ava's room. It appeared that Cass declined Eva's request to relocate from her room, and Eva declined Cass's offer to share it. Gren and Weg cleaned out the trash from his already small room, where they now both slept. Jadamara stood outside of her room and watched Sincret and a Painted Boy carry JV to her bed. When she peeked her head in, she saw the kitchen cot had been extended from the wall.

Sincret turned to her. "You can have your room back," he said.

He looks like crap, she thought. The blue veins creeping up his neck intensified as the day went on. His form had shifted again. A striking greyness had infused into his wild eyes while the blue and gold color of his hair had receded to just the tips, leaving a bright white in its wake. Where everyone else slipped into a sleepy exhaustion, his weariness took on a wired edge, giving him the look of an xene addict long deprived of sleep. Jadamara noticed that his appearance unnerved others aboard the ship as well. Still, he gave no explanation.

"I'm just tired. I'm going to sleep in the med bay tonight. If you or JV need anything wake me," he said.

He started walking away when Jadamara surprised herself by touching his arm. She said, "There's nothing the doctor can do for you. It's warmer in here, you should stay here." *Why did I just say that?* she wondered.

He looked surprised as well, "Oh. You're right but I don't think I'll be sleeping well tonight anyways. We have about five hours, make the most of it." He left down the hallway and Jadamara entered her quarters. She rummaged through her closet, found some comfortable clothes that hadn't been pilfered by the orphans and put them on. She took a moment to open a drawer and stare at her mother's red jacket – the jacket she had seen her wear almost every day of her life till she passed. It was one of her mother's possessions she could not let go, nor had she been able to bring herself to put it on. Just knowing it was still preserved calmed her down. She walked out and looked at JV who was lying down on her bed with his ingevein raised above him.

"You'll be glad he's sleeping in the med bay. I've never heard a worse sleep talker," he said. She sighed in response and dropped to her cot, falling immediately into a dreamless sleep.

She awoke to feel the ship already moving and see JV gone from his cot. She jumped up, pulled on a green jumper and fastened the brace over it. She arrived on the bridge to find the midday crew at their stations. Through the window ahead of her, Jadamara saw light beams bouncing off a black lake. The white walls that once surrounded the peripheral windows were gone and Jadamara guessed they had entered a large cavern.

"Good morning, Captain," Gren said with a wry smile. Jadamara guessed he meant the greeting to undermine Sincret's position. She looked around waiting for a reprisal from Cass, but she was absent from the bridge so none ever came. Sincret hovered over Isla's console. If he registered the slight, he didn't let it show.

Jadamara was too tired to make any more of it so simply responded, "Good morning, Gren."

"Here," Isla said as she pointed at the screen. "It's stable, thermally heated, the water is shallow…" her voice trailed off.

"Sure," replied Sincret.

"Sending coordinates," she said to Gren. His smile disappeared, Jadamara imagined holding any expression with his bruised face was an effort.

The view in front of her pivoted and the *Spear Throw's* nose bent downwards and accelerated until the banks of white writ-sand appeared. The ship swung around again, this time to become parallel with the shore and descended. Garvis spoke into the com alerting the ship's inhabitants to prepare for another landing. Jadamara sat herself in the empty Captain's chair and within the minute a loud moan erupted from the ship as it settled into the sand. A wave of relief washed over the deck's crew and behind her Jadamara heard cheering through the door.

Sincret smiled. He squeezed Isla's shoulder and grasped hands with Creline then Garvis. He beamed at Gren and Jadamara. "Okay who wants to go for a stroll?" he asked.

Jadamara and her former crew exited the *Spear Throw* behind most of the others. She walked beside JV and the two Painted Boys carrying him. Lights shone from the *Spear* Throw but did little to impede the thick darkness in front of her. She took a hesitant breath and tasted salty, slightly chilled, air.

JV said quietly, "It has been a long time."

Jadamara's vision adjusted, she saw the inhabitants of the ship lined up along the shore murmuring to one another, their prior enthusiasm stifled by the uncertainty of the shrouding darkness. There was nothing to see in vast emptiness, save for the orange glow of a river of lava far in the distance. Jadamara fixated on the river, trying the make out the patterns that ran along its banks, but despite her prolonged squinting, she could not decide what she was seeing. She turned her focus over to her other senses and became aware of an echo beyond the sounds of the nervous orphans; the drumming rumble of a great unseen waterfall. Her body felt lighter to her as well. She recalled the lessons from her education regarding the properties of writ-stone and the energy fields that emanated from it, which kept gravity stable throughout most their world and the labyrinth inside of it. A stable, but not perfect, grounding.

She turned to JV who had raised himself up on his left arm. He peered at the orange river in the distance and said, "This is a biopocket child. Your father named this place Glade's Embrace. The jungle you were staring at, it draws life from the thermal heat and water drip."

"Is this place dangerous?" she asked.

"We did not stay long enough to find that out. This particular system of tunnels leads to a dead end at the Great Lava Flows; not much property value to be found here."

Sincret walked past them, stripping off his clothes as he went until he was naked. He tossed them in a bundle on top of a boulder near the shore and stepped carefully into the water until he was waist deep. He turned and smiled to his crew, then splashed a handful of water at the ones closest to him. Hoots and hollers erupted from the lot of them as they charged into the water. The Painted Boys set JV down hastily and did the same. Jadamara sat next to him and went through her stretching routine. She felt the accumulated acid mobilize and work its way out of her stiff muscles. She groaned in satisfaction and savored her freedom from the confines of the *Spear Throw*.

Gren, the twins, and Weg looked onward at the fanfare. Gren stood with his arms crossed while the pilot picked at his hands in a meekly fashion. The twins whispered to each other, Jadamara could not see them well but wagered they were both blushing. Gren and the twins started for opposite directions, no doubt to seek some privacy, but Jadamara called out to them, "Stay together!"

Gren pointed down the shore, they activated lanterns and the three of them walked away together. Weg approached Jadamara and JV. "Would you guys like some help?" he asked.

"Sure," she replied. He didn't end up being much help, but after they stumbled into the water, the task of moving JV became easier. She released him and looked at Weg who stared for a minute. Jadamara removed her clothes down to her underwear and did the same for JV. Weg stood idly. She dragged JV a little farther into the dark water. It was not as cold as it looked, but she shivered nonetheless.

"Gah," JV said. He struggled for a moment, forgetting what they were doing. She never asked how he had managed until then without her. She assumed the Painted Boys performed most of his personal care. Dealing with the rotten was difficult work no one wanted to take on, Jadamara included. She loathed herself for her weakness. Still, his paralysis worked in his favor to stifle his involuntary spasmic movements, making him less accident prone and covered in significantly less feces as he lost control of his bowels. *He may be the first person to die of the second rot with dignity,* she thought. *When his mind finally unhinges, his body will bind him. But not his words.* She had no intention of hearing from JV the slander she had taken from her mother before her end. Yet for the moment, he simply stared up at her as she rubbed his neck while keeping him afloat.

They made their way to an area where a boulder rested in the shallows between them and the rabble. Once they were settled, Weg appeared from behind the boulder, an embarrassed look on his face. The lantern highlighted the scars covering his body. She ran a rag over JV, trying her best to keep him afloat, while Weg held their lantern close. The water was lukewarm but she couldn't shake a chill which rose from a nagging feeling of vulnerability. She paused to look around yet saw nothing but black. The gurgling of her drowning ward brought her back to the task at hand.

"Sorry," she said, but the sound of splashing continued, this time coming from the other side of the boulder. Ripples of water reached her and she lost her footing in the moment of panic and splashed into the water, almost taking JV with her. A hand grabbed her wrist and steadied her. She shook it off and wiped her eyes. It was Sincret.

"Sorry I didn't know anyone was here," he said. She rubbed her wrist. "You shouldn't be so far from everyone," he warned. He caught sight of JV. "Oh, I was looking for you. Are you all set then?"

"I want to go back," he said, shortly.

"Okay," Sincret replied. He met eyes with Jadamara, saw her icy glare and moved past her. He lowered himself deeper into the water and crawled towards the shore while lifting JV beside him. Weg stumbled next to them. Jadamara was glad for the moment alone. She dunked her hair, strained it, and scrubbed fiercely at the grime and sweat which still clung to her body. After a few minutes, she felt much better and a little more adventurous. She eyed the boulder beside her, found a footing and pulled herself up it. Once at the top she hugged her body for warmth and peered downwards. All in all, it was a very busy scene. She decided to stay and watch it for a while.

Most of the water faring children had left the lake and were drying themselves on the shore. A group of climbers maneuvered around the outside of the *Spear Throw,* evaluating the damage from the stolen loader which remained lodged in the skiff port at the rear of the ship. Painted Boys carried body after body out of the vessel, where they deposited them at a group of scrubbers in the shallows who passed them down a line then back to the stretchers. Jadamara guessed these were the severely rotted Uncut who occupied the other three cargo holds besides the med bay. She noticed a line of four motionless figures draped in white cloth. Several older girls brought them into the lake, one at a time, to clean their bodies.

Why even bring them along when they were so far rotten? She wondered.

She spotted Gren and several Painted Boys running a tube from the aft of the ship into the water. They sloshed into the lake with effort, Gren had never needed to fill from a body of water before but Jadamara was relieved to see he had the sense to seek an area deep enough to take in water and not the dirt. With a yelp and splash he disappeared downwards, then crashed back through the water's surface as quickly as he had descended, gasping and coughing. The Painted Boys seemed amused and braced themselves as he pulled himself back up by the tube. He pointed outwards then leapt from the shallows with the tube and swam farther in, towing it beside him. Jadamara smiled to herself and watched his ungraceful journey.

By the time she returned to shore and dressed, a large group had gathered around the four figures draped in white cloth lying motionless on the sand. The sweet smell of lightning oil drifted through the air and hung about in Jadamara's nostrils when she approached. She stood at the periphery of the circle with the older individuals, she noticed Cass amongst them, a solemn look on her face and her hand clasped around her right forearm. Jadamara's eyes returned to the funeral ceremony and Sincret who stood in the center of the circle.

"Palas, Candrine, Paluck, Gorivine. Find life in the wilds of the next world," he said. "Yield not to fear, fortune favors the brave." Jadamara had heard the service before. The Ehtlentin farewell was simple. Palas, Jadamara guessed, was moved away from the others. Isla walked towards the figure and began her eulogy.

"Palas was my sister…" she began. Jadamara turned and left quietly. Memories of her mother's funeral returned to her and she sought solitude. She walked to the shore and gazed out at Gren and the Painted Boys who were about fifty meters in the lake retrieving the tube. *The retractor-extender must have been damaged by the loader*, she guessed. A fire erupted as the pyre was lit behind her and the lake shined like it had not done before. She could see through the water a great way out, a sea of lobular lights shined back at her. The sight was beautiful and perplexing. The gems glowed yellow and danced back and forth, slowly drawing closer to shore, closer to Gren and the Painted Boys.

It took Jadamara a moment too long to realize what she was seeing.

"Come back!" she screamed across the lake at Gren. He looked up only to be dragged backwards under the water. Jadamara ran into the lake as fast as her legs could carry her. The gems quickened their approach to the shore, dark shadows now visible behind glowing, unblinking eyes. She heard screams behind her and turned to see the children swarming towards the ship in a mad panic. She returned her gaze to where Gren and the boys last stood but only saw white sprays of water. Glowing eyes closed in on her from the sides, she began backing away towards the shore, terrified and feeling sorely out of her element. She felt at her waist where her confiscated knife would have been. She turned and sprinted back towards the *Spear Throw* as quickly as she had come.

She caught sight of a pack of figures swarming onto the shore after the orphans. When they ascended from the water, the shadows stretched, giving rise to bodies much larger than their original shapes that remained hidden in the shallows so well. As they rose their snakelike swim turned to a profoundly fast run that was part hop and part gallop. Light from the *Spear Throw* glistened off their oily black coats and shining teeth. Painted Boys surrounded the ship, spears pointed outwards, steadily advancing towards the army of creatures as orphans retreated past them. Screams from youths still in the water and down the beach echoed and the creatures greeted the sound with siren howls of their own, which multiplied among them until it was all Jadamara could hear.

She was close to the shore now but the swarm cut off her path to the ship. She looked back and saw eyes almost upon her; she pushed herself forward. Blossoms of blue light from thrown spears were accompanied by deep booming sounds and exploded flesh. Several more spears flew at the creatures, creating an opening which Cass led a charge through. She fired her pistol madly around her to expand it. The creatures' necks stretched out to snap at her or weaved to avoid her blasts. She looked up and shouted something at Jadamara but it was lost in the howling cries.

Jadamara reached the shore the same time an immense pressure on her back pushed her over. The heavy weight expelled the breath from her lungs and pushed her face against the sand. Her vision disappeared, she tasted the salt in her mouth, but felt what strength she had left instinctively lift her body up. The weight rolled off her and she scrambled forward for a moment before a pain struck through her ankle and she felt herself pulled backwards towards the water. She kicked and struggled then turned to face her attacker. The creature released her ankle and crawled on top of her again. She extended her hands to push back on its slippery torso, but its neck stretched to make up the difference. She screamed and swept her own head back and forth to avoid its snapping teeth. Her grip slipped past its slick hide so she swung her fists wildly at the creature's snout. The monster only became more determined and caught her balled hand between its teeth, bit down hard then released. She withdrew and covered her head in her arms as it cocked back its head to launch at her again. A red flash from Cass's pistol illuminated the view through her forearms and she smelled smoking tissue. Another flash. The creature dropped its head onto her, burnt blood spilled from it onto her jumpsuit.

She pushed the body away, revealing more creatures encircling her. More red flashes flew by and the creatures howled then diverted their course. She clawed at the sand wishing her breath would return to her, and dragged herself until she could manage a crawl. She swung her head about to check around her. The army ahead was dispersing under the thrusts of Ehtlentin spears. Down the beach the squad of beasts that hounded her moments earlier tore at the draped deceased, the white sheets now shredded and stained red. Beyond them she could not make sense of what she saw: a tornado of light and fire with Sincret dancing at its center.

A hand grabbed the back of her jumpsuit and pulled her up. She stumbled but kept her balance and pulled herself the rest of the way by the waist of her rescuer. She saw gleam of a Painted Boy's sword clutched in a bloodied hand beside her as she rose. She didn't need to look any longer to know it was Gren. They sprinted the rest of the distance to the *Spear Throw* where Cass and KB held position. They sent another volley of red light around the pair hobbling toward them. Gren and Jadamara passed hordes of creatures dragging child sized bodies into the lake, most of them motionless but some still clawing at the ground.

They reached the ship. Gren urged her in, but against her better judgement Jadamara turned and searched the shore. The *Spear Throw's* engines whirred loudly behind her and expellers sent sand flying outwards from under the ship. Three more orphans passed her before she caught sight of Sincret running towards them.

"Fuck!" screamed Cass when it became clear the creatures would outpace and surround him. She made to run towards him but Jadamara snatched her arm and pulled her back. KB let out a high-pitched scream – a massive creature four times the size of the others ascended from the lake and hurtled towards them with unnatural speed. Its smaller counterparts snapped their teeth behind it, urging it forward.

"Oh gods," Cass said. More colossal shadows rose along the waterfront, one after another they slithered from the shallows then bounded towards the ship. The Painted Boy next to Jadamara activated his spear for detonation. It hummed and he launched it towards the closest beast. It landed short, a blue explosion sent a flurry of sand and smoke upwards. The creature burst through it howling a mad, hideous cry that put Jadamara's hair on edge. Cass and KB peppered it with shots that evaporated into puffs of smoke, leaving blackened holes along the creature's thick hide but doing nothing to slow it. They began backing into the landing ramp. Sincret appeared beside her, white haired and wounded, but somehow alive.

"Let's go!" he shouted. The four of them scrambled up the ramp which lifted behind them, but the first behemoth was upon them, wedging itself into the entry of the ship. Its neck extended forward, powerful jaws stretching open, closing on KB.

"Boooooop Booop!" it rang as it lifted into the air. The contrivance aimed downward at the creature and let off three blasts, two of which landed then dissipated as well.

The creature shook the contrivance violently then slammed it against the wall. KB dropped to the floor and the creature forced the rest of its body into the loading bay. Another's head filled the space behind it, holding the door open. Jadamara crawled backwards but the pain in her ribs halted her progress. The creature found its target. She searched around herself wildly for an escape. Sincret and Cass lay on the floor as well, though closer to the room's exit.

It is too far away, she thought hopelessly.

At that moment, she felt a force pull her from the metal floor, through the air, and over to the second deck. She accepted the unexplainable event without question and braced for a landing that would likely hurt. Her deadly trajectory changed midair and instead she landed against Sincret with a soft thud and a grunt. The creature shrieked in frustration and swiveled to follow. Jadamara opened her eyes to see Cass on the floor, unconscious and clearly afflicted with a deadly level of rot. Sincret's entire torso and arms were ridden with bleeding lesions from where the creatures bore into him.

He raised his left hand upwards and white fire swirled into existence around his fingertips. Jadamara became aware of a tingling in her hair and cheek. A force pulled her towards the light and she thought, *This is a pretty sight to end with.* Then the light disappeared. An exploding force reverberated in Jadamara's bones and toppled her and Sincret over. Smoke and gore exploded over her, the room darkened.

CHAPTER 6
Glade Jadamara

Jadamara awoke to the sound of a wailing baby. She could not tell how long she had slept, or if she had slept. A burning sensation coursed along her exposed limbs. She probed the tender skin along her arms and reached for her legs but could not manage to reach past the pain in her torso. Her eyes crept open.

She was on a cot in a curtained space of the medical bay. Beyond the sheets, she heard pandemonium and the Doctor issuing orders to control it. Jadamara lifted her head and found Sincret two beds down from her. The weight of her gaze stirred him awake. They looked at each other, both came to the same realization that they were alive, and sank back down into their cots. Sleep overtook Jadamara again and she fell back into it.

She awoke again some time later to a quiet room. The Painted Boys on either side of her were asleep. Sincret rested on crutches at the far end of the curtained area and spoke to the Doctor. He caught Jadamara's eye and gave a sympathetic smile. Culus noticed his distraction and turned, his face lit up as he did so. Jadamara couldn't help but return the smile. Sincret pulled the curtains aside and awkwardly hobbled out. The Doctor came to her side.

"Hey," he whispered. "How are you feeling?"

It took her a moment to respond, she felt no pain, only the softness of the cot below her and the breeze of recycled air moving around her. "You probably know better than I do," she mumbled. She tried to raise herself but he ushered her back downwards.

"You re-fractured two ribs," he told her.

"I left your brace on the beach," Jadamara interrupted. She felt strange.

"Aw, that's alright." He chuckled then continued. "Those creatures' bodies were coated with a paralytic, and highly toxic oil. I used Brenner's base to raise the pH. The burns go too deep for ointment to sooth though, and I'm reserving local anesthetics for the children. I put in seven stitches in your hand and three in your ankle, you will need them out in five days." Jadamara raised her arms above her and stared at them. "You are concussed again. All in all, you're not going to want to be aware of any of this for the next week. Here is something to take the pain away." He placed a vial of crystalline spheres next to her bed.

He's giving me xene salts.

"Take one crystal twice a day or as needed. I've already taken the liberty of giving you one about an hour ago. Don't take more than three crystals in a day. Jadamara, I mean it." He saw her suspicious expression. "Really, it's the same thing as the Omphala brands, a little less selective in its effects maybe, but it will do the job. Don't let the kids find it, they love this stuff."

"You got it," she replied, turning the bottle in her hands.

"There's more," he piped. "I need help. I've known these kids for a long time. They've suffered more than you know, but they are losing it right now. Between the injured and rotting on the ship, I have my hands full. Your man Gren insisted he command the bridge, thank the gods. JV is manning communications after Garvis poisoned himself cooking the creature that got inside." Culus rolled his eyes. "And I mean just cooking it too." He motioned towards a blanketed lump with a bright red face peeking out. The boy's nose and cheeks were inflamed and yellow mucus caked his eyes shut. "The little ones seem to like Weg, which is good, but there is no hell-storm like an upset adolescent Uncut, and there are many on board. It's got to be you." He waited while Jadamara caught up.

She sighed, the xene salts blended her thoughts together and she seemed to lose her words as they formed. Finally, she replied, "Yeah, no, that's fine. I'll keep them in line but I won't play mom, and first you undo whatever you did to lock my ingevein."

"Deal," he said. He removed the tool from his own ingevein and touched it to hers.

"JV is on the comm you said?" she asked.

"He was insistent," he replied, then more quietly, "his second rot has begun in earnest." When he finished with her, he went into his private tent and returned with a worn book. He sat on her bed again and brought his ingevein close to hers. A thousand crystals stored within it stirred awake to bend and cleave the writ-phenomenon drawn from its core. Ribbons of yellow light spat gently from the projector into a stasis field above his blue display, where they anchored together in circuit to create meaning where none existed before. The dancing illumination hovered from his wrist to Jadamara's upturned hand. She held it as the readouts on her fingertips scanned the data-bit he had given her. *It accesses the book,* she knew. She connected her own prints to the codes entry point, the locks around the tome unsnapped when she ran her fingers over them. As her thumb touched the first page, words sprang up from it.

In This City.

"My brother wrote it but never signed it. This is one of the last copies, it may be the only one, take care of it," he said. Jadamara shuffled through the pages. "JV told me your mother raised you in Corala." He looked at the dual redness of her hair. "Read what my brother had to say about your father's city and its people."

Jadamara made for the bridge as soon as she was in the hallway. She was slow to move but still quicker than she expected. The air was cool again and the ship was quiet. She silently passed the blanketed mass of children which had reformed in the main cabin. A flood of sadness swelled within her as she remembered those who never made it back to their fortress of security. She tried to push the thought away, but it was too fresh. She remembered the howls from the creatures as they hunted down the screaming children; she remembered their bodies being dragged into the lake.

She arrived at the bridge door and shook herself back to the present. Cots had been strung around the perimeter of the space. When she stepped in, Gren swiveled around in the captain's seat and scanned her up and down. The bridge crew glanced sideways at her.

He shook his head. "Nope."

Jadamara searched for JV and found him directly interfaced with a console at the communication station. He smiled and looked relieved.

"You need to rest now child," he said sloppily. Jadamara began to formulate a rebuttal when she realized the origin of his fractured speech.

"Exactly. You and the boy-genius just sit back," added Gren flippantly.

It took most of the bridge crew to separate Jadamara from Gren and remove her from the room. By the end of her uncoordinated assault on her first mate, JV was laughing so hard it seemed his whole body had regained movement. Isla stayed in the hall a moment longer after the others returned to the bridge. JV's cackle could be heard outside the door.

"We'll find you if something happens," she said and handed Jadamara the dusty tome she had abandoned. Jadamara could see the tears forming in the young girl's eyes though, and her hysteria abated at the sight of it. She choked on a laugh and knelt to hug the girl.

"You'll be just fine," Jadamara assured her.

"I'm scared," she whimpered.

"We are in a scary place, but we won't be here forever." She released the child, who sniffled, but seemed mollified.

It was only a few meters to her cabin. The door slid open to her, the lights were dimmed and Sincret snored softly on his fold out bed in the kitchen space. She undug the xene salts from her belt pouch and hid them within the wall, certain that she would not be taking them again. The adaptive equipment that allowed JV to sleep in her room was gone. Her bed was clear of the plastic partition that caught his waste, and looked inviting once more. A blue and silver glimmer sparkled at the center of it; her dagger. She touched the casing delicately, then drew the blade and danced it through her fingers. At last she caught it in her palm and felt her hand's strength against it, as well as the sting around her stitches.

She sat on her bed and felt alone.

Sincret's breathing quickened, silver plumes of mist spurt from his mouth. For a long while, Jadamara stared at him and wondered if he would wake himself. His last breath sputtered off then he stopped breathing completely. She waited, for what she felt like was an appropriate amount of time, until she stood up and slipped over to him.

It can't be the rot, she thought in disbelief. She wasn't sure how she felt about him succumbing to it at this point. He stole her ship, murdered one of her crew, yet also saved her life, and now trusted her with his. She could not explain the intuition that led to his success, or the fire he created from nothingness to obliterate the lake creatures; to deny she was curious would be a lie. She almost believed he would find an escape from his inevitable demise, yet he seemed as lost as any of them.

She peered over him. He did not react to her presence at first, but soon his eyes made a slow journey to her. He breathed again.

"Do you ever die in your dreams?" he asked.

His question took Jadamara aback. "No, sometimes I come close," she replied.

He pulled himself up from under the blankets and leaned against the wall. He rubbed his shoulder when he saw her staring. She waited, he decided to keep talking.

"He cleaves me in half, starting right here," he said, pointing to the skin he had been holding.

"Who cleaves you?" she asked.

Sincret looked authentically fearful. "I'm not sure, a man

with half a face. His eyes are on fire, then so am I. I burn, and wake up."

Jadamara hung on to the corner of wall between her and him. He looked like he wanted to say more.

"How do you feel when you wake up?" she asked.

He looked up again, as if surprised. "It depends on what I wake up to," he pushed himself up further, "you're easy on the eyes."

She scanned quickly over his body and instantly scolded herself. He was very attractive as well. She noticed the Ehtlentin symbol for "remarkable" painted on the proximal part of his left forearm. Her own father was painted "exceptional" and traded to Captain Gendine Jadamara of the *Spear Throw*. However, her father had taken his Captain's last name and was given the *Spear Throw* upon his death, where Sincret murdered his master and left his body slumped in a closet. That mark meant only his potential, not how he would use it. Her eyes lost interest and fluttered away.

"Goodnight," she said as she turned.

He sighed. When she was wrapped in her blankets he finally responded, "Goodnight."

Jadamara awoke the next morning to a metallic banging at the door. Sincret shot up from his bed but could not leave it. His expression twisted as he felt around his back. His wide eyes moved from his fingertips up his scabbed arm. Attempts to control his breath faltered as he prodded around the chemical burns. The door opened. A badly damaged KB rolled in haphazardly and belched out a series of tones. Long spindly extensions leapt from its body to roughly lower a table from the wall. It placed two plates of food and two cups of water on it, then reversed the way it came.

Jadamara broke into gasps. The burning on her skin made her want to tear it off altogether. Sincret clambered to the floor and began digging into a cabinet. He pulled out a vial of xene salts. Jadamara found her arm much more resistive to entering the wall space than the night before but also reclaimed the substance she discarded and swallowed a bitter crystal. She then stored a half dozen other crystals in her ingevein for intravenous injection later.

For the better part of a week, Jadamara bounced around the ship feeling unneeded and unnoticed, despite neither being true. The engines sputtered erratically throughout the voyage; a traveling embolism kept the ship's engineers running to release pressure around the vessel. Creline's voice sounded the alerts and proved, Jadamara thought, a soothing replacement for Garvis's hoarse yelp and JV's discordant commands. Ava rallied several of the more erudite orphans to help her retake inventory. Eva rounded on the rotting and wounded, who filled two of the four cargo holds; three if one counted the med bay. She lingered beside Cass longest. A group made up of warriors, engineers, musicians, children, and anyone seeking to converse occupied the main cabin, though the liveliness had left their words. The temperature spiked at midday, sending them all to seek cooler compartments.

Jadamara received an alert from the bridge on her ingevein. She arrived to a frowning Gren. Sincret stood with his arms crossed and his usual thoughtful look. Gren motioned to a projected image from one of the *Spear Throw's* hull cameras.

"We are being followed again," Sincret said. "It's a different ship this time. It's not showing up on radar but Isla snapped a picture of it."

Jadamara couldn't determine the make of the ship in the image, but there was one there.

"It looks Alliance. We should put the ship down," she suggested.

The crew looked at each other wearily. Sincret nodded and continued staring at the image.

"We need to do it now. It's about to get very hot," he said.

The corner of Gren's upper lip raised, he looked at Jadamara and shrugged. *Just a man doing his job once more. We're all friends then I suppose.*

They landed on a barren scape of writ-stone. As the *Spear*

Throw moaned and settled, so too did the bridge crew. Isla stretched and slumped over her station. Creline slinked off to bed. Jadamara activated lights on the hull to signal a parley. Sincret walked off the bridge, rubbing his hands. She followed.

The two prepared for the meeting they hoped would happen, and they hoped would happen peacefully. Jadamara pulled on a labyrinth-strider overcoat over her insulated jumpsuit. Sincret dug into a cabinet that used to hold cooking pots for the kitchen and tugged out an elegant metal case. He pulled a sky-blue cloak from it, but hesitated to unfold it. He finally snapped out of his reverie and shook the material loose.

The door opened, a boy Jadamara did not know waved for them to follow him to the bridge. They arrived to see the dust erupting from under the vessel that had pursued them. The ship had Alliance markings though it looked designed offworld, and showed signs of aging as well as recent battle. The body appeared large enough to contain either a squad of soldiers or a living space, while the cockpit indicated a small crew. The vessel had landed facing them, its two large wings folded over itself to make an "M" shaped roof. Jadamara guessed the wings contained the generators that masked the ship; she wondered what other equipment the vessel possessed. A light turret mounted on the starboard hull swiveled forward as a ramp lowered from the body.

Gren turned to the pair of them, looking doubtful. "I'm not so sure about this, but at least you don't look like a threat."

"Neither do they," said Sincret, hovering over Isla's console. "It's an observation vessel."

"Well that's good to hear, should we expect another one of your renowned first impressions?" asked Gren. Jadamara had the same question.

Sincret gestured to himself in an exhausted manor. "Like you said."

Elusive as always. Jadamara touched her blaster then her knife, focused into her ingevein and used its internal network to analyze her body. The act alone made her feel she regained some control of herself. Even still, the xene salts took away some sharpness to her coordination along with her senses. She needed to be as alert for the meeting as she could manage.

She was relieved to see the escort of Painted Boys waiting for them at the loading deck. Gore from days earlier still stained the floors and a salty rotten smell hung in the air. They approached the busted ramp, Jadamara noted its bent piston. She found the expected shriek of it opening to be everything she hoped it would not be.

Warm winds whipped at them once outside, bringing with it the smell of heated rock. Sincret's cloak shimmered with iridescent light and now appeared much more capable of breaking the hot winds. Jadamara activated the cooler on her suit. She looked back at the Painted Boys, it appeared they wouldn't be following them after all.

They walked down the ramp and around to the front of the ship. As they crossed its shadow, she stumbled, surprised by the hundreds of lava falls that demarcated the Flows and the blasting wind emanating from them. She got her footing and looked back at Sincret. He strapped a mask across his mouth and nose, gill like holes appeared around his collar. He furrowed the cloak around him to reduce its drag. A vision distorting veil drew down over his face. It took Jadamara a moment to realize it was anchor shielding: the smallest shield projection she had ever seen. *Another stolen asset*, she expected.

They pushed forward against the wind towards the metallic vessel. A figure walked down its boarding ramp. Reflected orange waterfalls danced upon her armor plating, blossoming and falling in upon themselves as the images warped with each step she took. A large black pillar followed behind her.

"What is that?" Sincret asked.

"It's a black box," she replied, "it's an Alliance protocol. There's a chance you won't be allowed here."

"Oh," he said. The way he drew out the words made Jadamara suspect he had heard of it before.

The black box floated from the scout and towards Jadamara, coming to a halt halfway between them. The pillar dropped onto the ground and layers of writ-shield sprung from it creating a bubble of safety where the meeting would take place. Jadamara walked closer until she felt the push of the field against her. Black boxes were essentially hyper intelligent contrivances with tattle-tale personalities. When set to neutral, a series of checks and balances made betrayal under its shield nearly impossible. However, that had not stopped her father from being murdered underneath the protection of his.

She reluctantly unstrapped her blaster and extended it to Sincret, it would be disabled if it passed through the shield. She took her knife from its sheath and cut her thumb with it then stretched the bleeding digit forward. Finally, she tossed the knife and its sheath through the field. She felt the force in front of her weaken and she pushed through the barrier. Sincret moved to follow but it closed behind her. He made a quizzical face. She shook her head and shrugged. The black box recognized her DNA and encryption on her dagger. Sincret would have had no reason to register with the Alliance systems, and without being identified, could not participate in the parley.

The anchor field disrupted almost all sound from passing outwards, as she moved closer to the center she knew he would have difficulty seeing her. The black box's writ-shield was grounded now, drawing energy from the massive writ-stone vein they stood on, rendering it practically indestructible to either of their ships' weapons. The Alliance officer entered from the other side. Jadamara searched for her knife but she eventually assumed the black box took it within itself. The Alliance officer approached. She removed her helmet, her hair had been tied into a tight knot underneath.

She evaluated Jadamara then said, "I am Lieutenant Eylea Denthor, Alliance Communications."

"I'm Glade Jadamara." She paused. "Captain of the *Spear Throw*. You've been following us for a while now. Why didn't you try to make contact earlier?"

"The Psyperials took Retine and Ehtlentin, I have no way

of knowing if you are a spy," she replied. Jadamara pondered the name. *Psyperials.* Hearing it somehow made the invaders more real to her. Eylea noted her expression and continued. "How much do you know?" she asked.

"Almost nothing besides what the orphans on the ship have told me. I saw them chasing down ships leaving over the surface, I hear they did the same in the labyrinth," said Jadamara.

Eylea nodded. "They did. Your ship has a knack for evading their patrols. Why come here?" She nodded to the wall of lava in the distance. Until yesterday, when Sincret completed the route, Jadamara had only suspected they were rounding on the Lava Flows. They were not relatively far from Ehtlentin anymore, but the magma created an impassable barrier between them.

"We're looking for something," Jadamara said. Eylea grew weary but also seemed to relax at the same time. Jadamara reminded herself to be forthcoming. "I'm Captain of the ship, but I'm not in charge. The boy waiting outside, Sincret, appropriated the *Spear Throw* to take him and his…" she paused, "followers, out of the city." This seemed to disturb Eylea.

"The orphans," she stated, for confirmation. Jadamara nodded. "Where would they even go?"

"Omphala maybe, or Corala if they were fools." Jadamara had gathered as much from the crew. She hesitated to share anymore.

Eylea laughed. "Ambitious, Omphala cuts all of their citizens. They would never accept them, but they may now. Either way, there is one way out of this network and that massive war pyramid occupies it. But not for long, the Alliance fleet is on their way." Jadamara expected as much, but did not feel as convinced about their success as the woman in front of her. She had been with an Alliance officer for a time when she made port in Omphala. Like the rest of the city, he enjoyed drinking, singing, and watching Omphalympian matches. To do his four favorite things in a day meant it had been a day well spent, and they spent many together.

An expired government worked tirelessly to provide the exquisite freedom their people savored, while keeping them blissfully ignorant to the mounting signs of their failing regime. The offworld power called the Ohwen, who helped build Omphala during the Great War, departed and left behind a cultural metropolis with no backbone. Every year another conflict too distant to diffuse escalated, corrupt politicians slipped through the law, and labyrinth cities under their rule became too dangerous to govern. The woman in front of her had the heart of her people, but also their presumptive attitude that the Alliance was too big to fail; that everything would work out.

"I intend to wait for them, I recommend you do the same," Eylea said. Jadamara considered the advice, Eylea turned to leave. "They'll be here in a matter of days. I am going back to the main corridor. I probably won't see you again, good luck." It struck Jadamara that she accomplished nothing in the time since they began talking. There were a hundred half-starved, injured Uncut on her failing ship.

Maybe she realizes it's pointless or she may just be a coward. "I understand you want to fight, but anything you can spare will help us."

Eylea turned. "I take vengeance on my enemies, I don't mull to them. Your ship is filled with criminals and traitors."

Jadamara searched for the meaning to her words. "You've spent too much time alone in that ship spying on us."

Eylea looked as if she had heard that before. "I have nothing to help you with: no medical supplies or rations, no technical components that would serve your ship. The Alliance will make their move soon and I will be there to give them information and advice, just as I have done for you."

A claw stretched from the black monolith and dropped Jadamara's knife at her feet. It deposited a jeweled booklet onto the scout's open hand as she walked away. Jadamara considered that the Lieutenant may be right after all. *The Spear Throw would barely limp out of the labyrinth as it is.*

The writ-shield retracted as the pillar rose, the influx of wind blew Jadamara off her feet.

She searched around for Sincret as she pulled herself up. *Maybe he went back to shelter.* It would be the simple explanation, but she knew better. She slowly turned her head towards the Alliance vessel. It was running through lift check. Jadamara scrambled to her feet at the same time Lieutenant Eylea began sprinting towards her ship. The black box turned on its side. It sped past Eylea and up the boarding ramp.

I'm too slow, she realized. She pressed into her ingevein to deliver a dose of stored xene salts. She felt the residual pain disappear from her body and pushed herself to a sprint.

Jadamara's limber suit served her well in the race. She caught Eylea at the rising ramp. Eylea threw herself into the opening and Jadamara rolled in after her. Before either could get to their feet, Sincret was above and over them, landing on the far side of Eylea. He grabbed her by the collar and brought his elbow down on her neck. His arm span worked for him and he stopped her swings short. He pinned her arm and brought his elbow down again on her shoulder. She screamed and grunted as her other arm connected with his torso. He came down for another strike but exploded backwards and landed against a wall console. The crackle of electric voltage from Eylea's taser ricocheted about the cabin. She rolled her shelled body over and clambered on top of the seizing boy.

Jadamara threw herself at Eylea as her fist reached the apex of its journey upwards. The weight of her body smashed into the woman and they both slid to the far side of the room where they regained their balance. Jadamara proved quicker again. She gripped Eylea's weaponized wrist with one hand, while the other twirled her blade from its sheath and to the Lieutenant's throat.

"Why?" Eylea rasped.

"Curiosity," Jadamara replied after a moment's thought. The taser on Eylea's wrist overheated under the commanding hack of Jadamara's ingevein. The device caught fire then burned out just as quickly. Eylea's eyes widened but did not venture against the knife pressed against her neck. A writ-shield leapt from Jadamara's ingevein and over her hand. She clamped it down on the smoking sleeve and put out the last of the flames. She looked down at her catch, then at Sincret. He rocked back and forth on the ground until he managed to unfurl and pull himself up.

"Thanks," he said. He stood up and looked uncomfortably at Jadamara. She stared down at the woman.

She is a disappointment and I am out of my mind.

"Any more surprises?" he asked Eylea while he rubbed his ribs.

"Yes," she answered.

"Me too," he said.

Jadamara interrupted her assessment of the woman to shoot Sincret a look of venom laced impatience. He jumped to, climbed up the ladder to the cockpit and sat in the crescent shaped pilot seat. "Well communications are still down on the *Spear Throw's* end. How do you do that light signal thing?" He didn't wait for anyone to answer but instead grabbed his cloak and lowered the boarding ramp. He ran outside and returned several minutes later with the five durable Painted Boys jogging behind him. They took hold of Eylea. Jadamara sat on the ship's pullout cot and felt she had earned a rest.

The initial rush from the xene tapered off quickly, lulling her into sleep. She laid down and soon Sincret's words phased in and out of understanding until she ceased registering them entirely. She slept soundly and barely stirred after they moved the ship closer to the *Spear Throw,* after successfully convincing Eylea to pilot the craft. Jadamara awoke and kept with momentum to swing her legs over the bed. She sat up and rubbed her eyes. Painted Boys stood staring at her. They began chiding her, speaking in Ehtlentin street urchin tongue she didn't fully understand. She sighed in annoyance and cracked her knuckles as she rose, stretched her arm across her chest and cast the boys an irked glare.

"Isn't there something you should be doing?" she asked.

Eylea glared down from the pilot platform.

She looks none too happy, Jadamara thought. *Coerced, but unharmed.* She looked beyond her and realized the ship had moved while she slept. The boarding ramp was open and a stretch tunnel connected it to the *Spear Throw.*

Sincret walked through the tunnel and up the boarding ramp. He acknowledged Jadamara with a tilt of his head then held up three fingers to the boys. "Two of you hang back." Without discussion, two of them moved towards the ramp. "Hey." He grabbed the taller one, Paridine, by his arm as he passed. The massive twenty-something year old Once-Cut dwarfed Sincret by comparison. "Gren knows the plan, make sure he follows it." The boy nodded but Sincret didn't release him. Instead he looked towards Eylea. The weight of his stare sent her back to her display. "Be ready for surprises," he whispered. The boy nodded again and Sincret let him go. Jadamara sighed once more.

"Are you coming with us?" he asked her.

"What?" she asked.

"Oh, right." Sincret wore the same sheepish expression Jadamara remembered from their first encounter. *He's nervous.* "I am going to take this ship into the Flows. I thought maybe you would like to come. These guys are coming." He motioned to the three Painted Boys: Creline and two others who usually lingered near Sincret.

Jadamara looked around, the boys had brought several crates on board, now strapped to the walls of the living cabin.

"Food, water, measuring equipment, thermal repellants..." he trailed off. He untucked a cloth sack from under his cloak. Jadamara recognized it as her personal care bag. He tossed it her way. She caught it and cocked her head to the side to express her thoughts about his invasion of her privacy. He met her with another nervous smile. "I can't tell you how long we may be in there or if we will ever come out, but we can't wait here any longer."

Our parley generated more attention than he hoped - doubt-

ful it will matter all the way out here. Her gaze lowered towards the ground as she contemplated the choice. She instinctively ran her fingers over her knife and thought of the doctor, of JV who slipped farther into the second rot each day, and the growing list of chores to accomplish on board the *Spear Throw*; some monotonous, others impossible. She felt guilty when she realized she would rather face the molten death of the Flows than return to the ship. She knew she wouldn't even return to collect the rest of her things, and wondered if Sincret anticipated that.

She motioned Sincret to the cockpit. He looked pleased, but not overly-so once he noticed her impatience had not lifted during her nap. He climbed up to the cockpit where Eylea and Creline were already waiting. Jadamara found a port which she could access the ship's data and functions through her ingevein. She pushed into the network: it was small, disorganized, and accessible – all the elements she did not expect to see with an Alliance vessel that seemed so well equipped. The ship's history, locks, and deeper data stores were absent or destroyed. It appeared to her that Sincret's novice hack of the ship had done more harm than good, or that Eylea had deleted the data. The labyrinth map she found was more comprehensive than most, but still showed them in uncharted territory save for the newly mapped trail which indicated Eylea had followed the same path as them to the Flows.

If this had fallen into Psyperial hands, we would have been found out, she surmised.

Hundreds of data points flashed in front of her indicating the ship was running through its lift-off protocols. She pulled away from the network and climbed up to the cockpit. The ship began lifting away from the *Spear Throw* and for the first time Jadamara could fully appreciate the damage to her ship; the loader remained lodged in the skiff port, bands of rust streaked across the hull, one of the rear engines was visibly shot, a gash on top of the ship replaced the node the communication module once occupied.

Not to mention the lesion on the belly of the ship letting in the hellish climates, she thought.

The ship continued to rise and rotate away from the *Spear Throw* and towards the pillars of fire.

"How are we going to do this?" Jadamara asked.

"Slowly?" Sincret replied in a sardonic tone. "Or maybe very quickly? Do I look like I've done this before?"

Jadamara exhaled and shook her head.

"What kind of shielding does this thing have?" she asked Eylea.

Sincret answered instead, "The same as the *Spear Throw*: vector and globe. You ought to..." but Jadamara was already down to the cabin again. She strapped herself into the seat behind the desk of what she now realized to be a secondary control board. She ran a physical wire from her ingevein into the port. She remained only partially aware of its presence and focused her attention on learning the shield controls in front of her.

The globe shields needed little oversight, they would respond to incoming projectiles unbiasedly. The vector shields struck from the anchor lenses towards projectiles to detonate or deflect them before they ever reached the globe layers. She found the functions for the vector shields and the measurement tools to monitor the environment around the vessel.

"What do you call your ship?" Sincret asked.

"It doesn't have a name," Eylea replied.

They flew along the wall of lavafalls until they found an opening between two giant streams and slipped through into another cavern. Lava oozed down from the chamber and surrounded them completely save for the cavern ceiling above them. The ship made a circle around the cavern, coming to a stop near a glowing flow. The ship hummed, Jadamara sensed the wings were folding overhead as they did when the ship had landed before the parley. She bent over the desk and stretched for the headset that was just out of reach. Her torso throbbed in resistance but she managed to grab it and secure it on her head while stumbling back into her chair.

"Whoa, what's going on. What are you doing?" she asked.

Sincret's voice buzzed on the other side. He seemed to be having difficulty also. "Oh, here we go," he finally said. "We have to punch through here."

Jadamara smacked her head. The two other Painted Boys shuffled uncomfortably behind her.

"I know where we're going!" buzzed Sincret through the headset again, Jadamara guessed he was responding to Eylea or Creline. "Vector shields forward," he said more clearly to Jadamara.

She angled the vector shields forwards and primed them, then routed globe shields to fixate on top of the ship. She approved of the decision to raise the wings as she noticed the latticed shield reinforcement the smaller surface area allowed for.

"Hit it," Sincret said.

Jadamara sent the vectored anchor energy forwards and through the lavafall. The ship pulled forward at the same time and punched through the opening, but not before the lava descended on them again and sent the shields' alarms whooping. She heard cursing on the other end of the headset, but the ship appeared alright. Jadamara accessed the cameras again. Another long expanse of cavern lay ahead of them, streams of lava drained from openings in the cavern ceiling, cascading down into a river of fire below them. The shields worked to keep the heat from reaching the hull, but even still Jadamara felt the temperature rise inside the cabin.

They picked up speed. Eylea wove the ship between lava cascades, Sincret searched for their opportunities to move deeper into the Flows, Jadamara monitored the systems, and the Painted Boys moved around nervously. As they moved further into the Flows, masses of lava began flowing not just below and around them, but above as well, occasionally swirling in arcs midair as it bent around gravity anomalies. A particularly powerful blast from the bubbling river below shook the ship. Jadamara could hear the hiss of pipes moving coolant through the walls and to the scorched belly. She cursed herself for being so focused on the fire falling from above to foresee the boiling bursts below. She equalized shields in both directions, then quickly angled vectors upwards to deflect a fireball plummeting towards them.

The shields' sirens alerted her again of their depleted state. She felt a tap on her shoulder. Gardinidine, one of the Painted Boys, handed her a canteen of water. She hadn't noticed them unload the crates or undress. He and the other occupant of the cabin, Karvine, were dripping sweat. She turned around quickly and felt glad to have her climate controlled suit, but even still she felt the sweat aggregating into drops on her forehead.

"How are we doing?" Sincret asked.

"The temperature around us is enough to melt this ship," she replied, "I can't guarantee we will be able to use the vectors much longer. We need to find a place to cool off."

She heard him conferring with his co-pilots. "Give what we've got to the globe shields, no more punching holes. We get to see why Eylea was given her own ship."

Jadamara transferred all the energy primed in the vector shields to merge with the globe and diffuse around the ship. *That should help with the heat also.* She decided that dying in a fiery ball of twisted metal would be punishment enough for agreeing to this misadventure and she didn't need to feel like she was in an oven leading up to that moment. She transferred a percent of energy to cooling the ship's interior and administered a dose of xene salts into her body. The feeling of weightlessness and adrenaline returned to her. She sprung from her seat and took in the cool filtered air. She unsealed her jacket from the leggings and slithered out of it. Sweat glistened on her arms and she felt the perspiration lose its heat to the coolness of the air swirling around her. She climbed up to the cockpit. They were arguing.

"Do you feel like indulging in any other creature comforts?" asked Eylea through grit teeth to her when her head appeared.

"Not everyone has coolant suits," Jadamara replied. Creline panted in the back seat but seemed to come out from his acidotic state as if on cue.

"So hot," he panted.

"There." Sincret pointed ahead to a towering writ-steel cliff that partitioned the massive flow of lava into two streams. Jadamara climbed over the center console to look closer. A triangle of dark shadow within the cliff hinted at the possibility of an inlet.

A cave, somewhere we can get out of this storm, she hoped. Eylea pushed the ship forward. As they approached it became clear just how massive the cavern's entrance was, but also how turbulent the flow of lava became against the writ-steel banks of the cliff. The river below them quickened pace and kicked up a storm of crackling orange lightning as it fell in waves upon itself. Jadamara could hear the thuds of residual voltage upon the bottom of the hull. The vessel's rattling ceased as it passed out of the storm and into the cave.

The temperature gauge confirmed that the cavern was insidiously hot. They hastily moved deeper into it. Eylea seemed nervous that a hemorrhage would leak onto them at any moment and kept her eyes upwards searching for the deadly glow. None ever came though, and they dove yet deeper into the cavern, and upon a discerning sight.

"What the hell?" Jadamara whispered.

Eylea slowed and fixed the lights to capture the image. "That is a surprise," she said simply. Racket from the Painted Boys below echoed upwards as well.

A massive Ehtlentin battlecruiser rested below them: a relic from an age long passed. Its hull was littered with scorched lesions and blasted welts. It looked as though it crashed violently into its resting place and melted into the cavern floor, the rear of it breaking from the front to rest at a different angle upon the uneven rock. Eylea swept the viewsceen to magnify the image when Sincret interrupted her.

"Let's keep going," he said.

They pushed onwards. *This is impossibly far for a writ-steel vein to stretch into the Flows*, Jadamara thought. The cavern narrowed and took on a red glow. She looked upwards and saw the slow creep of lava contained by the many facets of an enormous ruby crystal. It slithered ahead lighting the path before them.

"This is a crystal shoot," Jadamara said. "A writ-crystal tube, and we are traveling through it."

"Auspiciously so," said Eylea.

Sincret and Creline looked at each other, they did not understand her accent. Even Jadamara who learned Ehtlentin through Omphalic translations had difficulty understanding the woman at times.

Jadamara saw buildings ahead, growing larger as they crept forward. Soon, she made out turrets and several rows of ramparts, all blasted. More ships lay scattered around the walled chokepoint, this time unmelted. The observation ship's lights reflected off the silver metal scales of the larger frigates that had fallen upon the walls, and was swallowed by the blackened holes that tore through them.

"Where are we?" Eylea asked.

"A forgotten place," Sincret answered. He sighed and leaned back. He took a moment to think then looked at Jadamara. "This crystal is unlike any most people will ever see. We are floating through a pyruvutase crystal. A big tube of it." He started laughing, then a look of horror passed over him. The ship approached the melted gate. On either side, where the writ-steel met the cavern wall, sat two massive turrets which spanned from the cavern floor to the ceiling. Barrels upon barrels of artillery protruded from them. The exterior of the buildings showed no signs of damage, but the few holes blown through them indicated the fighting had occurred inside.

"I've seen wreckage like this before; those blast holes are from Mongrelai boarding crews," Jadamara said.

They passed through the twisted hole in the gate. They could see the turn of the cave ahead and a light glowing beyond it. The scene immediately below them was more of the same; fishy Ehtlentin ships punched through with holes or burst open from inside. Anything more detailed than that was hard to make out, and part of Jadamara did not want to find out what more she would see. The light which bounced from the distant end of the corridor had an artificial whiteness to it. As the observation vessel angled around the corner, they saw for themselves what their scanner had already gathered.

The light was indeed artificial, and shone dimly from an enormous array of lights which promised so much more potential. Overgrown crops, now dead, covered the ground below. Ahead, a facility had been carved into the rock against the far wall and a massive orange dreadnaught sat abended in the plaza before it. Signs of battle traced up the steps from the courtyard to the structure's entrance. Fallen snubfighters and craters littered their approach to the structure. In the light, she could make out the ships scattered across the ground and was certain they didn't all belong to the Ehtlentin defenders.

Sincret started breathing heavily. Jadamara turned to see him wipe away the beginning of tears. He continued the motion into a stretch, all the while fixated on the derelict Mongrelai ship, aware and avoidant of Jadamara's eyes. "This is it then, fuck," he said at the climax of his spread. "There are things here that can help us."

Creline stared at Sincret as well, alarm apparent on his face, and terror.

"Sincret," he whispered.

Sincret nodded, "Yeah, I know."

Creline's shock turned into a smile. "The Dreamer," he said, "what a bad joke."

A smile flashed on Sincret's face too. "Remind me to rub this in Cass's face when we get back."

So he dreams of more than just being murdered, Jadamara suspected. She felt like she knew what she needed to know. Eylea did not.

"What is this? Where are we?" she asked.

Sincret ignored her. "Land near that vessel," he said.

His response perturbed her. She released the controls earning a glare from Sincret. The ship came to a stop and hung in the air below the great array of lights. Eylea swiveled her seat around and seemed unfazed. "I'm not scared of you, boy."

Sincret leaned back and looked at Creline who leaned forward. "You flew this ship through the Flows, skillfully I'll add, but you don't want to land it?" he asked.

"I don't want to land it near that." She nodded to the dreadnaught. Jadamara found herself agreeing with the Lieutenant.

"That's a Mongrelai warship," Jadamara said, staring down at the behemoth. She doubted Sincret didn't already know, but when he didn't say anything she looked over to see him slowly nodding, deep in his thoughts again.

Creline pointed at a blasted building, erect enough to shield their ship and large enough to fit it. "There," he said.

Eylea sighed, and dropped the ship towards the skeleton of rubble. She mumbled to herself unintelligibly. The ship descended quickly and Jadamara felt her stomach leap. The *Spear Throw* she had grown used to was a slug of a vessel, any quick moves were liable to blow a stabilizer on the best of days. Eylea seemed to relish in the maneuverability her small craft granted her. Debris littered their landing zone but Eylea lowered them into a space which had been relatively spared. The torched walls of the building seemed to rise above them as the ship settled. Sincret searched through the various data points the ship had collected since their arrival to the room.

The air outside was filtered and breathable. Gravity was stable, though a fair bit heavier than on the surface of the planet. A final rumble signaled their journey through the fires of the Flows, and the emptiness of the tunnels had ceased. *At least for the moment,* Jadamara thought. She knew eventually they would need to return the way they came.

Eylea unstrapped her belt and grasped her hands on the armrests as if to rise, then thought better of it when she saw Creline's eyes vigilantly monitoring her moves. *Always on guard.* Jadamara had been the recipient of his discriminating surveillance for the past weeks. To have it released from her gave her a sense of... something. *Am I part of this crew now? Am I that eager to be double crossed?* She thought of Eylea's comment about her contentment with imprisonment. *Sincret opened the ship to us. He realized then that we would not survive if we didn't work together, the same goes now.*

She took one last look out the viewport in front of her. *I am in an ancient chamber within the Flows, gazing at a sight no one has seen for hundreds of years.* Sincret had taken her here. She could have lived and died with her life story the same as countless inhabitants of the surface. She knew without a miracle her story would end the same way her mother's had. *This boy may be my ticket to break the cycle. If the Alliance Historic Council could just see this, surely that is worth the price of a second cut.*

Her mind wandered far into the fantasy before snapping back. She gave Sincret a look, suddenly overwhelmed with an urge to have him. He looked at her quizzically, sensing her conflict and hesitation to return to the cabin. Finally, she exhaled and slid down the ladder.

Sincret followed her down, then Eylea with Creline close behind. The Painted Boys had already armed themselves with short spears. The crystals glowed dimly blue. *Almost out of charge, but still sharp*, she thought. She pulled her jacket off its resting place on her seat, and back over her tank. She zipped it up her chest and around her waist, Sincret shrouded himself in his cloak, the Painted Boys put on their weaved coats.

"Ready?" Sincret asked. They nodded in response. He looked around for the release handle. "Um."

Jadamara pulled up the ship's functions on her ingevein and the clamps securing the ramp snapped open. It lowered then unfolded to reach the ground. A faint fog billowed up the ramp before they moved down it. Sincret was the first out followed by Creline and Jadamara. Gardinidine and Karvine followed last with Eylea between them. They climbed over the rubble surrounding their landing zone and through a hole in the skeletal wall. Once through, they surveyed the Mongrelai ship in the distance. Carefully, they approached it from its starboard side.

Massive dirty rectangular orange plates covered the ship,

with numerous brown plates that intermittently broke the arrangement. Bends in the plating around those spots indicated that the panels were placed to reinforce lesions in the hull. A grey double-barreled cannon mounted near the front of the vessel seemed out of place. The nature of its embedment hinted that it had also been an afterthought to the design of the ship. Along the same side but closer to the rear of the dreadnaught, the paneling ceased and the hull fell in upon itself to create an alcove. Within the space, large claws, magnetic pads, and a windowed control cabin accommodated the docking of smaller vessels. The more Jadamara scanned over the ship, the more apparent it became that the owners of the eclectic dreadnaught did not care for aesthetic tact. The harsh contrast of the ships components conveyed a different message.

The Mongrelai had been a subject of interest for Jadamara since she was a child listening to the stories her mother and JV told her about the spacefaring warriors. When she began her education, she poured over the videos and accounts of their invasion. They waged war upon the planet for 30 years. In their wake they left civilizations, populations, and almost all evidence of their occupation obliterated. Ehtlentin was one of the last cities they took. The Alliance, which sprung from the necessity for unification and became reinforced by the offworld Ohwen, drove them from the mountain just days after they conquered it. The Mongrelai worked quickly to erase the history of the city, but failed to do so entirely. For years, curator analysts scoured the corpse of Ehtlentin. The discoveries they made represented nearly all the insights Jadamara had read about Mongrelai culture. Soon after losing Ehtlentin, the barbarians left the planet completely. Omphala became the seat of control for the Alliance, and a new age dawned. For all anyone knew, this dreadnaught was the last remnant of the Mongrelai's incursion left on the planet.

She began to truly comprehend the enormity of the relic as they drew closer to it. It stretched 1000 meters in length, and towered eight stories above them; the front third of the vessel

STAR STORY BOOK ONE: ANCHORED

rose two stories higher still, creating a spine-like protrusion at the top. They proceeded downwards along the wide street and lost sight of the ship as buildings, boxy and concrete unlike those of Ehtlentin city, blocked their view.

Evolving signs of death appeared as they cleared the last gap between fallen buildings. Their approach put them in the path of blasted craters and skeletons draped in melted scale armor. They could clearly see where the dreadnaught's cannon blasts had swept forward towards the grand staircase in front of the ship, leaving a torched trail along its path.

"C'mon," urged Sincret as Eylea and Jadamara fell behind.

They passed through the scarred terrain. When they reached the ship, their path redirected to walk alongside it. The grizzled vessel seemed even more imposing up close. Jadamara silently speculated about the arsenal that once was, or may still be, present within the intimidating mass of metal. It was clear the ship had once housed at least a squadron of snubfighters, though Jadamara did not consider their beastly three manned crafts in the same classification as the Alliance single manned ships. Hatches appeared every hundred meters. Whether they were simple exits or launching points for the signature landing pods their foot soldiers dove into cities with, Jadamara could not tell.

The courtyard tile had cracked and caved under the force of the ship's hasty landing. The indention reached its greatest depth as they arrived at the head of the ship where the contest for the staircase had begun. More torched skeletons, all armored in Ehtlentin scale plate, littered the blasted steps. Some of them curled against barricades while others appeared to have attempted to retreat before their fiery ends. Despite the sterile feeling of their environment, the smell of decomposed carcasses drifted past them.

"Wow," said Creline simply. His eyes swiveled up and down the staircase which ended 30 meters above them. The Painted Boy named Karvine moved to flank the group, while the other, Gardinidine, remained behind, his eyes fixed on Eylea but clearly distracted by the scene around him.

They kept moving forward until they reached the base of the stairs. They looked back at the ominous ship they now seemed to be in the direct scope of. A massive grey rail gun, buried in the vessel, poked a few meters from an enormous cavity in the front of the ship. On both sides below the gun, large metal ramps extended to create a bridge from the dreadnaught to the cracked ground. Jadamara could not see more than twenty meters inside the vessel, where darkness beat out the dim light. She shuddered.

There's the entrance, she guessed.

The Mongrelai had set up their own barricades around the ramps, equally blasted as those on the staircase but absent of corpses.

Jadamara looked at Sincret. His mouth hung partially open and his eyes drooped sleepily as he surveyed the staircase. He broke his stare and his eyes slowly made their way to Jadamara. *He looks awful,* she thought.

"You ought to rest," she said. He shook his head slowly. She took his arm in her hands, he jumped but did not pull away. She unlocked the seal of his jumpsuit and peeled his sleeve back. Thick blue veins from his rotting teslac ran throughout his arm.

"I'm just tired," he responded.

"So was Cass, the rot will win out if you don't have the energy to fight it." She scowled at him. He closed his eyes and sighed, his body began to sway as if giving into exhaustion upon suggestion. Jadamara became aware of his soldiers' eyes on her and his arm still cupped in her fingers. Sincret's eyes burst open and darted nystagmantly to regain focus. He squeezed Jadamara's forearm in return, willing energy back into his body. He pulled away from her, his hands rose to wipe the drowsiness from his eyes.

"Hundreds of years ago, Ehtlentin's city shield was considered impenetrable. It protected the city for thousands of years, until the Mongrelai found a way to bring it down. I was apprentice to a Norrin Dimeric, an offworld shield engineer hired by the Ehtlentin Council to restore them. When we looked inside the shield generators, we found what everyone else had; massive pyruvutase crystals with no power source." He took a breath. "But, there was an energy relay, indecipherable to everyone else except my master." He chuckled again. "Which is ironic because it is enormous. We are standing in the facility that houses it." Sincret turned to Creline and began speaking in Ehtlentin slang.

At first, Jadamara couldn't fathom how energy from this deep in the Flows could reach the city. As she thought on it though, it made sense. Writ-phenomenon was as fluid as the stone it emanated from. When anchored to solid points, such as a large body of writ-stone, its physical properties manifested as solid barriers. Though she had never heard of such a technology, it stood to reason that energy transmitted through the fluid writ-lava could reach Ehtlentin like a boat is carried by water. *And a power strong enough to send that signal would have to be drawn from a massive energy source such as the Flows, and channeled by the crystal around us.* The mental exercise exhausted her, she wasn't sure if her estimate was even close, but was too tired to explore the concept.

Karvine and Gardinidine pushed Eylea away from the stairs and retrieved a pair of handcuffs from Creline's backpack. She growled and pulled away.

"What is this?" she asked. "If you think you will get that around my wrists, you'd best be prepared to have yours broken." Her response did not surprise Jadamara, but the aggressive twist of her intonation did.

We took her easily enough, Jadamara thought, yet the Alliance officer's eyes blazed with violence.

"You haven't inspired us with confidence, they will be on only until we return," Sincret answered.

"If you return," she said, backing away from the Painted Boys. Karvine and Gardinidine moved at her from two directions in coordinated fluency. Karvine's fist aimed at her torso while Gardinidine dropped low to tackle her waist. Karvine's fist arrived first and met Eylea's hand as she chopped it away then she swung a wide hook that never reached him. Her body lurched back as Karvine took her to the ground. He crawled up her, pinning down her legs with his. Her elbows flew at his face, landing three times until her head jolted forward and bit down on him, pulling away with a bloody ear in her mouth. Gardinidine fell upon her. He pinned her shoulders to the ground and attempted to clasp her hands down as well.

Eylea's knee came up between Karvine's thighs and landed in his groin. The force and pain pushed him over her and clumsily into Creline. Gardinidine picked up the fallen handcuffs and threw himself onto her. He fell backwards a moment later with Karvine's knife protruding from his gut and a look of shock. Creline's foot landed against Eylea's face, then repeatedly against her torso until she stopped moving.

Gardinidine pulled the knife out from his body, Sincret clasped his hand against the bloody spot in his weaved jacket. Karvine lay clutching his groin and moaning. Jadamara twirled her dagger into a reverse grip and approached the crumpled woman.

Creline secured the handcuffs around Eylea and pulled her up. Her breath sounded bloody and weak but she was still conscious. When he had her on her knees, she jumped upward, the crown of her head catching him under his chin. Her hands drew the blue scimitar at his hip as he stumbled backwards, and in one motion she swung it around to Jadamara who raised her dagger between her and the arcing blade. A clang resonated from the meeting of the crystal weapons and Jadamara put enough distance between them to anticipate another attack. Eylea raised Creline's blade again as Jadamara reached for her blaster. The savage look burning in Eylea's eyes became diluted with fear. Blood trickled from her mouth and nose, and the look on her face told Jadamara she knew there was no beating the weapon trained on her.

But she knows I'm not a killer.

Jadamara's eyes flitted towards Sincret as he rose from Gardinidine and made for Eylea. Eylea saw the draw of Jadamara's eyes and swiveled. Her blade came down on Sincret but her downswing wavered just long enough for his hand to clasp her throat. She choked in his grasp yet managed to rotate the blade into a perpendicular position, ready to sink it into his back. She spat out an unintelligible sentence then dropped the weapon but kept her hands raised in surrender. Sincret continued pushing her backwards by her neck. His hand separated from her throat, yet her labored breathing persisted. She dropped to her knees and clutched her stomach, heaving the contents of her last meal on the ground. Jadamara looked between them and saw the subtle bending of light between Sincret's fingers, and faint iridescent waves washing over Eylea.

"Sincret!" Jadamara shouted, "she surrendered!"

Her voice seemed to frustrate him, he swept his arm to the side, sending the officer sprawling to the ground with the same telekinetic force which had saved Jadamara days earlier. The residual force emanating from his hands almost blew Jadamara over as well.

Where is that power coming from? she wondered, astounded again by Sincret's supernatural display.

Eylea phased in and out of consciousness and Sincret fell backwards, exhausted. Jadamara stayed focused on the crumpled officer. She side stepped in an arc around her, arriving by Gardinidine's side. He groaned and tenderly touched his wound. Karvine was on his feet again, still clutching his groin. Creline's hand clasped against his mouth as blood oozed through his fingers. He removed his hand quickly enough to spit out a bloody mucous bolus then returned it, wincing as it contacted his lips.

She managed to do a number on us, Jadamara thought. *So why did she hesitate when she faced Sincret?*

Jadamara lowered herself over a pale Gardinidine. His breath was light and rapid, every movement sent flashes of pain across his face. Sincret knelt beside him wordlessly. His face was a mix of concern and rage. His eyes were grey again, but behind them Jadamara saw fire. He touched Gardinidine on the shoulder then picked up the bloodied knife by his side. He rose again and walked towards Eylea who had regained enough sense to realize what would happen next.

He sunk the blade into her stomach.

She coughed a word that sounded like "wait" but was lost to the throaty gargle that followed.

Sincret removed the blade and stepped back. For a moment the cavern was silent, even the sound of Gardinidine's panting ceased. They watched her writhe on the ground.

"Sincret," Jadamara said, but he did not acknowledge her. Instead he walked by her and spoke to Creline.

"Fix him as best as you can." He handed him the knife. "When she stops moaning, stab her again." Sincret dropped the knife in Creline's open hand, who nodded and returned to digging through his bag.

Jadamara stared at the officer twisting on the ground and felt sick. She sensed the weight of her own weapons in her hands, and the weight of her decision on her mind. She sheathed them and approached the woman, then thought twice about it. When she turned back, she saw Sincret staring at her. The warmth had left him and the coldness of his grey eyes seemed to give him insight into her thoughts. Jadamara sighed and looked down for a moment then met his eyes again and shook her head in disapproval. Without a word, he turned and began climbing the stairs.

She looked back once more at the officer who had slunk herself over to a pillar, leaving a trail of dark blood that stood out against the white of the stone. *You fool,* she thought.

Jadamara covered the first flight of stairs in three strides then looked back at the Painted Boys. "We may still need her. Stab her again if it makes you feel better, but keep her alive," she said. Creline looked at her and blinked. Then, to Jadamara's relief, nodded. She walked at a steady rate until she caught Sincret a quarter of the way up, walking beside the wall that rose alongside the stairs.

"You are such a dumb ass," she said, hoping her crassness would ease the tension. It did not.

"Fuck you," he said.

"Does this white hair, grey eyes thing happen exclusively when you are being an asshole, or what?" she asked.

"Fuck you," he said again. "Give me that look that you gave me down there once more and I'll plant a dagger in your gut."

They reached a platform halfway up the climb, the Painted Boys disappeared below it. Sincret lurched to the side as Jadamara threw him against the wall. He buckled underneath her as she kicked out his legs. She put her dagger to him. "Threaten me again, and I'll swipe this dagger across your neck." He looked at it, then at her. Slowly, he drew his hands from his cloak and sprinkled a purple powder line across the blade, then ran his nose along the glistening crystal, inhaling the xene, leaving only a faint blemished residue behind. His eyes rolled back in his head and he began laughing.

"Then do it and get it over with. You won't. I know it. Eylea knew it. You know it." Jadamara only half listened to him, her focus was on her knife.

"You don't need my help getting killed," she said absently. She sat back and focused into her ingevein, seeking the euphoric release of xene salts into her own circulation but no rush came to her.

She withdrew her knife and opened the compartment where she stored her salts. Sincret squirmed underneath her. "Not so fast," she said, then moaned. Her cartridge was empty. "Damnit."

Sincret's eyes were still rolled to the back of his head. She took the vial of powdered salts from the pocket he withdrew them from. She had never taken them in through her nose, doing so felt like a misuse of the medication, but she laid out a line on her knife all the same and proceeded as Sincret had. The burst of pleasure hit her mind harder than it ever had before, making her sway forward and back. Every turn of her spine and stretch of her muscles sent shivers running through her.

She felt an observer of her own actions rather than the agent of them. She restrung her legs around Sincret and pressed her hips to his. She drew her knife across his cheek. He did not wince or open his eyes but inhaled deeply as blood leaked from the cut. Jadamara's tongue licked the dark red from his wound then moved into his mouth. Their lips pressed together and remained so until the metallic taste had all but disappeared.

When they finally parted, Jadamara pulled his lower lip between her teeth until his eyes opened and she released it. She raised herself from him and offered him her hand.

"C'mon," she said. He took her hand and she pulled him up. She touched his cheek. "If anyone asks where you got that, you tell them it was from me. If they ask why, you tell them it's because I hate you." She sheathed her knife and began ascending the stairs again.

"Alright," she heard Sincret say behind her.

They arrived at the top of the stairs. Beyond them two dozen bodies laid sprawled against the ground in front of an enormous gold and silver gateway embedded in the cavern wall. The bodies were not just Ehtlentin this time. Amongst the numerous scaled corpses and scorch marks, Jadamara saw three armored Mongrelai figures on the ground. She jogged towards the nearest one, then stopped short when she realized the danger of her haste. She inhaled sharply.

The Mongrelai was humanoid, about six feet tall, with a wide build. A heavy blue weave jumpsuit covered its body with red crystal plate armor over it, exposing only the joints needed to allow movement. Scorch marks riddled the crystal and darker stains spilled from the singed holes in the weave. Along both its arms, screens, blades, and other instruments of death had been integrated into the armor, giving the warrior the eclectic, yet deadly, appearance like the dreadnaught it had arrived in. The weave ended at its neck where it disappeared underneath a silver helmet inlaid with a single horizontal band of dark crystal glass where eyes would have peered through. Jadamara wanted a closer look, yet part of her feared that even now, the warrior would rise to meet her in one last violent act of tenacity.

When she did not pull herself away, Sincret approached

behind her. "We need to keep moving," he said. "Our friends..."

"Yeah," Jadamara interjected. "One moment."

She moved forward and knelt beside the body. Her left hand lightly touched the ruby chest while her right hand snaked up the weave around its neck and underneath the helmet. She heard Sincret croak her name as she fumbled for a divide; some way to remove the metal piece. Her fingers brushed over a protrusion inside the rim of the metal and a light glowed from within it, showering her hand in a red glow and excruciating pain.

The pain pulsated up her arm, the agony of it stealing her breath. She inhaled laboriously and withdrew her cramped, twisted hand. She was aware of Sincret peering over her, trying to see what had happened.

"Ouch," she said finally. "Okay don't try that." She waved her hand to loosen the tensed muscles, but the movement exacerbated the knotted ache, and rubbing it only had the same effect. She backed away from the crystal man and turned to see Sincret observing the once magnificent doorway which had been blasted in.

She approached behind him and gazed down the long hallway that dove into the cavern wall. The doors were warped inwards but no sign of soot marred the gold and silver that still gleamed in the dim light. Beyond them, the corridor's floor, walls, and ceiling had been carved directly from the cavern's crystal walls, and their dark matte surfaces eventually gave way to the deep red crystal they had glimpsed along their journey. The corridor wavered and shifted, lines of iridescent colors flashed for milliseconds at a time, giving sight to the writ-shield that stood between them and the hallway within.

Sincret approached and stretched out his hands, feeling the repellant properties of the force field barring their entrance.

"Well?" she asked.

He unclipped his cloak from where it was doubled up over his shoulders and it billowed outwards, wrapping around his body. He then raised the hood over his head, and his arm to his shoulder, inviting Jadamara into the space within.

"It will be tight, but we can both fit," he said.

It suddenly dawned on Jadamara. "So, this is your secret to breaking and entering?" she asked rhetorically.

He flared the cloak. "Functional and fashionable. Let's go."

Jadamara pressed against him and hoped her brevity conveyed her discomfort. He didn't waste any time either and soon they were both totally enveloped by the cloak.

"Okay, slowly," he said. They shuffled awkwardly through the doorway. Jadamara felt a pressure on her right shoulder as it pressed against the field, then a heavy force downwards as they proceeded through it.

"Whoa, that's... Whoa," said Sincret as he struggled underneath the force. Jadamara felt him ready to collapse upon her when they ejected from out of the other side of the shield and tumbled onto the floor. They looked at each other for a moment, then down the hallway which ran a great distance into the crystal. They rose and continued forward. Instead of the blasted craters evident outside, the walls of the corridor were melted away where blasts had sunk into the crystal, yet the pair found no bodies accompanying the signs of battle.

They were twenty meters from another gold and silver door, warped inwards as its predecessor had been. Sincret's eyes remained focused ahead. The light from outside began to fade behind them, and the dark walls swallowed the rays from the glowing rods above before they had a chance to illuminate their path. Only a blue glow from the other side of the bent doors showed clearly where their destination lay. Sincret pulled at the door, willing it open just a bit farther to slip through comfortably. Jadamara jumped when she entered and removed her blaster.

The room was large, octagonal, and lined with screens which continued to run data points across their blue surfaces. In the center of the room sat a single cylindrical console and a Mongrelai resting against it, legs folded and hands placed on its knees. Beyond the hulking metal figure, a host of twenty corpses, Mongrelai and Ehtlentin, had been laid out and incinerated, their armor husks all that remained.

Jadamara suddenly noticed Sincret's hand stretched in front of her. His eyes were closed and head bowed in deep thought.

"Wait," he whispered. Slowly, he looked up and to a far wall where an explosive charge blinked ominously, then his eyes were drawn back to the motionless Mongrelai and a similar, though larger, explosive by his side. He moved delicately to the wall first and removed the metal casing with a toolkit from the inside of his cloak. After a moment of tinkering with the device, he exhaled and relaxed, then nodded to Jadamara who remained where she stood even after he disarmed the second bomb next to the Mongrelai. Sincret sat on his knees next to the unmoving warrior.

The air hung still in the closed space and Jadamara became faintly aware of the soot stirred by their presence. She brushed a wisp aside and slowly crept towards Sincret. He raised his hands hesitantly, as if figuring out the correct journey they should take to the Mongrelai. Jadamara was relieved to see it wasn't breathing, then thought twice about her sense of security as she realized she didn't even know if they breathed at all. But the figure did not notice Sincret's hesitant hands hovering in front of it. Finally, his fingers touched the outside of its helmet, traced over the mouth region and the grooves which must have facilitated its speech. Jadamara gulped and took a step forward as his hand slid under the helmet, but stopped herself from interrupting him.

The same red glow emanated from under the helmet, but Sincret did not withdraw his hand, instead his fingers seemed to be probing over the box that Jadamara had touched earlier. A second later the red glow disappeared and the sound of air escaping through the tight gap cut through the silence. Sincret clasped either side of the helmet and slowly raised it.

The face staring back at them was his own. *But not exactly his,* she realized. The high cheekbones and well-shaped jawline were uncanny in their resemblance, as too was the sense of familiarity she felt looking at his resigned expression. However, instead of green eyes cut through with veins of hazel, the man had vertical slit pupils like those of the snakes native to Corala which blended into the colorful buildings and frightened Jadamara as a child. When she looked closer she saw hints of grey seeping outwards from inside his pupils, eventually giving way to bright yellow iris. The unnatural white of his hair, which also appeared intermittently on Sincret, did not completely cover his head, but started at the roots then morphed to the dull blonde that cropped the top of his short haircut. The presentation was enough to send shivers through Jadamara, and the eeriness was made more morbid by the man's gauntness which she had seen on the faces of starving orphans back in Ehtlentin. *He starved to death,* she guessed.

Sincret sat back and sniffled, then pressed his hands against his face and shook his head. *Nothing prepares a person for this, and I don't even know what this is.* She did not understand how she could be seeing what she saw, it was clear to her that Sincret felt the same.

Without looking away from the man, he said, "We stormed this place. The journey, the fighting, reaching this point – I remember it through a veil, but the loneliness of being trapped, alone, that is vivid." He wiped tears away and suddenly looked his age. Jadamara wanted to move closer but he got to his feet and slouched against a wall opposite of himself. Within the minute, he had fallen into an unintentional sleep.

It's about time, she thought. She felt tired as well and uncertain how long it had been since she had a proper rest. She looked around the room and surmised she would not get one here. Though there was another door against the far wall, silver and gold like the others, she decided not to enter it; not to leave Sincret or the safety she assumed would be compromised by journeying alone. Instead, she sat a meter away from Sincret and watched him sleep.

CHAPTER 7
Glade Jadamara

She dozed in and out of sleep herself, but snapped to occasionally and looked over at the snoring boy next to her. A short time later, she awoke to see him standing by the console staring at her.

"You may be excited to learn that we are sleeping a mere hundred meters away from possibly the largest active energy field on this planet. The shield we passed through doesn't just seal the entrance, but runs around the entire installation to contain it."

Jadamara wiped crusts from her eyes and climbed up the console beside her. "A shield, containing the power for a shield?" she asked.

Sincret nodded. "We can't blame… me… for staying," he said, gesturing towards the corpse beside him. "There is no way to take the shield down anymore, only to switch the energy between the relays here and those within the city."

"So why not just wait a few days for their attack to finish then send the energy back to the city?"

"I don't think it's that simple, at least not anymore." He flipped idly over the glowing screen, it's colors reflected against his face: blue, purple, and red. He looked towards the small door Jadamara had noticed earlier. "There's a communication console somewhere through there. I will see what I can do about it, but no promises. This stuff is old, completely backwards from what they use in the city except for the language. While I'm looking at that, I think you should check on the others."

"I don't want to leave you here," she said. She had a hard time looking at him.

He smiled. "I won't be long, it'll be pretty obvious if I can fix the comm station."

Who are we going to reach anyways? The Spear Throw's communications are busted, it's doubtful they would have repaired them in the time since we've been gone. But as she thought on it, she remembered all the ways the orphans had impressed her already and couldn't help but hold on to some hope that they could reach them. She thought of JV and forced away the visions of how the second rot would steal his cognizance, how it had already begun stripping the coordinated movement he had left to him. Her decision to abandon him had started to weigh on her as their journey into the Flows went on. *Every minute we are away is a minute I lose with him.*

She left the way they came. Sincret used the cloak to tunnel a passage for her through the shield and she descended the grand staircase. She arrived at the bottom to the motley crew in the state they had left them. Gardinidine's torso had been wrapped with the bandage now soaked through in yellowish blood. His face was still perfused, but as Jadamara knelt next to him she smelled the foul stench of splayed organs around his wound. Eylea stooped against a pillar where she had pulled herself, her hands and feet bound. She had been bandaged as well, once around the gut, and again around her head covering a bloody stain where her right ear should have been. It was then that Jadamara noticed her missing ear dangling from a strand of twine around Karvine's neck. He gave her a depraved smile and continued sharpening his knife against a tempering stone.

She summarized their journey into the installation to the three boys, but left out finding the Mongrelai with Sincret's face. By the time she finished, they could see him descending the staircase. He had switched out his dock jumpsuit for the blue-green weave underlay that had encased his Mongrelai counterpart. It seemed to fit but he had removed some of the crystal plating to lighten the burden. His cloak billowed outwards as he descended, giving vision to a new malevolent pistol strapped to his chest.

"Eylea's ship can't handle another trip through the Flows. There is only one way we are going to make it out of here," he said when he reached them. He pointed to the Mongrelai dreadnaught. He gave Karvine his old pistol. "Stay here. Keep this trained on her, if she moves, kill her." Then he looked at Creline and Jadamara. "You two follow me, I'll lead."

They approached the front of the ship. The closer they got to the massive rail gun, the more insignificant Jadamara felt against it. When they reached the ramp on the left side, the vessel's towering presence pushed down on her even further. Their proximity to the interior of the ship did not lift the shadowy curtain that grew from inside it. Creline dug through his backpack and pulled out two lights. The darkness swallowed the faint glow almost immediately, hidden objects appeared from the outskirts of the aura only when directly centered. Sincret tapped the screen embedded in the weave over his left arm and a bright pale light burst from a bulb on his shoulder, illuminating the cavernous interior of the ship.

Jadamara could not explain everything she saw. She recognized the mounting rack that hung above them, alongside the cannon, and wondered where the snubfighters it once housed had gone, then remembered the wreckage below them on their journey through the tunnel. She imagined the chaos and death this war machine must have brought with it. Nets along the outer wall held cargo in place, beyond them several doorways appeared and another directly ahead of them. They reached the door at the end of the walkway. Sincret's hand brushed over the screen and it turned red. He then drew a design on the pad and the red light became replaced by a green hue. Still, the door needed to be pried apart by Creline before it opened to them.

They entered a hallway on the other side. It felt cramped and the yellow lights that activated with their motion made the shadows in front and behind them shift with their movement. Sincret seemed to know where he was going, but more than once the group found themselves facing dead ends. Along their routes, Jadamara noticed remnants from its previous inhabitants: sleeping quarters, a cantina with shelves lined by various bottles containing colorful liquids, and even simple bathrooms. Everywhere they went, tattered cloth hung on walls with symbols scratched into the metal around them. They squeezed out of the narrow maze of halls into a large square clearance whose ceiling reached eight levels above them. Rusted walkways lined the walls and spiraled up as far as Jadamara could see. In the center of the room was a very old looking elevator. Sincret walked into it.

"Hell no," said Jadamara, even Creline held back.

Sincret growled and stomped off to the staircase.

The journey upwards took them longer than she expected. The stairwells in the walls only rose two or three levels at a time then ejected them onto walkways where they wound about until they found another way to climb higher, occasionally resorting to groaning ladders which stirred after years of stasis. Doors and open spaces lined the perimeter of the walkways. Some appeared residential, but others gave the impression of store fronts with tools of their trade behind them: rotten food, weapons, clothes.

Dust coated almost everything. They shook it loose from the rafts, sending the puffs through the rectangular holes of the walkways as they moved along them. The grey powder broke apart and hung in the central space before it had a chance to settle anywhere else. The yellow light above them struck through it, the sight alone made Jadamara want to sneeze.

By the time they reached the top deck, they were covered in the grime as well. Sincret brushed himself off, seeming a guest who didn't want to track it into another's home. The final hallway stretched towards, what Jadamara guessed, was the bridge of the ship. The final door crept open with a grinding shriek.

"The command deck," breathed Sincret.

Inside the room, a large circular table was sunk two meters into the floor, encircled by a random mix of antique equipment. Beyond, against its walls, periscopes viewed through meters of mirrors and writ-glass to the outside. The machines hummed to life as they approached, the fury of their resurrection spat out plumes of dust. Jadamara covered herself. Once the storm finished, she felt the current of air and pin-pointed it rising from the cooling fans below the equipment.

"Behold, the Mongrelai Empire," she said sarcastically. The whole ship astonished her in its unapologetic hodgepodge de-formity, but this room was truly its apex. The fans that sent the dust flying cooled the large wire veins that ran through the floor below them. Metal cords flexed and twisted to escape the bridge in rivers. Shelves of large, crystalline discs lined the walls of the deck. Sincret pulled one off a shelf, blew the dust from it, and inspected it thoughtfully. Jadamara had seen the technology before.

"These are crystal discs, or CDs," she said, pulling out a disc and flipping the ancient technology in her hands. "People used them to store recordings."

"And programs," finished Sincret.

As she looked around, Jadamara saw a theme. A plain looking metal case and a ingevein port were hard mounted onto every piece of the vast array. She could not find any trace of a wireless ingevein network but felt her heart leap all the same. Creline wiped off dust from a console, she did the same. Sincret found the seat that seemed to resonate with him and they began exploring. Jadamara didn't understand a single image on the screen, or the next three machines she looked at.

"I can't read Mongrelai," she looked at Creline and asked, "do you read Mongrelai?"

He shook his head.

Two dozen holographic images hovered in front of Sin-cret. He instinctively swatted at the close commands as they ap-peared consecutively.

"Nope," answered Sincret as well, then distractedly, "It's, uh, there's a lot going on here." Finally, the holograms ceased but still a few hung before him. Jadamara walked behind his seat.

"For a guy who doesn't read Mongrelai, you read a lot of

Mongrelai," she remarked.

Creline approached his other side. "What's up?" he asked.

"Nothing good. We will likely die here or within the Flows," Sincret responded.

"So, the same old," said Jadamara.

"Yes, and as usual it will be my fault. But even more so because I'll be piloting this time," he added.

"But you'll pull through, because it's you," said Creline nervously, "right?"

"Ummm," hummed Sincret. "I'm not terrified when I look at these charts which vaguely resemble diagnostics. So that's good!"

"Let's do this then. I'll get the others," Jadamara said.

Sincret jumped up, "I'll get them. Do you think you can fly the observation ship into the top dock? It should be open."

"Sure," Jadamara agreed hesitantly.

Creline said he would explore the ship for anything useful, if they promised to come back quickly. Karvine volunteered to guard Eylea. They split ways at an exit on the side of the ship closer to where they had landed. The journey back alone to Eylea's ship felt longer than when they had come and Jadamara jogged most of the way. When she booted up the Alliance vessel, it scanned over the waking Mongrelai dreadnaught, providing her with more data points that she could make sense of. She did note that the vessel had a surprising proficiency at reading Mongrelai technology, listing ship components she had never heard of.

She lifted the ship from the skeletal building that had hid it. She flew the damaged vessel carefully, and lowered it into the dreadnaught's docking bay. Creline already had magnet locks primed to keep it in place. He secured the fasteners, then giant metal doors closed above them leaving them in darkness. He delayed finishing his progress until dull yellow bulbs blinked to life.

"We are leaving now," he said as she descended the boarding ramp.

"Do we have everyone then?" she asked, expecting a simple yes.

"Karvine is watching Eylea, Gardinidine..." he trailed off. Jadamara felt robbed of her relief. Her mind flashed to the events of the day, but the most pronounced was the way Eylea worked the knife to open Gardinidine's abdomen and the confused look on his face as he held together torn organs and hemorrhaging vessels. "Where is he?" she asked darkly.

"Sincret wants us on the bridge. We need to get going," Creline deflected. She begrudgingly accepted she wouldn't get an answer and journeyed with him through the foreign region of the dreadnaught in silence.

Sincret acknowledged their presence when they arrived but said nothing. The screens in front of him had multiplied. *At least he's practicing,* she hoped.

He sat himself up in his chair, looked at the pair of them. "Let's do it," he said confidently.

Moments later the ship rose. Nothing exploded immediately, but the stress of the liftoff sent tremors throughout the vessel. Jadamara imagined its components falling off as they ascended, leaving them with just the bones of the aged relic. Artificial gravity took hold and created a slightly lighter pressure on her joints. She felt the ache in her ribs dissipate to some degree. The ship shuddered again, forcing her into a seat next to a periscope.

"Shields? Weapons? Communications?" she asked.

"It's all here," Sincret replied. "I loaded CDs into most of the controls. I think they're just going to do their own thing."

Jadamara felt uncomfortably useless. She turned to Creline who had silently slipped into the seat next to hers. He delicately wiped the dust away, using a cloth wrap instead of his hand.

"Did you find anything good?" she asked.

"Loads of weapons, loads of armor, I think some food. Then a lot of large stuff, a few damaged crafts in one of the rear hangars," he answered. A haunted look passed over him. "Most of the doors were sealed." He flexed his hand and winced. "There are also a few open rooms you don't want to see."

The ship rotated around to face the way they had come. Jadamara felt the force of acceleration as the ship lurched towards the tunnel.

"Whoa, my bad," said Sincret.

"What's with that blinking yellow screen?" asked Creline.

"Ummm, that one is for the hull breaches, but those parts of the ship are sealed off." He closed the tab. As soon as he did, another screen arose, red this time. "Oh, come on."

Jadamara turned away and searched for an ingevein network again, but gave up on the fruitless venture. The ports she could hardwire into needed an adapter to work with her ingevein. She found another distraction looking through the periscope, but the view through it did not raise her spirits. They were moving recklessly fast.

Minutes later they left the pyruvutase crystal shute and entered the wilds of the Flows. Once they cleared the stormy bank, lava poured on them from above, below, and occasionally sideways. Their ship was too large to avoid all the geysers, but the shields seemed to hold against the occasional spattering of magma. Sincret pushed the ship forward and again Jadamara felt sickly acceleration. Though she had no way to be sure, she was certain they were moving well past the speed of the Alliance communication vessel. She shifted to another periscope mounted on the front of the ship, just in time to see a flow of lava burst onto the window. She felt the vessel groan and sink under the weight.

"What was that? That was lava," said Creline nervously to no one in particular.

Jadamara leaned back, the lava covering the window was not going anywhere, she switched back to her previous scope and angled as far towards the bow of the ship as it could go. They crashed through five more magma rivers before arriving at the broad glowing curtains that separated them from the labyrinth, and the *Spear Throw*. With a last mighty crash, they cleared the

116

fiery Flows. Creline cheered, Jadamara wiped her brow, and Sincret slowed the ship. He reclined his seat.

"That was super easy," he said with obvious elation, though half the screens in front of him had turned red or yellow.

"That was the best, worst flying I've seen. Where were the barrel rolls?" Jadamara asked.

He laughed, then leaned forward to cycle through screens again. Creline dug through his bag and pulled out some of Garvis's nutrient bars. Jadamara forced one down her mouth, breaking it up and drowning the pungent flavor with the water he extended to her.

"I'll look for the *Spear Throw*," said Sincret.

"We'd better go check on Karvine," Creline said to Jadamara.

She nodded. They left the bridge and descended two flights before jetting off down another hallway, this one barren of flags and inscriptions. They rounded on the only open door at the end of the hallway into what served as a brig. Four cages lined the wall to the left of them, all empty, and Karvine on the floor, encircled by a pool of his own blood. Creline dove onto him and checked his vitals. Jadamara withdrew her pistol, confident this time she would pull the trigger on Eylea if she got the chance.

"That bitch," whispered Creline. He pulled Eylea's ear from Karvine's open mouth, closed his eyes and crossed his arms. Despite his efforts, the young Uncut still looked as tense and eruptible as he had when he was alive.

Jadamara knelt and aimed her weapon down the hallway.

"We should get back to Sincret, maybe he can find her," she said. *If she hasn't already found him.*

They made their way to the bridge slowly, Jadamara probed around each corner with her blaster, Creline followed her in reverse, prepared for an attack from behind. They reached the bridge and Sincret immediately became aware that something was wrong. His eyes widened as he inferred the nature of their alarm and the need for their military style entrance.

"Oh no," he murmured.

"Can you find her?" Creline asked.

"Karvine?" wondered Sincret.

Creline shook his head. "Dead."

Sincret dove into the holograms, cameras around the ship fed him video intel. Jadamara leaned on his seat from behind and scanned over the images with him. None of the cameras they accessed gave any hint of where she might be.

"She'll have a harder time hiding when we have a hundred people scouring the ship," he said, frustrated. Then he grit his teeth, "The *Spear Throw's* communication is still down, but they are broadcasting a distress signal. They aren't far."

"So why do you look so nervous?" asked Jadamara

"Why are you not nervous?" he replied evasively. "It's a distress signal." That was the end of it.

They started moving again. Jadamara felt comfortable walking around the bridge and did so as they approached the source of the distress signal, which she hoped was being used as a beacon to guide them rather than for its intended use. They swung around walls of stone, Sincret finding the straightest lines to move them along quickly. It seemed to her that he enjoyed controlling the vessel, especially now out of the Flows. He experimented, to Creline's discomfort, with the potential of the dreadnaught's mobility. They crossed beyond a wall shadowing the starboard side of the ship when Jadamara saw lights flashing upon the ground. The *Spear Throw* was tucked under an indention in the wall, hiding behind two large pillars of stone.

The ship was aflame.

Three beetle-like vessels adorned in red lights hovered in a semi-circle around the bastion of defense which had been erected around the crumbling ship. They seemed unable to penetrate the fortifications poised around the crash site. *A grave. Still, smart of Gren to land there,* she thought. She focused harder through the periscope and enhanced it. The scene was obscured by smoke and arcs of light. She saw crew from the *Spear Throw* climbing over the ship's carcass to find further shelter behind it. Around the pillars, Painted Boys shot blue light from their spears and dispersed under plumes of smoke shot by approaching Psyperial contrivances.

"We've got to do something!" she screamed.

Sincret swung the ship to face the battle and a thunderous boom erupted from the rail gun below them. Jadamara's heart dropped when she did not see the shell leave the ship, but a second later, the farthest beetle vessel exploded in a fiery storm and fell to the ground in pieces. The other two ships retreated, and from behind them, three snubfighters swooped down upon the fortified *Spear Throw* and sent a volley of bolts that chipped away the pillars shielding it. The thud of the gun mounted upon the starboard side of the dreadnaught pounded rhythmically, spitting out yellow bolts towards the snubfighters who had followed their strafing run on the *Spear Throw* with a low approach towards the dreadnaught. Sincret lowered and accelerated towards them. The shields crackled as they ate the battering of bolt blast from the trio. The Psyperials managed to dodge the dreadnaught's return fire, but broke formation upon seeing Sincret's commitment to run through them on his way to his fleeing comrades.

Creline ushered Jadamara out of the bridge.

"You got this?" he hollered through the door.

"Yeah! Exit on the starboard side," replied Sincret.

They leapt down flights of stairs at a time to get to a pod exit near the ground. Creline seemed to know where he was going. They paused at the door until Sincret's voice buzzed over the speaker next to it.

"Get them in here!" he yelled as the hatch opened to them.

Creline went out first. Sincret placed the dreadnaught between the *Spear Throw* and the beetle ships, giving him and Jadamara a straight sprint to the pillars which the Painted Boys, and now other members of the crew, had fortified with detached cargo containers and other blast fodder. They defended the line desperately.

A cloud of smoke passed over Jadamara and Creline.

She found herself stumbling, distracted and braindead. Creline pulled her forward and covered her mouth. The rudimentary barrier only partly filtered the gas choking her, but she felt her mind clear. They climbed the hill upwards towards the pillars where they could clearly see the assaulting Psyperial contrivances. However, the machines saw them as well. Bubbles filled with the noxious smoke sprang from their guns; the projectiles exploded around them and released a haze that overwhelmed her senses again. Motion and direction twisted into nausea, both she and Creline crumbled, coughed and clutched the ground to work out the debilitating fog.

Jadamara felt sick. She felt her strength misdirected, disjointed and jerked. Clawing on the ground gave her some sense of gravity so she breathed against the stone below her and willed consciousness back into her mind. The smoke dispersed, drawn away by the current of air flowing through labyrinth. She opened her eyes to relative darkness, save for the blue lights shooting down on the contrivances and the explosive aerial battle taking place above them.

The *Spear Throw* defenders' formation scattered into motion. A man in a writ-steel cuirass over leathril padded armor launched himself from the defending line towards the rows of advancing contrivances. The Psyperials altered their formation in response. The machines spread out then folded themselves into boxy forms with weapons in front or held above them. With a blade in one hand and his father's hand-cannon in the other, the man who Jadamara now recognized as her first mate Gren, progressed towards the Psyperials with a tympanic concert of blaster fire. A volley of spears arced over him to light the ground in front of him in blue fire and dust.

Jadamara's stumble formed into a jog, then a sprint up the hill to the next rocky cover. She reached it at the level Gren had stopped and curled behind a stone that was quickly disappearing under the white thunderous blasts from the contrivances targeting her. Her finger twitched on her own blaster trigger, but she held it still and waited for her chance to move again. From the

Spear Throw defensive line, a black pillar puttered forth behind Gren.

My black box? she wondered confusedly. It was half blasted, from where her father's murderer had ripped through its defenses, but still retained some function. She had not seen it since burying it in the *Spear Throw's* storage years ago. A shield sprang from it, reaching downwards in a dome to cover Gren and the glowing rock that separated him from the contrivances.

Bolts snapped against the shield and crackled into nothingness. The gaseous iridescent bubbles burst against the dome as well and washed over it. A crooked grin formed on Jadamara's face. *Resourceful*, she thought. She became aware of the patter of feet behind her. Creline was at her back, waving a stream of orphans and wounded down the side of the hill, towards the dreadnaught. She looked back to Gren's distraction, relieved to see a host of Painted Boys moving to reinforce him behind the cover of the shield. Then to her horror, a pounding bombardment of light from above shook the ground, sending the Painted Boys off their feet. She leapt from her cover and persisted towards Gren only to be diverted to another rock for cover.

Blasts from a Psyperial snubfighter sent up a wall of dust that punched through the fleeing crew. One skilled pilot broke off and turned at an impossible angle to avoid the blasts from the dreadnaught, then rounded out the way it had come.

Jadamara tore her eyes from the scattered line and back towards Gren. A Psyperial layered in black cloth walked towards the domed shield. Without a pause, it lifted a glowing hand. A hole opened in the shield and the malevolent Psyperial moved forward. Bolts from Gren's blaster sprang out of the opening to meet it. The lights diverted around the creature or were swallowed by its robes, then the shadow disappeared into the shimmering barrier which closed behind it.

Enough sitting around, thought Jadamara.

She leapt from behind her cover and diverted diagonally uphill. She looked back to see the black box's shield collapse entirely. It seemed to eject Gren from it as it did, sending him scrambling up the hill with the cloaked creature in pursuit. The Painted Boys above him struggled to stand, concussed from the earlier volley. They raised their weapons but did not attempt a shot around Gren's hulking figure.

That thing is using him as a human shield, she realized. *Gren either doesn't realize it or is too panicked to care.*

Her trajectory bounced inwards across the hill once more, attracting the attention of the contrivances below. White bolts thudded around her.

They are using stunning bolts, she realized with some degree of relief. The concussive charge could still be lethal to Once and Twice-Cuts though, and the cloaked warrior had yet to use a weapon. Its sinister appearance gave Jadamara the impression that its methods were not as humane.

Gren turned and let off more blasts towards the creature which was almost on him. Orange fire blazed to life from the dark figure's hand and showered the space around them in a flickering glow. At the same time, Gren's gun was yanked out of his hand and thrown down the hill. Even at her distance, Jadamara heard the familiar growl he purred during dangerous situations in the past. Situations, like this one, she had not been proud to have put them in. The wavering flame emanating from the creature's hand fell in upon itself and blossomed into a solid crackling bar of light. In its hand, Jadamara could see it clutching an orange crystal from which the blade emanated. She ran as fast as her injured body could take her.

Close enough, she decided.

She drew her pistol and let loose three blasts towards the cloaked Psyperial. It moved the bar of fire between itself and each bolt. The blade grew bulbous where the bolts landed, twirling in an acrobatic display above the dancing shadow, then towards Gren who had reversed direction to charge at it. The three bulbs of light left the blade's tip as one. Gren lurched back as the blast exploded against his chest. When he hit the ground, he made as if to put out the fire still smoldering in his cuirass, but his arms soon fell to his sides.

The creature's silver, flame-shaped mask rotated to stare at her. She struggled against Creline who had caught up and pulled her back upwards away. He screamed at her but she did not hear it. Down the hill, the dreadnaught's mounted cannons pumped yellow bolts towards the sweeping fighter that managed to slip in once again to disrupt the fleeing flow of youths. The Painted Boys could do nothing against the fighter, but formed two lines, the handful of frontward boys adorned in gas masks from the *Spear Throw*. They traveled in a phalanx to meet the metal infantry that continued to fire gas bubbles and white bolts towards the line snaking into the dreadnaught's entrance hatch.

Light crashed around Jadamara and Creline until they reached the top of the hill. She ran past nurses unloading the rotten from a detached cargo hold and found Culus Kell yelling down the hill. She ran behind the perimeter of Painted Boys, but stopped when she saw what Culus had been screaming at. Eva began the mission Jadamara intended, and had launched herself against the shadowy creature which walked over Gren. Her sister Ava ran past Jadamara, but she snatched the girl before she reached the barren descent now made unpassable by the contrivances. Eva however, was too far gone to hear her pleas to return and she disappeared through a haze.

"Stick together" I told them.

She tugged Ava around towards a sheltered approach that would lead to her sister and Gren, then broke diagonally hoping to catch the cloaked warrior before it arrived at Eva. They made it close enough for Jadamara to let loose another volley towards the creature, this time aimed at its feet. Ava aimed her pistol at the same time and Jadamara heard the satisfying thud of energy into a soft target. The creature toppled over and down the hill in a tangle of its own robes, its uncontrolled tumble turning into a cartwheel which soon revolved it back onto its feet. It clutched its side, but continued its march forward. Jadamara leveled her pistol once more before being driven back by explosions of light from reinforcing contrivances.

The creature swept its hand in an arc around it, lifting a veil of dirt into the air. From within the cloud, she heard Eva scream. A moment later the girl's body flew upwards above dust and hung in the air. Her screaming ceased, as too did the blasts from the hill. A silent second later, a plume of fire erupted below her and enveloped her body in a fierce blaze. A scream formed but was burned away by the torrent so ferocious that it stripped her skin, muscle, and voice in an instant. The flames withered as they struggled to find fuel on her flesh, so the creature slung her smoking remains to the top of the hill where the last of the *Spear Throw's* crew cowered. Then it jumped from the cloud, following the course of her corpse over the incline until Jadamara lost vision of it; however, screams echoed beyond the hill long after she turned away.

"We have to go *now!*" Creline insisted. The defenders' bolts stopped from above them but the Psyperials' continued to whiz by from below. The three doubled back to the sheltered approach they came from, Creline tugging Jadamara who in turn tugged Ava. The line of orphans had disappeared into the dreadnaught, and a similar burnt arc they had seen at the shield installation had been burned into the ground around the vessel. She did not see any contrivances or the larger metal figures which had stormed the area earlier.

We've won? She realized, unbelievingly. The question shocked Jadamara. Sincret had created more chaos than she realized. Now five separate guns mounted on the dreadnaught sprayed multicolored flak bolts over the area around it and upon the hill where the Psyperials had taken cover.

JV, she thought sadly. She knew in her heart that he was not on the dreadnaught, but still atop the hill they fled from. In their panic, they had abandoned most of their medical personnel near the *Spear Throw.* Jadamara paused and looked back. *I left him, twice. The man who sacrificed more for my family than anyone else, the man who I promised everything would be okay.*

Ava pushed her through the hatch and Creline pulled her from the other side. The door slammed shut, and Jadamara slammed her balled hand against it in turn. Then she hit it again, and again, and continued until the sides of both her hands were bruised and each pound shook a louder scream from her. Her assault finally surrendered to pain. She sank against the wall and drew her knife with quaking fingers. She slit a line in her palm and watched the blood drip in the wake of her blade. *I deserve this,* she believed, but Ava stopped her short of any further mutilation and wrapped her arms around her captain.

The fire of Jadamara's rage gave way to the emptiness of lament, and she was left with a hole she knew she would bear the rest of her life.

CHAPTER 8
Getaeight

<u>In this City – a transcription from Culus Kell to Caleb Kell following the Pazish rebellion:</u>

I arrived when blue skies failed
Red fire licked black earth
Clouding the sky with ash
It lit a sister
It lit my sister
Fed
But did not survive on her flesh
Missed her
And you
And me

New Psyperia: the massive, ancient city sat upon a mountain surrounded by blue sea, crowned by a pyramidal epitome of the Psyperial's abnormal occupancy. A network of grey platforms rose in mushroom patches over tangles of docks around the circumference of the island. They gave way to writ-stone buildings fortified with emplacements from the *Omedegon*. Gold and black turrets looked over the walls which striated the city.

Getaeight's shuttle passed the minefield of anchor brakes suspended in a great array surrounding the city, dotting upwards into the wisps of clouds. Heavy air traffic buzzed about the mountain. The shuttle cleared the shore and sailed into a canyon that put them below the buzz. The shadow which the *Omedegon* cast over the mountain promised doom but delivered a reminiscent comfort to Getaeight and the other Psyperials still growing used to the sun's bright blaze. He wondered if he would ever get used to it. Their ascent steepened until the shuttle dove over the Rim and sent their nociception amiss, turning the scraps of breakfast in Getaeight's stomach. Finally, they arrived back home from their days-long campaign to take Corala.

He looked back from his cockpit console and watched lines of officers march out. *Diplomats, spies, some downtrodden defectors.* They had been brought to negotiate a vassalage, and succeeded. *But their people paid the price of blood defending the Corala long before we arrived.* Upon their orders, the hungry allies the Psyperials found across the world swallowed the city in a ravenous incursion. The city that had once been a colorful mix of nature and civilization now stood as a ruin; its government handed over to the Mulgtai, a bordering nation who shared no love for the Coralans.

Getaeight reported as much to Admiral Visparion when he debriefed at the rebuilt Rim fortress. The structure had been repurposed to coordinate Psyperial operations in the city and abroad. He retraced the path through the buried chambers they seized weeks earlier, now in peace. In their vast emptiness, he felt as the architects intended: small. Within the courtyards, platoons of Ehtlentins trained with Psyperial sergeants. An odd coupling that was new since Getaeight's departure.

The council chambers had been reorganized into a communications center as well, though it only moderately resembled a military operation. Maps illustrating Alliance fleet movements illuminated the faces of nervous onlookers who crowded around them. Noise, orders, and requests tumbled through the air meeting Getaeight's ears in half coherent tangles, as disordered as the sight of the operation would indicate. Admiral Visparion had already been briefed when he received Getaeight's oral account.

"Good work, Lieutenant. Battlelord Aemon asked me to send you to him next." Getaeight turned to leave. "*Straight* to him." The comment stopped Getaeight.

"Sir?" he asked.

"You've been informed the insurgency murdered three officers the last three days?" Visparion asked rhetorically, then looked back at his charts. Getaeight had heard the news, and though disappointed, was not surprised by it. The battle to keep New Psyperia had already begun, just as Aemon predicted. He expected the cells of insurgency would ramp up their attacks until the Alliance arrived, then they would rear their heads long enough to be severed.

Getaeight nodded politely to Visparion's back and left. He wavered at the dock, but took a single manned ship directly to the *Omedegon*, into the hive of tunnels penetrating the ship, and towards the hangars located within. He jumped down from his ship, walked over the scaffolds, through the bustle of inquisitive deck officers, then down to the wide rectangular exit at the hangar floor. A shadowy figure waited for him.

As Getaeight approached, he began making out the long lines sewn into the writ-steel mask that gave it the impression of crescent bags below metal eyes. The mask's expression was the embodiment of age itself: a mouth twisted into a gritted nervousness, metal eyebrows raised as if watching a child venture too close to danger. However, by the time Getaeight arrived the elderly façade had broken. The Shadowed rose half a foot above him, dark cloth laden with writ-stone particles draped over his wide shoulders and upper arms, leaving exposed armored gauntlets which glowed purple beneath jagged, black obsidiron casing.

Paudochton the Shield, Getaeight knew. He smiled when he arrived at Aemon's Shadowed Hand and protector. Paudochton the Shield bowed his head and turned, sweeping layers of black and grey over the gleaming obsidian floor as he did. Getaeight reflected on their relationship. He had grown familiar, even comfortable, with the man over the recent months though they had never exchanged a word. *Not due to a lack of my trying*, he thought. They journeyed through the winding hallways to Aemon's chamber in the heart of the pyramid.

Massive metal doors opened to the grey hall. Aemon sat at the far end of it, a shrouded figure on both sides of him and an Ehtlentin boy knelt at the base of the stairs below him. The taller figure that stood beside his master was Kentochten the Striker, Paudochton's nest sister and Aemon's second Shadowed Hand. The other figure was a sight Getaeight had still not grown used to - behind Aemon's right shoulder was a woman draped in layers of black lace, a woman the officers had come to call the Shrouded Lady. She swayed and twisted in a disjointed dance. The thickness and deep hue of her robes stifled her involuntary movements, but her head tilted wildly as she leaned down and whispered into Aemon's ear.

The kneeling boy rose, bowed and exited towards Getaeight and Paudochton. Brown and purple opalescent locks spanned from his head down to his jaw, framing a handsome face marred with a scar that stretched from scalp to chin over the right side. A blue tattoo painted over the gash traced down his face with it, giving it the marked appearance of a bolt of lightning. Getaeight wondered what had given the mark; he inferred from the boy's eyepatch that the injury had not spared his eye. He found himself staring a moment too long, but the young man seemed interested in his appearance as well. The boy nodded when he passed but Getaeight did not return the gesture. He did notice, however, the tattooed paint in the boy's skin glowed in the dark between the beams of light shooting down from the ceiling.

He is from Retine, he realized, as only the inhabitants of the labyrinth city were tattooed with luminescent paint. The Uncut had fared even worse in the Ehtlentin mining city of Retine than they did in the slums. The orphans lived, toiled, and died in the crystal mines that supported the city. After the Psyperials secured Retine, droves of them shuffled from the caverns. As many laid dead inside, though not due to wounds suffered during the decisive battle, but from their enslavement.

Getaeight saw the bodies stacked in his mind, deposited

throughout the crystal tunnels and slouched inside their tents. It was the first time he saw the rot, but far more of the orphans had died of body wide hemorrhaging caused by the reactive particles around them. Now, amongst the piles of corpses Getaeight saw this boy's eye staring back at him; within it, fiery ambition and frozen resolve.

A caged animal seeing the light for the first time, he reflected. He grimaced at his quick judgement. *Or perhaps a saved soul.* But something continued to nag at him until the sight of his master above swept the thought from his mind.

The Shrouded Lady left through the doors beside the throne that led to Aemon's quarters. Paudochton took his place by Aemon's side opposite of his sister. The other half of Aemon's Shadowed Hands, Kholo of the Frost and Plamya the Flame, were absent from his side, having accompanied Kyphothree on her mission to find the criminal, Sincret.

"Welcome back," Aemon said as he lifted himself from the seat and motioned Getaeight to follow. He jogged up the flight of stairs to the throne, then down the identical flight behind it to catch up with Aemon. The space at the end of the chamber was meant for discourse. A fire burned in the far wall. A red and gold rug covered most of the room. A table set with food stood in the center. Aemon chose a comfortable seat in the corner of the room surrounded by bookshelves. He held out his hand for Getaeight to take the other. A contrivance set down two steaming cups between them.

"You seemed distracted when we conferenced last," the Battlelord said.

"You're right, sir. I'm sorry sir," Getaeight replied. His head buzzed with acceptable excuses: *Lack of sleep, illness, travel sickness,* – and less acceptable truths – *Yearning, restlessness, conflict.* But Aemon did not solicit a reason from him.

"You are composed, wise, and dedicated, Lieutenant. You were sent to me because your mentors saw the potential of your future, and they were correct in doing so." Getaeight could not help but smile. His master had only ever complimented his performance, never his character. "But even still, they underestimated you. When you arrived before me, I sensed the writ-phenomenon manifesting around you as it does only too rarely in our people. Even now I feel your teslac reorganizing itself within you, just as you must feel it." Getaeight gripped his aching forearm. It had been sore lately, but that had been the case on and off for the last year. "Let me show you what I see."

His master looked away, then back to him, and slowly moved his index finger above his steaming cup. Getaeight felt a sensation pull him upwards from his seat, which skidded backwards on the ground until it bumped against the bookshelf behind it. His sense of balance faltered and the sensation of spinning made his stomach turn again. He instinctively reached out his hand as if to grab on to an invisible support in front of him. He was surprised when he found one.

He felt an unseen liquid running through his fingers, it's current changing with the movement of his hand. The soreness in his right arm opposed the soothing sensation on his skin. He tapped into his mind's capacity to acknowledge the pain, then shut it out. He lowered his arms to his sides in an anatomical position with his palms facing forward. As he meditated to stifle the soreness, he became aware of the fluid energy coursing over his entire body. The calming effect of the river flowing around him broke as he realized that it was now his perception perpetuating its motion. The energy loosened from its tight spiral into wild revolutions, knocking over the cups and books around them, before expending itself and returning to the nothingness it had spawned from.

Getaeight looked at Aemon, unable to hide his surprise. *Or is this fear?* The ability to control writ-phenomenon came only to those who possessed with the writ-gift. Individuals manifesting the writ-gift were picked away from their normal lives and trained for one purpose, to become Shadowed. Getaeight knew the test sealed his fate.

"There is no one on this world, Psyperial or not, who can teach you to writ-bend. You will be instructed at the Shadowed

Temple just as the rest of us have, and when you reach the age to take a name, you will join me again."

Ten years from now, Getaeight thought. *I can wait that long to find my name, I can wait that long to discover my heritage, I can wait that long to learn my genetic makeup, but I cannot wait that long to return to this world.*

Aemon studied the young man in front of him. "You will leave tomorrow. If you have questions, now is the time to ask." Getaeight shook himself back to the present. He had so many questions, but they were lost to him now. Only one remained: the thought which had lingered in his mind since the night of the Nun's procedure.

"Are we related?" The question dominated his thoughts since his and Kyphothree's conversation. Asking it filled him with excitement and dread. The literature he searched indicated the de novo genetic mutation that he assumed gave him his albino appearance was a rarity, arising once every other century. The cases he studied indicated the trait disappeared after birth for many, whereas it persisted for him. He couldn't explain why Aemon's appearance changed only that night, but he couldn't deny the significance of their shared semblance, even if it only was for a few hours.

Aemon smiled mysteriously. "I won't know that answer until your name day," he lied. Getaeight didn't believe him, he remained silent. "Wipe that question from your mind, Lieutenant, it will not serve you to think on it anymore."

Getaeight bit his lip. The Psyperial development system removed bias from their society, or so he believed. He had four nest parents and seven older nest siblings. For sixteen years he lived, tested, and grew with his family. He loved them, and when they said goodbye for his military rotation, he cried. Now, he ruminated on his master's decision to send him away and doubted it was motivated by a lack of teachers onboard the *Omedegon*. Suspicion arose from ashes of the trust he had walked into the chamber with.

"Why can't you teach me? Why not any one of the

Shadowed onboard?" he asked.

"To serve our people you must be with them, you must be one of them. Our world is harsh, it's unrelenting, but from its challenges we learn to trust each other and we find our family in every citizen. If you stay here you will forget who your family is, and if I allow you to stay I will be betraying mine. You will go to the temple and learn how to use your traits to benefit our people."

Getaeight found Aemon's answer paradoxical from start to finish.

"My family is here though." He was sweating now, angry. "And with all due respect, I don't think Shadowed slaughtering the elderly benefits our people. I'll have nothing to do with it." He had grown bold, but his courage sunk away as the spiteful words left his lips. He lowered his gaze. "My apologies, sir. I know this is war."

Aemon stared at the fire for a while then said, "We eradicated the surviving Twice-Cuts because without the teslac network in their brains, most of the Shadowed cannot search their minds. We've kept that information secret to keep our enemies off balance. As for your family, 12,000 of your brothers and sisters who have not reached their name day are returning with you." Getaeight closed his eyes and opened them when the silence became uncomfortable.

"The gateway is closed," he stated.

"It will open for you, just as it did when we arrived," Aemon replied without further explanation.

Getaeight departed from the heart chamber disturbed and distressed. He found himself walking towards the cargo dock instead of his quarters, half hoping control of his emotions would return to stop him before he ever arrived. But he did not waver from his path. Once cleared to enter the dock, he searched the manifest and found a hauler he could sneak aboard. Contrivances and door clearance insured he would not be able to enter the hauler. He decided it would not stop him, but when he stared down at the two story drop onto the top of the vessel, he thought twice about trying.

Operations on the *Omedegon* ran at all hours, but the dock was relatively quiet. Getaeight took a deep breath after scanning the area and let loose from the rails behind him. The lift of his stomach reached its peak just before his feet slammed into the metal hull. The force buckled his knees, taking the air from him and sending him tumbling down the smooth back of the ship. His fingers searched in futility for anything to stop his descent until they clasped the openings in a vent that left him dangling from the side of the vessel. He followed the grating and other handholds until he swung himself from the body of the ship to its neck, where he stuffed himself into a nook he hoped would hold him during the journey to the city surface. He waited for someone to climb up and retrieve him, but no one did. His muscles relaxed as the hauler's engines roared to life, then tensed as the next step of his defiant act began.

The flight to the surface was cold, colder than Getaeight had ever felt in the city. Even after he arrived and the wind abated, the chill hung in the night's air. He felt it on his ears and nose, while his uniform sufficiently shielded the brunt of it. Sneaking out of the surface docks was easier than sneaking in, as security policy was still more concerned with Ehtlentin infiltration than Psyperial defection.

As Getaeight walked the five kilometers to his home, the wetness of the cold sunk into his uniform and sent shivers through his body. The fog that should have lifted into the air met the hulking presence of the *Omedegon*, which had changed the very climate of the city, and sunk back down into the crater of the mountain. It filled the streets and masked Getaeight's trek, though he still made the sojourn to his house carefully.

Quantine will be there, he believed. Whenever he needed her, she appeared. *She will know I've returned.* Getaeight grimaced at the thought. Her knowledge of Psyperial operations was too concise to be coincidence. *Now, with officers dying...* He did not want to complete the deduction he had been content to ignore until now. Yet, the thought rolled over in his mind nonetheless.

He did not know what to expect, and anxiously drafted scenarios. Alarm cut through him as the prediction that terrified him most rose to the forefront of his mind: *She's betrayed me.*

He stood at the door of his home and pressed his head against it for a moment, collecting his thoughts. He pulled his taser from a pocket and kicked himself for not bringing a pistol. The door opened and he entered an empty house. No feminine figure sat upon the railing behind the wispy window drapes. No naked body laid on the bed ready to be taken.

He leaned over the counter in the kitchen and rocked back and forth on his heels, inspecting the distinct differences between the home he left and the one he arrived at. It became clear a struggle had taken place inside the apartment. He ventured onto the balcony and dread filled him. Upturned furniture suggested a fight, the blackened gash and crater-like burns on the balcony railing signified a Shadowed's involvement. Getaeight backed away from the marks. When he turned to the door inside, he saw ashen scorches along the walls that could only have come from a blaster.

Fear and grief overwhelmed him, but he refused to believe Quantine had been taken or killed. *If she had been captured, I would be in the Omedegon's brig. If she is dead...* He shook his head with certainty. She was an acrobatic artist, stronger than she looked and devilishly clever. He imagined her leaping from the balcony as she had many times before, but this time a flurry of black cloth following her over. His heart raced, the walls threatened to suffocate him, so he left the home he would never return to.

He walked down the stairs outside but paused on the last one. Strands of purple hair peeked out from a crack under the handrail. His fingers glided along their smooth texture. Even in the dim lit street he could appreciate the opalescent shift of purple as he twirled the hair around his fingers. He pulled, and just before the tensile strength of the fibers gave way, they released from the railing's grip, dragging a folded note with them.

Getaeight's eyes widened. He walked into the closest alley

and pushed his body flat against the stone. He unfolded the note hastily. It read:

[I am alive, I am waiting. You know where to find me.]

He harkened back to an evening they shared discussing futures that could never be.

"Nothing has changed," she had told him, "the powerful still occupy the rim of the city; they still decide our futures. When you slaughtered the Once and Twice-Cuts, you erased the history of our city. Now it is your people drafting orphans into your army, it is your people taking our food, it is your people bringing the Alliance down upon us!" She left angry that night, but before she did, she kissed him. "I can hide us until the fighting starts, then we can leave. Come back to Deep Home with me, please."

The request was as impossible then as it was now, but it gnawed on Getaeight as he made his way back to the docks. *What is important is that she is alive. My leaving will keep it that way.* He did not conceal his return to the *Omedegon*, but convinced the deck officer a mistake had been made, knowing the formal inquiry she submitted would not reach conclusion until after he left the city. Before stepping into the shuttle, he took a last look at the colors radiating from the sunrise beyond the Rim and finally accepted that his future had been decided for him.

Hours later, he departed from the *Omedegon* in an armored transport filled with cadets and scientists. He looked out the window from his seat in the broad cockpit at the identical vessel soaring downwards alongside them. Two more like it trailed behind and a dozen more had already departed into the labyrinth. Next to him, the once talkative pilot silently plotted their course, having received the hint Getaeight's brooding attitude conveyed. Their route would take into the labyrinth and the gateway to Old Psyperia like the others, but first they needed to stop at the docks kilometers away from the island to load wildlife and geo samples onboard.

The sight ahead gave urgency to their mission. Specks of the Alliance fleet peppered the horizon. Having lost their foothold in Corala, the anchor capable fleet had no other recourse but to cover the ocean from their base leagues away. They had done so with surprising speed. The ships jumped just outside of the Psyperial anchor brake field an hour earlier. Above the city, unseen through the blue of the atmosphere, a second space faring fleet was coming down upon them. Skirmishing had already begun at both fronts, Aemon intended to draw them closer before sending forth the legions hidden within the *Omedegon.*

A blaring alarm rang over the radio, the information came in codes.

[Surprise, target marked, unknown, large, attack authorized.]

The pilot became distracted and switched the screen in front of him from pilot functions to radar, hoping to find the location of the infiltrate.

"Stay on target," Getaeight ordered. He had the radar in front of him as well. The readings put the ship directly behind them, moving with speed towards a large cavern outlet a level below. Getaeight ran to the side of the hammerhead cockpit and looked out the window backwards to the cavern to confirm the gate sealing it was still closed. It was, but he waited in anticipation anyways. The gate was writ-stone, barred with writ-steel reinforcements. It could not be penetrated so easily. *Either they are trapped, or well-armed,* he suspected.

As the latter thought passed through his mind, writ-stone blasted from the mouth of the cavern, but the writ-steel skeleton remained. Familiar flashes of green and gold light lit the dust. From it, a brown and orange dreadnaught pierced through the writ-steel bars, bringing a torrent of dirt with it as well as a host of Psyperial snubfighters. Other Psyperial fighters descended from the Rim and still more spewed forth from the walls of the city. Artillery fire rained down upon the dreadnaught from the mountain walls, narrowly missing the convoy of transports. The barrage exploded short of the dreadnaught as its vector shields leapt to meet the incoming shells and missiles. Yet the persistent fire broke through and flames swathed the hull of the ship, giving it even more of a hellion look as it plowed forward.

Getaeight swiveled to move back to his seat, but a shimmer caught the corner of his eye and he returned to the window. He couldn't explain what he was seeing, when he could, he couldn't believe it. Broad bands of light erupted from the massive shield generators scattered throughout the city, covering the mountain in a shifting bubble of iridescent light. The shields came together at the top of the mountain, converging on the towering presence of the *Omedegon*. Light as bright as the sun erupted in an unnatural storm of instability where the city's shields met the *Omedegon's*.

Ships that had launched to pursue the fleeing vessel became caught within the field, either exploding against the massive expanding shield, or routing just in time to peel away. Artillery blasts stopped short and an eerie silence lingered in their absence. All the while, the orange dreadnaught sped onwards, its cannon sending volleys of yellow light backwards at its remaining pursuers who had not been trapped in the shield's ascension. It gained speed and turned its course upwards.

The comm buzzed with chatter regarding the newly formed barrier, then suddenly ceased. From the silence came a great roar outside, as the city's shield generators detonated simultaneously in plumes that swallowed the city, the mountain, and the *Omedegon* in blue fire. More eruptions from shield generators at the base of the mountain sent balls of fire and debris upwards, while a cascade of blue plasma flooded down from the Rim. The city became shrouded in smoke and flames that reached up, covering the *Omedegon* as well. Getaeight trembled and searched to make sense of what had happened.

The pilot worked the comm stations to find a channel still functioning.

STAR STORY BOOK ONE: ANCHORED

"... falling back. Alliance in pursuit. Full retreat and regroup near the mountain. Transports forgo platform pickup and fall back to the gateway."

The squad of transports pivoted to the rendezvous point. The pilot gasped as the city aflame came into view and fell into the surreal stupor that had taken Getaeight. Getaeight's terror turned to outrage. Uninhibited and commanding fury rose from the shimmer of a thought.

Quantine.

He pointed ahead at the rising dreadnaught. "Follow that ship!" he shouted. The pilot fumbled at the controls.

"Sir?" he asked. "We have orders."

"Follow that ship, now!" he repeated as he moved into his seat. He liberated the pilot from his controls and the burden of defying the order. Their ship angled upwards to catch the dreadnaught. The view ahead became lost in the smoke trailing the ship, but their instruments told them the danger they were running headlong into.

"Those are Alliance ships, sir!" the pilot yelped, pointing towards the sky. Getaeight remained in quiet focus, pushing the engines while tracing the ship with an anchor marker.

You won't escape me, he thought.

Lights erupted as the dreadnaught met fire from the descending Alliance fleet. Snubfighters peeled off to avoid the ship ramming through their formations, and swooped around, sending volleys of bolts upon the dreadnaught as well as the transport on its tail. Alarms lit the dashboard but the shields held steady for both vessels.

"Cannons, missiles; fire," he ordered into the headset. "Fire everything at that ship." He marked the vessel and watched as green bolts and comet tails leapt forward. *Three, four, five.* The bolts burst against the dreadnaught's shields and broke them with a final snap of light. Turrets embedded on the rear of the dreadnaught sprayed flak backwards towards the missiles. Two detonated in the trail of metal, two were punched through by vector shields, and the final three landed against newly formed globe shield, which again erupted in color after the impact. A cannon mounted on the side of the dreadnaught swiveled backwards.

Getaeight rolled the ship and soaked up the blasts along the belly shields. They had risen well above the city. They charged ahead while other Psyperial crafts fled backwards, floating gun platforms disintegrated around them, and immense ships lowered from the cover of clouds just beyond. *Not clouds, though, steam. This is unprecedented.* Getaeight looked between the window and his data streams. His eyes saw a silver domed fortress, floating within a cloud of its own making. The instruments on his ship didn't register the domed vessel, or even read interference - just the presence of a very hot cloud. Blue light lit the misty plume as artillery fire poured from the massive vessel onto smoking peak of the city below. Within the haze of soot, the great pyramid responded with its own barrage upwards. Caught between the war machines, light and fire encircled the two ships.

"Sir..." Their tracker detected an anchor tether launching from the dreadnaught. *Not much time.* Getaeight traced it. The tether reached outwards, beyond the atmosphere and moons then became lost in deep space. He didn't need to know their destination, he only needed to lock his own tether around the vessel to drag behind it. He paused for just a moment to consider his options. *We stand a better chance to survive this if we anchor jump out of the battle with them, rather than turn back now*, he convinced himself. However, the circular mass of the cloud vessel eclipsed the sun, threatening to cut off their escape. Before covering them entirely, an opening amongst the smaller ships formed near its edge. The dreadnaught sprung through it, along with the Psyperial shuttle soon after.

CHAPTER 9
Glade Jadamara

In this City – a confession by a Painted Girl during
the Pazish rebellion

I woke at our home as if I were dreaming
Shaken by the sound of our mothers' screaming
Murdered by painted sons in scaled armor; metal casks
Who shout "yes, sir" every time they're asked
We are tasked as collectors for our fathers, the bankers
Called free, but kept tethered like anchors
Yet my anger has unwound the oath I am bound
Now I truly see

Jadamara cringed as Sincret's maneuvers unfolded. Equipped with the seemingly indestructible vessel, they doubled back through the Flows and anchor jumped into the root of the labyrinth, just outside of the city of Retine, which harvested heat from the Flows to power their mining operations. As the dreadnaught pierced the fragile river above, magma rained down upon the city, melting through the scaffolds around the monumental purple crystal. They did not stay long enough to assess the damage of their unfortunate exit, as the destructive announcement of their arrival had mobilized a garrison of Psyperial vessels. They made two more jumps to the mouth of the labyrinth and the world beyond.

They caught the Psyperials off guard, but not so much that they could escape through the peak of the mountain. Instead, they took the largest of the accessory tunnels and sent missiles, bolts, rail magazines, and their own ship through the gate. The effort depleted their shields and shook the hull. When they emerged, their prospects did not seem any better. Then, Jadamara heard Gardinidine's voice croak over the speaker and Sincret's final command to his dedicated follower who had stayed behind at the shield facility.

"Now Gardinidine. Thank you," Sincret said.

With those words, a million lives ended.

Holographic images which displayed the city behind them distorted as writ-phenomenon escaped the disrepaired shield generators, blasting them open, and reigning fire down upon the city. Swaths of mountainside melted as plasma spewed from the generators, while flames and electric discharge reached into the sky. Hastily installed Psyperial towers teetered over as their foundations softened. Buildings which had stood for hundreds of years dissolved in a matter of seconds. Streams of plasma reached the coast and the eruption of steam veiled the city in a violent mist. The crew went speechless, struck by what had happened, feeling complicit in the momentary safety attained at their city's expense. Even Sincret swirled in his seat to the rear displays. Jadamara ran her fingers through her hair and curled them around the roots. She wanted to scream, to form a coherent thought; to do anything but look in silence at the act they had committed.

No, what Sincret committed. He kept us in the dark about his plan to avoid our condemnation, she knew. *He will receive it nonetheless.*

She tore herself away from the periscope, the bustle of curious orphans behind her fought for her place to see with their own eyes the destruction that ensued in their departure. She slouched against the wall and slid to the grate floor. One by one, the children pulled away from the periscopes and fell to the ground, or left. A young girl threw herself at Sincret, screaming, only to be swept up by Creline and removed from the bridge.

Poor Gardinidine, Jadamara thought. She was reminded of

Sincret's Mongrelai corpse. *Are you destined to die alone as he did? You just wanted what we all want; a chance to live.* Gardinidine's wry smile flashed before her eyes. He, and Sincret, had given them a chance to survive.

She could not deny that Sincret had given her that chance before: once by allowing her to stay onboard the *Spear Throw*, and again when the labyrinth creatures attacked. Her eyes ached as they searched for tears to expel, but she had spent them all on JV and Gren. *My life is not worth this cost.* But as the thought passed through her mind she sensed the dishonesty of it. She may have had crewmates alive in the city, but they seemed like distant dreams to her now; friends from another life. She had no ties to the city, or any way of knowing if it was truly still the Eht-lentin she had arrived at weeks ago.

The wall rattled behind her and a begrudging awareness of her appearance slunk into her mind. She exhumed her buried head from her arms.

"Ugh," she groaned and pulled herself up.

A sizable Psyperial vessel swerved in and out of the rear-view display. The dreadnaught shuddered again. The impact of missile blasts conducted through its welded appendages, so echoic that she could tell where they had been hit. The beating of their mounted cannon answered back. The hunter diverted course, so too had the dreadnaught. She found the reason when she looked at the forward display.

A flotilla of Alliance capital ships had appeared from the blue mask of the atmosphere: various boxy, grey slugs of Omphala, windblown shaped cruisers from the moon Arido, and a single lumpy shield carrier created in the submerged city of Tredent. The armada dove ahead of a great cloud moving at an impossible velocity towards them.

As the cloud lowered, the thickening air of the atmosphere pushed the vapor backwards, revealing a glistening, domed saucer within its mist. The saucer leveled out, threatening to intercept their path upwards while the Alliance vessels around its periphery dove down towards the city. Blazed trails from munitions burst downwards from the coalition of ships, and bolts of light rose from the pyramid to meet them. The wall of death swept towards the dreadnaught and its pursuer. Chaos abounded when it reached them.

Jadamara shielded herself instinctively as bolts rained down on the ship. She felt a pulling in her gut and heard the roar of the anchor reel accelerating. Time stopped as the reel cocooned the ship and everything in it in anchored energy. A wash of sensation passed over her and crawled through her sideways, making her shiver.

The passing melt of writ-phenomenon signaled to Jadamara that they were traveling at anchor capable speed. Displays around her blinked out of existence and the room darkened. A final rattle shook the ship. When it died, the sound of fearful breathing and whimpers replaced it.

Sincret moved first. He didn't look like he knew what to expect when he turned around in the captain's chair. He mumbled incoherently then said, "We are heading into deep space, the last place this ship had been to, a place I think we will find help. We will arrive in sixteen hours," and walked to the rear of the bridge.

Jadamara did not move to follow him out. A sense of duty, still new to her, compelled her to remain. *These kids need help.*

The youths had begun talking. Jadamara approached the deck overlooking the two levels of the control pit where most of the remaining children had gathered. They quieted and looked up at her expectantly. She debated telling them about the escaped, and presumably pissed off, prisoner lurking aboard the ship. *First thing is first.*

"We are safe here," she said, then corrected herself, "safe on this part of the ship. Paridine, tally the crew and take note of their condition. Kendiline, I'll show you apartments nearby to set up bedding. Creline, take some of your boys and set up a perimeter around camp." She addressed them all. "There is an Alliance officer on board. She attacked Gardinidine and killed Karvine. I'll lead the search party." The crew broke into conversation and dispersed.

"I will go with you," said Creline.

Everyone is exhausted. Eylea will be as well, she hoped. "Set up the perimeter and get some sleep," she said.

She followed her own orders. After directing the crew, she drifted around the upper levels of the ship looking for a soft place to lay down. She found a door close to the bridge, with a new green light illuminating the control panel. Her hand trembled as she inserted it into the green glow, but the door opened without objection. The apartment inside was compartmentalized by hanging sheets. The room had far less dust in it and the vibrant colors from the fabrics leaped out at her despite the dim lighting. She touched the materials as she walked through a hallway they created, all the way to a window ahead. Beyond the panes of writ-glass, comet tails came to life and died as particles hanging in space disintegrated against their shields. The sight was distracting, but her senses told her she was not alone.

CHAPTER 10
Sincret

In this City: a confession of affection by
Caleb Kell to a Pazish Nun

Years of wind and water have shaped this cave to be vast
And infinitely intricate
Much like your heart, I could spend a lifetime exploring it
And still be amazed by what I discover
Without light, I am bound to lose myself
But with you by my side I know I am safe
Without the sun, I will surely freeze
Yet your arms give me the warmth I need

Sincret exhaled in relief and stared at the woman he had grown fond of.

"Hey," he said.

"Hey," Jadamara replied, startled. His heartbeat continued to race, though to his displeasure, not with the rush of attraction. Her dreamlike appearance was blemished by nausea and thirst, but mostly a need for xene salts. She sat next to him and swiped her thumb across his cheek.

She has questions but she won't ask them, he knew.

"Sleep," she said slowly, and pushed him into the mattress. Her hands were unsteady. Like him, she still had the teslac network within her body, but the stroma within his arm had kept him ahead of their shared injuries. Even his oil burns from the week earlier had faded, while hers remained scabbed over. She massaged her fingers through his gold and blue hair. When his eyes closed, he heard her strip out of her mesh layers and lay on top of the sheets beside him.

She fell asleep but soon stirred from her hazy slumber, too aware of the cold sweat pooling on her that chilled the blankets below. What ensued was a battle.

She availed herself to one of his pillows and indulged in a majority portion of the covers. Fortunately, he wanted nothing to do with them. The dust rose from the shift of material and threatened to make him sneeze, but she beat him to it. She put her face close to Sincret's back, content to bask in his body odor as opposed to the musky sheets. Three blanket configurations later, a surge of nausea, which had steadily been working up, overwhelmed Sincret. He climbed onto all fours out of bed and heaved in the bathroom.

Hours later, he awoke spooning the roll of blankets he had wrestled away from her. She softly snored underneath a mound of pillows. It struck him as brilliant. *Not too hot, not too cold. Aerated...* He regretted using so much energy on his first thought upon waking. The effort sent his head spinning and he could not hold on to any thought afterwards. His mind grappled to comprehend the profoundly desperate situation that lay outside. Pain, regret, and above all else, a deep self-loathing, swirled together.

I feel like a toilet, he thought.

He dragged himself to the sink and retched in it again, then forced himself to look in the mirror. *Obviously withdrawing, hair is knotted, filth on my face, filth on my body.* He had looked worse. The first time his master banished him to the bottom level of Ehtlentin, the orphans had made short work of him. He literally crawled back to his master on two broken legs when the week was up. Now, he suffered by his own hand.

Despite the circumstances, he felt reassured his situation had improved. The woman he had woken up next to stumbled behind him. She was worn out, yet even in her tarnished state, she looked beautiful. The dual reds of her hair twisted upon her shoulders and around her neck, working with the curves of her body to lull him in. She had a strong build. He wondered if he saw in Jadamara what his master had seen in him. The line of thought ended; all thoughts ceased entirely and he began his ritual to purge the memories.

"Fuck, fuck, fuck," he murmured under his breath. *Reboot. Get it together.*

He jogged out of the door. Pedrine stood shivering outside, and Sincret doubled back quickly for every layer he could find. He reemerged fitted in weave and armor, draped in his Mongrelai shawl and his master's cloak. He tucked his pistol into its holster over the left side of his chest, then brushed out his hair and let it fall over the other side. His hood climbed over his thick lochs and he felt ready to handle what lay outside.

Ten hours to go.

The first hour was filled with bad news. Seventy-two on board plus their unseen fugitive. Injuries: substantial. Morale: abysmal. The survivors had gone through all but three gallons of water they had loaded onto the Alliance vessel. Sincret managed to bring some components of plumbing online but the water was thick with contaminants. The search party went out absent of Jadamara, whom Isla tended to.

In the third hour, Creline's search party returned with cases of what looked like water. When all conventional methods of opening the jugs failed, he and Sincret hid behind a barricade with their pistols and blasted one open. The jug blasted back and they wondered why they ever thought water would have been sealed in such a manner.

We must be delirious with thirst.

On the eighth hour, Creline led Sincret and a party of Painted Boys on another search mission for Eylea. Their route took them through the technical tunnels at the base of the ship. Their search pattern converged on a hatch at the center of the network.

"This was open when I found it," Creline said.

"It's closed now," replied Sincret.

"I closed it," mumbled Creline with a hint of shame.

"Why?" Sincret asked. Creline gestured to the hatch.

They descended into a cramped chamber where the ceiling stood four feet high. Sincret's light revealed a maze of trash and burnt opaque armor around them. Mounds of ash, human remains and torched machinery stretched out twenty meters in every direction, at times reaching up to the ceiling. Sincret choked on the dust and the realization of its biological origin. The scope of their investigation was reduced to searching for footprints and signs of disturbance in the ash. When none appeared after the hour, they returned to the orphans' camp near the bridge exhausted, filthy, and empty handed.

One hour left.

Sincret dragged himself to the door of his cabin but thought twice about entering and walked the short distance to the bridge where again he paused. A nagging guilt curbed his urge to hide. He turned back and walked the distance of the tunnel that led him to the tower shaft where his wards had taken residence. Blankets and bodies lined the levels of walkways but little else. The injured were tucked away, attended to by whoever was available in Culus's and KB's absence. Sincret spotted Cass through a doorway on the level below and climbed down to her. His arrival drew the eyes of several residents of the compartment, but the majority did not stir. Cass's red eyes were on him, and Ava's as well, who sat on her bedside.

"Cass," he said quietly.

She turned away.

"Ava," he said.

She looked up at him, the same question painted on her face as everyone else on board.

"Who are you? Why are you doing this?" she asked.

He knew how it looked. *The power that swallowed her sister in fire is the same that I create. Now that fact is poisoning the promises I've made. I'm holding everyone captive on board a dying ship heading to an unspecified destination. No one is holding me accountable, because they fear what I can do.* He wondered if that fear was founded. *How many others will die because of me?*

"I'm just me," he said helplessly, "And we don't have a lot of options, we haven't since we started, so we are following the thread that has gotten us this far."

"We…" said Ava doubtfully.

Every second he stood there he could feel her contempt mounting. Cass' silence concerned him too. She followed her own path, he wouldn't be the first person she killed for betraying her.

She is barely hanging on. The thought did not comfort him though. Half of the Painted Boys on the ship joined on her word. Without her by his side, their loyalty hung in limbo. The possibility of mutiny was palpable. Creline was his only connection to the cohort of warriors now, and Jadamara too. She made leadership look effortless, they trusted her word as much as anyone's. Even he found himself drawn to her command.

As if on cue, Isla walked through the door. She startled Sincret, which in turn startled her.

"I thought you were with Jadamara," he said.

"No. No, no, no, she didn't want me there," she replied as she moved past Sincret to an injured Painted Boy.

Garvis walked through the door behind her, shifting past Sincret and towards the injured Painted Boy Isla was tending to. The swelling on Garvis's face had quelled, but the blisters had scarred over and mottled the skin around his mouth, nose, and eyes.

"Captain," he said as he passed.

"Good to see you, Garvis," said Sincret. And he meant it. Garvis was one of the dozen on board who grew to age seven alongside him at Deep Hold orphanage. The same Pazish Nun had even pulled them from their mothers within an hour of each other. The simple greeting was enough to give him the courage to return to the bridge. He gave a last long look at Ava and Cass and hoped in some way it spoke apologies he could not voice out loud. He made his way back to the bridge.

He arrived to find the command crew of the *Spear Throw*

seated around the rim of the control pit. The intricacies of the ship's design still eluded him, but instinct pulled him towards the correct crystal discs to load into the various slots available within the pit. He blew them off one by one. *Rear vector shield focus, pursuant targeting protocols, broad range scanning*, he guessed.

He took a seat and pulled up diagnostics. They came up sluggishly, the circuits that controlled many of the functions were as rusted as the beams holding the dreadnaught together. The sheer number of redundant systems kept the vessel functioning, but they were failing one by one as if a clock counting down to their destruction.

Two minutes.

Quick and shallow breathing became audible behind him. Jadamara had taken a place by his side. The writ-tether pulling the ship reversed and began repelling it. He heard her groan as the gut turning lurch welled up inside her. The vessel decelerated and the shield surrounding it snapped open as they passed through the anchor. The invisible energy that made their journey possible returned to the anchor reel engine which it had sprung from, and the ship grew quiet.

An enormous gas planet floated ahead of them. Swirling purple clouds covered the surface and slowly melted into one another: a peaceful mask of the violent storms raging in its mass. A green moon peeked over the horizon, revolving around the giant as if to greet them. Red lights flickered on overhead.

"They followed us," observed Sincret. Another tracing appeared on the radar. "One behind and a new contact ahead," he called out automatically. The crew began mumbling. Jadamara squeezed his shoulder.

The vessel ahead was a third the size of theirs, but his scan showed thirteen bolt guns covering the hull, two blaster cannons on the dorsal aspect, and two larger cannons at the tail of the ship. Anchored energy sprung from fin-like protuberances on both sides, surrounding the ship and halting Sincret's scan. A moment later, ten of the thirteen bolt guns detached from the hull, and five more starship tracings appeared on the radar.

"Six ahead now: a frigate and five fighters. One behind."
Always between a rock and a hard place, he thought.

The new starfighters fell away from the parent ship like sucker fish leaving their host. Their flat bases facilitated their attachment to the frigate, an arthropod-like shell formed a sturdy half-oval on the other side, shielding fins extended on their sides, and a tail with two blaster cannons trailed behind. They were too large to consider snubfighters; Sincret surmised there was space for three or four bodies inside the cockpit alone. The enigmatic insight that had led him this far told him their ability to cling to vessels didn't extend just to their own. *The Mongrelai call it the board and blow,* he faintly recalled. *And these are most assuredly Mongrelai.*

A ping appeared on radar much farther ahead. Blinking, not reading as an object.

"They want us to land on the moon," he said.

"Can we jump out of here instead?" Jadamara asked.

"Not in time," he replied, "the anchor reel is still rewinding from our last jump." In another minute, they would be caught between the two. He powered down the weapons and sent what was left of the spare energy to their shields. The dreadnaught angled towards the moon, on a direct course to pass by the Mongrelai ships ahead. The ship shook as the first blasts arrived from their Psyperial pursuer.

The Mongrelai broke formation to pass over them and regrouped on the other side. The painful sound of bolts thudding against the dreadnaught stopped as the Mongrelai came together and soaked up the barrage which had been peppering their hull. The expected pounding of missiles also skipped a beat, and instead erupted in the silent void of space as they met Mongrelai flak bolts. The Psyperial vessel turned from its course to double back, but the three Mongrelai encircled it and lit its shields ablaze. The bridge crew cheered at the sight visible in the rear display.

More orphans flooded into the bridge, most of the same lot

who had witnessed their departure from Ehtlentin. Some reveled in the moment's celebration, some remained silent; the nervous gave in to familiar tics. Some simply held their loved ones.

"Everyone needs to strap in now. We're finding a place to set down," Sincret said.

Jadamara departed from his side and rallied two of the crew to alert the others and three more to secure the injured.

"Hurry," she called after them.

Sincret looked at the tactical display, and shared the image on the center projector of the control pit for the crew. The Psyperial had been routed again, and now made its course for the jungle moon as well, its engines all but destroyed. Three Mongrelai shepherded the Psyperial vessel, while the other two caught up with the dreadnaught and held place on their rear starboard side.

Where we've sustained the most damage, Sincret knew, though he did not intend to run anymore.

"We are all set," said Jadamara who reappeared behind him and strapped herself into the seat next to Creline. The floors shook as they entered the atmosphere and threatened to rattle loose from their fastenings. Flames distorted the viewscreens and periscope windows. An early sunrise appeared ahead and a green carpet covered the hills below. The immense foliage grew in size and detail until the ship scraped over the tops of the tallest trees that rose a hundred meters above the ground.

"Angle port!" yelled Jadamara. "You got this." Sincret had not spared a look her way since she arrived at the bridge. She turned back to the periscope but Sincret could hear the distinct sound of her praying under her breath. He saw the spot she saw, and angled the ship towards the patch of land devoid of trees. "Never mind it's too close. Can we go much slower? Or circle back? Or find another place?" Her voice grew louder as their descent continued. Sincret did not have the time or heart to tell her that they were in free fall.

"Here," he said as the ship dipped below the canopy and obliterated everything in front of it. Their path left a wake of gore: trees, foliage, and likely thousands of other lifeforms disintegrated.

"This is actually pretty nice," Jadamara stated, referring to the comfortable speed at which the jungle matter slowed them. They cleared the forest line too soon though, moving too fast.

"This won't be." Sincret forced the ship down and silently begged it to provide one last miracle for them.

A sharp pain in Sincret's jaw jolted him awake accompanied by the familiar taste of blood, but in lieu of pleasure, he was only made aware of the throbbing in his head. Every breath stirred him to consciousness. He became aware of the moist air filling him and his feet dragging behind him. He willed his head up. Jadamara walked beside him, flanked by her own escorts.

"So that's what that feels like," he said.

"Crash landing is a bitch," she responded as she shot him a sideways glance.

There is so much green around us, and in her eyes. Even her dark Ehtlentin skin was lightened by the pale green of her Coralan heritage, and now it showed true in the cover of approaching storm clouds. She had cut the knots from her red hair, now it brushed the top of her shoulders instead of cascading over them. Her belt and weapons had been confiscated, along with his cloak and blaster.

The Mongrelai deposited them in a line of their compatriots. Jadamara left Sincret's side, but not before helping him into a sitting position in the mud. He felt vastly alone as she walked away. The crew congregated around her, at least as much as the massive sentinels guarding them allowed. Three of the Mongrelai ships surrounded them; their rear cannons facing outwards, their front bolter guns trained on the captive orphans.

A Mongrelai approached, as large as the rest of them, but adorned in light blue crystal armor over a purple weave. A short blue cape hung over his left shoulder, and on it the emblem Sincret had seen painted over the walls of the dreadnaught. He walked towards Jadamara. She frowned and jerked her thumb towards Sincret. The sea of orphans parted and all stared at him. Even the injured on their stretchers did not look so pitiful. The Mongrelai exchanged glances and he knew at that moment they were sharing a joke at his expense.

He struggled to stand. The nearest Painted Boy relieved him of the burden and he rose to his feet as the Mongrelai leader stopped before him. Sincret instinctively reached out with his writ-gift, probing the creature's mind with his 6th sense, but only felt nothingness. *His presence is a void,* he decided. His unusual knack for reading others only ever failed when he attempted to gain insight into the minds of Twice-Cuts. He guessed the Twice-Cuts' absent teslac networks limited his capacity to read them. He still felt the presence of a teslac in the warrior, but like the armor encasing the man, he could not pierce it.

His static voice projected from his helmet. "Anata wa karera o komara semashita ka?" The question lingered in the air. Sincret had only a vague idea what the towering figure had asked. Yet he got the feeling it ultimately wouldn't matter. Time expired. He led Sincret around one of the feeder ships and through the entry underneath the tail. The inside of the ship did not look as eclectic as the dreadnaught, now sunk in the mud, but still very alien. A tinted window wrapped over them and allowed the passengers to see almost ninety degrees upwards if they stood in the middle of the ship. There was still a hardness about it, as if all comfort had been stripped away to an unnecessary degree. The Mongrelai dropped him in one of the six seats lining the walls beside the entrance.

Two more Mongrelai dropped Jadamara next to him, then leapt the entirety of the five feet separating the entry from the cockpit platform. The leader arrived last, the door closed behind him. The six rode in silence, except for the muffled voices of the Mongrelai speaking to one another through their helmets. The ship descended. Sincret fought the urge to stand, wary of their blue captor that stared at him. The same fear did not stop Jadamara who shuffled past Sincret and peered over the step.

"What do you see?" he asked.

"We just passed over the Psyperials. They looked like they were in a rush also," she answered.

The feeder ship landed on a hill overlooking the downed Psyperial vessel. The Mongrelai leader slowly peeled his stare off Sincret and opened the rear hatch once again. Sincret felt his edge coming back as they exited into the fresh air, though the fumes of burning metal fowled the breeze as stormy winds blew it their way.

Our ship may be broken in half, but at least it's not on fire. The Psyperial ship was sunk in the mud and riddled with bolt holes. A handful of muddy soldiers scrambled backwards from melted barricades between their ship and the Mongrelai. An array of colored bolts exploded around them as the Mongrelai lazily corralled the group into a corner, except for a young, white-haired, officer, who slid his way from barricade to barricade until the Mongrelai were forced to look for him.

Sincret could hear their leader directing them from his vantage point, but his voice became inaudible as the sound of another Mongrelai ship boomed overhead, past the battle and towards a fleeing Psyperial skiff making for the forest line. At the peak of its engine's roar, the Psyperial boy made his move. He hurled a mound of mud at the nearest Mongrelai which hit its mark, splattering over his visor. Two bolts from his blaster also landed against the Mongrelai, but to no more effect than the mud had. The boy fell backwards with a splash, barely missing the colorful crossfire that converged from around him. Their fortunes now reversed, the Mongrelai aimed at the Psyperial.

Three bolts started on target, but none arrived. Instead they fizzled into smoke as they passed through a shimmering barrier extending from the boy's hands.

A personal shield? No, this is familiar, Sincret thought. He could almost sense the cloak of writ-phenomenon that temporarily surrounded the Psyperial boy. The moment hung still as both soldiers evaluated what had just happened. A barrel rose from the Mongrelai's forearm, spewing flame. The Psyperial screamed as it engulfed him.

"No!" Sincret yelled, though he was not sure why. *This boy feels significant,* he knew, though he could not explain it. Jadamara furrowed her eyebrows but did not look away. The continuous spray of flames torched the ground, mud, and barrier alike. Another scream rang from the epicenter of the hell storm, this time projecting with the quality of a battle cry. Ground, fire, and the Mongrelai flew outwards from the Psyperial. The Mongrelai found his bearing midway through his flight. When he hit the ground, his body curled like a spring, ready to launch him feet first back into the air. As he did, a green bolt traveled the considerable distance between the boy's blaster and the Mongrelai, burrowing in his neck just as he became upright. The upper half of his body continued its return forward, but the bottom gave way. He slammed face forward into the mud, the slap of his crystalline corpse against it brought a second eerie hush.

A sound like a saw splitting wood cut through the silence as another Mongrelai ascended into the air. The leader called after him, alarmed.

He's yelling to hold, Sincret knew.

Crystals on the second Mongrelai's gloves and boots glowed red. They whirred loudly, working to keep his body afloat. The Psyperial rose to his feet but froze.

That must be terrifying, he pondered. *Poor kid.*

The Mongrelai did not share the sentiment. A missile shot from his weapon, moving as fast as the bolt fired by the Psyperial at the same time. The projectiles passed each other. The bolt sailed well over the Mongrelai, the missile detonated against the boy.

The remaining Mongrelai moved fast, rounding up the rest of the Psyperials who threw down the weapons and dropped to their knees. The sound of explosions turned their heads to a fire burning upon the forested hills in the distance. The flames died quickly in the storm, but before they did, the outline of the Mongrelai feeder that had passed overhead earlier lowered into it.

The rain had stifled the heat from their own explosion and the smoke around the Psyperial boy cleared. Sincret searched until his eyes found the ashen figure of what remained. The force of the explosion had blown mud, clothes and flesh from the right side of his body. His hand and the better part of his forearm had been completely incinerated. The organ body of his teslac was the only thing remaining, still clinging to the remnants of his stripped bone. The thing hovered above him as if he were quietly inspecting the obliteration of his appendage. Then Sincret realized that was exactly what he was doing. Nearby Mongrelai realized that the boy was still alive as well.

The leader ushered Sincret and Jadamara back aboard and he looked one last time towards the Psyperial.

His hair, his face, his eyes; but something more, something ethereal feels familiar.

The uncertainty only created more anxiety, he let his curiosity dissipate. He could not control the boy's fate, but he could control his own. He could keep his eyes open. He could plan.

CHAPTER 11
Sincret

<u>In this City: A reflection from an Ehtlentin soldier during the Great War</u>

A smoldering moon hangs in the sky
A torched ground below
I exist in between
War has taken me here

They arrived at an ancient compound that had been taken back by the jungle. It's roots and vines grew through the triangular buildings on the surface. The green weaved its way into brown rusted metal which lacked the enduring properties of writ-steel. The super metal rarely existed offworld. The qualities that made the material sturdy, also made it easily detectable. Whenever a source appeared, anyone with the equipment to mine it made it disappear.

Water slapped on the window overhead as they passed through a delta of waterfalls and into a passage in the cliff side behind them. Another ship crashed through the waterfall after them, bringing a torrent of water and wind with it. They traveled a distance that Sincret estimated put them beneath the structures on the surface. The tunnel ended in a hangar just large enough for two Mongrelai ships to swing about and land. The air smelled of water on rock and reminded Sincret of the vast caverns he explored in Ehtlentin.

They left the ships and entered a hallway. They winded

through the darkness, their path illuminated only by the lights emanating from the Mongrelais' devices. They ascended a narrow winding staircase to a hatch. It released at the leader's hand against the glowing pad. Beams of white, cloud-stifled light penetrated in a crescent shape and exploded through the hatch as the Mongrelai pushed it completely aside. Fresh air rushed into the stairwell as he did.

Sincret and Jadamara climbed up ahead of the Mongrelai into the sunlight and the hatch slammed shut behind them. The distinct grind of metal locking together screeched from the other side of the hatch and it became apparent to the two that they had been left in a prison cell. They adjusted to the inescapable flat light bleeding through the clouds beyond the metal bars which composed one wall of the cell.

A Mongrelai in opal armor passed the outside of their cage a moment later and stood sentry across from them. The pair instinctively approached the steel bars and wrapped their hands around them.

"These bars are the only thing in this place I've seen that isn't rusted," Sincret pointed out.

Jadamara flicked her fingers against the metal. "The Mongrelai took a lot of captives in the Great War, but they never gave any back," she replied.

He gulped. "No chance they all escaped, huh? I mean, they didn't even chain us." He gestured towards the iron links nailed to the walls.

"We can still use those if you'd like," she said absently.

He laughed. "Feeling better then?"

"New day, new problems," she said and continued staring ahead. "I'd say you should get worked up and bust us out of here, but they let us see this place from the sky and the ground just so it's nice and clear that there is nowhere to escape to."

"There's one place," replied Sincret, but he did not want to go back into space. The dread he felt waiting for the hull to blow away under Psyperial missiles was the newest of many painful memories. It seemed to grow worse over time as the comprehension how close to death in the icy void they had been set in.

I'll need to work through it, he thought. Then he remembered Karvine. The Painted Boy's fiery temper had been a liability from the start of the journey, and the reason Sincret had the audacity to begin it. *But for all his faults, he understood fear and how to move past it. Wrath for his enemies, trophies for his victories, and forgiveness for his failures. Eylea suffered the first two, but deprived him of the last.* He imagined his friend bleeding out on the ground, wondered what thoughts raced through his head before they stopped.

He released the bars and paced the cell, allowing himself to become angry.

"What do we do?" he asked her.

She didn't respond. Outside, a group of Mongrelai passed carrying several of the *Spear Throw's* rotting crewmates between them.

"What's happening? Where are you taking them?" she yelled at the closest Mongrelai, the one in jade armor who incinerated the Psyperial boy's arm. The crystal warrior walked on, yet as he passed, Sincret had an unexplainable sense that the creature was different from the other Mongrelai. The creature's teslac network remained closed to him, but another presence occupied it: a whisper of a foreign voice that seemed to share his body. Before Sincret could make sense of the feeling, the group passed. Jadamara cursed them fervently until the soldiers moved out of sight.

They heard screaming all through the day and night, screams they did not think the dying compatriots had been capable of releasing. One by one their distinct voices rang out. *Paginine, Calayine, Kegor, Cass, Tentilitine.* The list grew until dawn, when the purple glow from the planet above yielded to the sun rising on the horizon. In the absence of the gas giant's mass, the water which had been lifted during the night settled again upon the moon, clouding the sun until it became just a bright patch amongst its endlessly shifting grey. The blue Mongrelai leader came for them at mid-day.

"Step back," said the sentinel outside, speaking in omphalic common. The growing gravity made standing a struggle, but neither felt like losing what dignity they had by crawling so they trudged to the far wall. The hatch swung open with a loud clang and the leader sprung from it, just barely clearing the lip of the opening.

Even if we could get through the hatch, we wouldn't get far. The descent may shatter our kneecaps during the day, and it would be slow progress to navigate during the night. There are about three hours of normal gravity at sunset and sunrise that may make it possible, Sincret calculated. He had quietly probed the hatch with his sixth sense and debated whether his power could open it. He decided not.

Three chairs followed the Mongrelai up, he swung two of them at Jadamara and Sincret. They danced and skidded their way towards the pair until stopping neatly in front of them.

The hatch slammed shut, the Mongrelai took a seat. He looked at them each in turn, then his helmet hissed and released. The man beneath had brown skin and eyes, and hair as black as his slit pupils. He did not give the impression of an older man, but he seemed weathered beyond his age. He looked suspiciously at Sincret then sat back.

"I know your face, and you knew where to find us, which means part of my friend must be in there," he said, evaluating a clearly confused Sincret. "Or at least I had hoped. Who are you and why are you here?"

"I am Sincret, we came because…" he paused, "we had no choice, and we need help."

"You tortured our crew all night and didn't even figure that out?" asked Jadamara angrily.

"We didn't ask your crew any questions," he replied darkly, then waited to see her reaction which remained as veiled as when Sincret first met her. "But we did help them."

"So, are you here to help us?" she asked.

He pointed at the scar on her right forearm, the mark of her first cut. "It does not look like you need help, but there's always room for improvement." He regarded Sincret wearily. "Damaeon can attest to our methods. Or he could have, when he lived as one of us."

Damaeon. My true name, he knew. It felt right, more real to him then the name Sincret ever had. Hearing it spoken aloud shook memories loose, memories he had not made in this lifetime.

"But you are not Damaeon, just his shade returning with the bones of his ship," the Mongrelai continued.

"Sounds like providence. Don't forget the seventy halfrotten, half-starved children he brought also," Jadamara added. "He's kind of their prophet, so if you don't have any more questions, we can just get out of your mud stained shit hole and die in the jungle." Sincret cringed at the undiplomatic harshness of her rebuke. The Mongrelai only smiled and returned his helmet.

"This is no prophecy, and I don't have any more questions," he said, his voice made metallic by the helmet's microphone.

He was halfway through the hatch when Sincret cried, "Who am I?"

"You are Anchored, Damaeon," the Mongrelai responded, "anchored to this existence; reincarnated in the multiverse as well as a bridge within it. And that is not good for anyone." The hatch shut.

CHAPTER 12
Getaeight

<u>In this City: Lonely Mountain</u>

A lonely mist shrouds this mountain
It will not lift, it has always existed
Blanketing every building, enveloping every figure,
filling every corner
It is on my clothes as I walk down these streets
It is in my eyes as I search for a haven to escape it
The night tastes of wet stone
And the howling of motherless children reaches me
Through the mist their songs will echo
On this mountain they will fall
This lonely mountain

Getaeight wondered how he had made such a mistake. He wondered why the Mongrelai killed what remained of his faultless crew. He wondered why they kept what remained of him alive. He wondered when they would break what remained of his spirit. Wondering was all he could do until the screams rising from the building beside him died at dawn, and he felt certain the time arrived for answers. The blue Mongrelai leader appeared to deliver them.

His hulking shadow stood over Getaeight and intercepted the morning rains misting through the window.

"How do you feel?" he asked in Psyperial. The question and the dialect surprised Getaeight, but he didn't have the strength to answer. "You are dying," the Mongrelai continued. He walked around the table to inspect the teslac clinging to the bone of Getaeight's shredded arm. "Before you do, I have questions that need answering." He injected something into Getaeight's thigh, moments later a rush of warmth came over him. "Several weeks ago, your people passed through a gateway from your world, into this one. How long have your people known about that gateway?"

"Sixteen years," he answered. "We weren't sure it was a gateway."

"How did you find it?"

"Hadeon the Betrayer, the man who murdered our last Battlelord, stole an artifact vessel. Shadowed traced it to the gateway." The Mongrelai had gotten the same answer from the boy's predecessors, he began his real interrogation.

"But it did not open again until Aemon the Proven brought the *Omedegon* to it. He has secrets, what are they?" he asked.

The question rattled Getaeight. The Mongrelai moved to inject more serum, but Getaeight blurted out, "He is ..." another pause. *Don't say my father, don't say my father.* "...different." The answer fell short. Aemon served as the last Battlelord's Shadowed Hand. He had been away evacuating the capital when the Hadeon launched his coup. He coordinated the marines who saved the population, and though he could not save the Battlelord, he himself rescued the Elector Council from Hadeon's Shadowed assassins.

The remnants of the Council, the Shadowed Ministry, and the people's vote, raised him to Battlelord. His reputation thereafter, ascribed him the title Aemon the Proven. Since then, transparency had been the cover for his secrets.

He was not the first Shadowed Battlelord, but he was the first to unmask. However, he wore a hundred faces underneath it. He integrated the Shadowed into public service somewhat correcting stigmas the people held about them, but never revealed how they were taught at the Shadowed Temple. He built and baptized a military that served utility, yet he must have known he would need it on the other side of the gateway. He developed the facilities studying the anomaly, but he disappeared through it, leaving behind the people he swore to serve. It pained Getaeight that he did not know any secrets that gave him answers, only secrets that created more questions.

"What have you seen?" the Mongrelai asked calmly.

"Power no one else has," he thought of the Nun, "knowledge no one else knows."

"Examples."

"He doesn't need crystals to bend writ-phenomenon. He extracted a woman's teslac entirely from her body without killing her." He dug deeper, but found his knowledge of the man as limited as he expected. "His form changes when he exerts himself," he confessed, unable to control his words. He took a pained breath.

"Tell me more about that," the Mongrelai insisted.

"He glows… his hair and eyes turn…" A cramp knotted in the remains of his scorched teslac and traveled up his shoulder. "He's…" His heart beat against his chest and he choked on the words. "He's…"

"Calm, slow breaths," the Mongrelai said. Getaeight heard the words through the fog overtaking his mind, but did not understand them. More figures gathered around him.

"Get Patch. He can't die yet, and we can't risk turning him. Report when he wakes up, or gets worse," the Mongrelai ordered.

Getaeight awoke that night as the sedatives left his system. The Mongrelai lifted him in a cot and transported him to the structure where he had seen the Ehtlentins taken. Before ascending the stairs to the peak, he saw a pile of bodies stacked five layers high in a mass grave. Ehtlentins composed most of the mound, but he could spot a few of the Psyperials he brought with him intermixed as well. He closed his eyes as his guilt returned. Atop the structure, he felt Mongrelai hands lift him, straps bind him, and a sharp pain in his forearm. Wind rushed in through the ruined walls across him and swayed the new IV drip stuck into the body of his teslac. Pain and nausea spread until it wracked his body.

He could not close his eyes against the pain, so willed them to find a means to escape it. He searched the room and passed over a pale face just beyond the light. In most contexts, it would be the last face he would want to see before he died. But he felt overwhelmingly relieved to see it. The woman's dyed brown hair fell over her stolen Alliance uniform and she had recently lost an ear; however, her curious stare gave her away.

"Kyphothree," he mouthed through the agony. She continued to stare at his writhing, burnt body. She looked uncertain, concerned even. Her sympathetic eyes met his, but a wicked smile formed underneath.

"Kyphothree," he tried again, but choked on the words. Her face drew back into the shadows and he felt her presence leave him. "Don't leave me!" he cried out, but she did not return.

The pain burned within him, but now hate as well. The two fueled each other until screaming was all he could do to release them. He never realized the extent at which he could feel his body. Now, every cell in him cried out to him at once. Each reported their condition and complaints: broken capillaries and spilled organelles leaking under bruised skin, the itch of infection growing in his arm, the release of endogenous hormones attempting to alleviate his suffering or deliver him from the inescapable danger.

Organs failed and thought slipped away until only the faint breath of his will to survive remained. It wavered against the wind rushing through the wall-less room, like a candle threatening to blow out. In the last minutes of lucidity, memories of his life played out in front of him. Beautiful, simple moments: losing a stormboarding race to his nest sister Getatwo, sneaking out of the academy to explore the hubs of Old Psyperia, the feeling of Quantine's fingers dotting along his back. The memories came loaded with woe. His old home was unreachable, and his new one, a ruin. The woman he loved, murdered. The memories evoked a spectrum of feelings, but ultimately, sadness that they would be ending.

Ending with Kyphothree's smile, he thought.

With great effort, he nurtured the life left in him, the flame growing brighter to beat back the darkness in his mind. He spread it further through the maze of pathways extending outwards. With every push, he mastered the chaos inside him; listened to its message. The knowledge he learned worked itself into a new conception of what it meant to be alive.

Breathing, heartbeat. He gasped, then searched further to find the worst of the damage. Arteries shunted blood to revive organs, buffers increased to manage his acidotic blood, and fat stores broke down to provide energy for the processes. He experienced the biological miracles happening within him, but as he drew back the veil of their mystery, the ethereal writ-phenomenon he once sensed within and outside of him departed. His concordance with writ-gift unraveled, until it split entirely, and only the feeling of it lingering just beyond reach remained.

His body and spirit broke, and the mosaic reconstructed from their remnants was not quite the same, but grew stronger each second. The flame of passion that crafted his new self burned out, and the world felt cold without it.

CHAPTER 13
Glade Jadamara

Night came, and with it the screams of the Psyperial boy. The Mongrelai brought Jadamara and Sincret to a shower where they cleaned off the filth of too many long days. They gravitated towards each other under the crush of the cold water, giving in to urges which they could no longer deny. Despite the circumstances, and possibly because of them, it was the best shower Jadamara had ever had. They both knew it could be their last.

The sentry outside gave them all the time they needed, but eventually the cold water drove them to the door. They found it unlocked, and passed through side by side, hoping their clothes were nearby. Before they could step into the hall, a bolt of white light impacted against them and sent both backwards into the shower. The blast left a ringing in Jadamara's ears and the world spinning around her. She rolled over to keep from drowning in the falling water and blindly crawled away from it. She found a corner and wiped the streams off her face.

Eylea strode into the room and crouched over Sincret, a silver spidery contrivance adhered to the ceiling over her. Its red eye glowed through the water towards Jadamara. Eylea dragged Sincret through the doorway, the spider followed her out. After a moment, she returned alone to the corner Jadamara feebly attempted to climb up.

"The wisest thing to do is kill you, sorry," she said. She stood over her and raised her blaster. Jadamara raised her arms, and to her shame, begged for her life incoherently. Eventually her arms gave in to fatigue when no bolt landed. When they unfurled, the woman scowled down at her. The light on her weapon switched from green back to white. This time the blast knocked her out completely.

She awoke wrapped in blankets, lying on a cot in a room she did not recognize. Mongrelai moved busily around her, all helmeted except for their blue leader who sat next to her. All things considered, she did not feel so miserable. She felt a familiar warmness and became aware of the xene salts in her system.

"Ugh, not again," she said.

The Mongrelai did not understand until she yanked the IV out of her thigh. The leader scrambled to bandage it. "You will be in a lot more pain soon," he said.

"It's not worth it," she groaned and lay back. "Sincret?"

"The woman who stunned you took him and escaped in the Ohwen ship you brought with you," he said.

"What Ohwen ship? You mean the Alliance ship?" she asked.

"It bears the Alliance sigil, but it is of Ohwen design," he answered.

Jadamara groaned. She had heard more than a few conspiracy theories surrounding the reclusive Ohwen people.

"I know you may not want to, but please listen. Pieces are moving on a board that has remained static for 300,000 years, in a game that we have lost control of. The arrival of the Psyperials in your realm, and the behavior of the Ohwen, have made it clear it is time for the rest of your people to comprehend what is happening, and what is at stake." Jadamara wondered who 'her people' really were anymore.

"This story begins an unfathomable amount of time ago, with a people much like you and I, living on a world much like your own. Their civilization suffered through a war between two dimension transcending beings, the Angels and the Enemy. As the war swept towards their system, the Angels offered the people a means to escape the destruction brought by the Enemy. They selected four members from the First People's society - their most cunning scientist, their fiercest general, their resilient emperor, and a worthy citizen – and embedded teslac organs in their arms. They were the first to bear the teslac organs, and were thereafter named the First Four."

"The First Four then passed through anomalies constructed by the Angels. As they did, their physical bodies shifted into writ-form, where their spirits hung imperceptible, but omniscient. In that state, they watched the war unfold and consume their planet. They witnessed the suns that had once warmed them burn out, and distant galaxies collide. They waited as the universe collapsed in on itself, then with a big bang, exploded outwards to regenerate itself anew. Even then, they continued to drift in the writ-dimension, spectators – countless times over – to the physical universe's infinite cycle of reorganization."

"Each reorganization of the universe created worlds that existed in previous generations, and worlds that would exist again. Inevitably, some cycles gave rise to massive planets of writ-stone revolving around two suns, like the world the First Four had once called home. As these planets came to exist, the First Four perfused all matter and dark matter in writ-phenomenon, preserving the essence of each universe down to the last micro particle. By doing so, they created a perfect mold of each universe. Each of the First Four held a mold in memory, waiting for the cycle when they could rejoin the physical dimension."

"A time came when the universe manifested in a manner identical to the one they had left behind. They watched history unfold as it had before, from the creation of biologic life, to every foolish decision made by it thereafter, until the events of the Enemy's arrival culminated in perfect copies of themselves passing into the Angels' anomalies. As their copies left the physical dimension, the First Four reemerged to inherit their lives. The molds they created entered into physical reality as well, filling with matter drawn from beyond our universe. The four anomalies changed their conformations, each one becoming a gateway to one of the new universes the First Four had manifested. Each gateway became anchored to a member of the First Four, ensuring that as long as that leader survived, the gateway to their realm would as well. The unique nature of the First Four's teslacs allow them to shift into writ-form upon their death, and be reborn in another body, essentially binding them to existence as long as there are teslac organs their writ-spirits can inhabit."

"A great many people implanted teslacs and fled through the gateways to the new universes. The Scientist led the exodus into your realm, which we call The Whole Realm. However, those who followed her, and their descendants, would be cursed for doing so. The Prince gathered the aristocracy and fled to the Undying Realm. He promised the political elite lives free from the decay of age. The General retreated to the Cold Realm, vowing to create a weapon which would one day destroy the Enemy. Now, his realm is devoid of biologic life. The Citizen embarked to the Cracked Realm, alone, and waited for the day he could see his Angelic lover again. The people who journeyed to his realm found it rife with astronomic hazards, and sparse in planets. Their tenacity to survive is evident in their descendants, the Psyperials, who have created a utopia from the ruins of their fractured world."

So, the Psyperials are not from the labyrinth, at least not the labyrinth in this Universe, Jadamara thought.

"Though many fled to the parallel realms, some stayed behind in the First Realm to fight the Enemy," the warrior continued. "We are the Mongrelai, and we have been fighting for over 300,000 years."

He allowed Jadamara to contemplate, but she only thought about how much she missed her old life. Wars that lasted for millennia, living anchors, and interdimensional physics seemed like the stuff of dreams. She wanted to wake up.

"You called Sincret Anchored, is he one of those spirits?" she asked.

"Given his reincarnation, I am certain he is Anchored, but I cannot say that he is one of the First Four. He was conceived in the Cracked Realm by two Mongrelai in my tribe while we orbited Psyperia. I took him as my son after his mother and father died. I brought him with me here when our tribe cycled to this realm for the harvest. That was over 200 years ago."

The word harvest made her stomach turn but she ignored it for now.

"But you said there was only one gateway connecting this realm to your realm, so how did the Psyperials end up in Ehtlentin?" she asked.

He smiled, she had arrived where he hoped. "It can only mean a new generation of Anchored have been born, and their genesis manifested gateways connecting the parallel universes. So that leads us to the question: who are they?"

"Sincret," she answered.

"It's likely he is one of them," he said. "Five parallel gateways have opened in the last thousand years, meaning there are five new Anchored, born from the First Four, living in your realms."

She thought on it. "So now your secret is out, and you can't keep us isolated."

He shook his head and leaned back. "It's worse than that. The only goal the First People had was to survive the Enemy coming for them. The war ended for your people when they passed through the gateway but not for us. The Enemy went on to destroy our homeworld. It took 200,000 years to drive them out of the system, but they still lurk in our realm, waiting in deep space or a far-off star system, no doubt building their strength. Every day the war is kept in our realm, every day your people live, is a victory. But that security expired. The Angels haven't been seen since our world was destroyed, our universe is collapsing in on itself, and the Enemy are looking for the chance to escape to a new one. If we cannot contain them, and they make it into your realm, they can now transverse these new parallel gateways to infest the others."

"Isn't one universe big enough?" she asked sarcastically.

"They see what the First People saw: a chance to perpetuate a civilization that can survive even the collapse of the universe. And they will get their chance soon. For the last 2,000 years, we haven't just fought to keep the Enemy out, but also to keep the inhabitants of the Cold Realm in."

"You said there was no life in the Cold Realm. Are you keeping out ghosts?" She bit her tongue. The xene salts left her uninhibited, but not uninhibited enough to miss his frustration.

"Contrivances overran it millennia ago. They call themselves the Virion and the only living things there are the prisoners they bring back through their parallel gateway from the Undying Realm."

"So, the Virion attacked the Undying Realm through a parallel gateway, just like the Psyperials attacked ours?" she connected.

"Yes," he said, then added, "but their war has raged for 800 years and already eradicated most of the Undying population. The Enemy is powerful, but only a few of their warriors remain - the Virion have become a much more urgent threat."

"What I've told you is taught to all Mongrelai on their first day of rebirth, so they understand the importance of the war they've inherited. But as I've said, the board has changed and it is no longer just our war. You know about the gateway between your people and the Psyperials, but more recently another gate opened bridging your realm with the Undying. The Virion will find the path to you, and they will spread through the worlds of this realm like wildfire. Unless your people prepare for them, and even then, your only chance is to fortify the gateway, or destroy it."

"So where is this second gateway?" she asked, though she knew the answer was irrelevant.

"Beyond the edge of the solar system; two months' travel by conventional anchor, and even then, we can only approximate its location somewhere in the Ohwen Empire's territory."

"There is no way the Alliance or any other world powers would spend the resources to search for an alleged gateway in deep space," she said frankly. "And even if they did, they wouldn't spend the resources to keep a garrison there. I assume you can't destroy the gateways or you would have. So really, what is the point?"

The Mongrelai smiled. "We don't know how to destroy the gateways, but it has happened before. 800 years ago, three gateways closed simultaneously. We believe Sincret, or the Psyperial leader Aemon the Proven, may know how."

Jadamara nodded. Sincret's instinct, drawn from knowledge learned in his past lives, had gotten them this far. *He saved us more than once already, who is to say he can't save us again?*

"You believe me?" he asked.

She nodded again. "If you told me this a month ago, no. But I've seen too much to doubt it now. What happens next?"

"You and your crew are free to decide what happens for yourselves. We open the First Four's gateways once every 15 years to trade and communicate with the First Realm. Tomorrow the gateway from your realm to the First Realm will open and our tribe will cycle home. You may go with them as initiates or ambassadors, either way, you will be tested. You can stay here; the compound will be abandoned but is well provisioned and there are vessels your engineers may be able to repair. Or we can drop you in a populated system between here and your world, where you can find passage to Omphala." The options seemed appealing to Jadamara. "Or you can come with me back to Ehtlentin and retrieve Damaeon."

The memory of Sincret's gaunt face within the shield facility surfaced, and sent a chill through her. She pitied him.

Wherever he ends up, it will not be good. Eylea had the last surprise, but I'm sure there are more in store for him. She thought about the spidery contrivance that followed the woman into the shower. She had seen the unique metal coating before. *She has a working artifact,* she realized, remembering the ancient technology on display at the Omphalan Museum of Science. She snapped back to the Mongrelai waiting for her.

"I can't speak for the others, but I'm with you. How do you know he is in Ehtlentin?" she asked.

"The Ohwen stealth systems on the vessel you brought allowed Sincret and his abductor to slip past us, but we tracked their anchor tether," the Mongrelai answered.

"That doesn't make sense, she should be going to the Alliance headquarters in Omphala."

"She is going to the Psyperials in New Psyperia, as they call it."

"She is Psyperial? Those bastards." Rage filled her as the revelation dawned on her and she found another reason to hate the invaders. "What are we waiting for?"

"Only for you." He put on his helmet. "Your crew is already on board."

He returned her blade, blaster, and belt, then handed her Sincret's cloak, pistol, and the trappings of his Mongrelai incarnation. They walked outside the compound where the large arthropod vessel rested and the even larger dreadnaught beyond it. Five smaller bottom-feeder ships coated the hull of the first ship, as they had when they first encountered it. The last two were perched in the docking bay of the dreadnaught.

"We call them feeders," said the Mongrelai, gesturing towards the vessels whose double barrel cannons had been trained on her days earlier. "This is the *Resolvement*," he said as they passed the first vessel. He pointed to the dreadnaught, "That is the *Herald*."

Jadamara was impressed they had salvaged the ragged ship, at least to the point of moving it. She became nervous as they kept walking towards it.

"We barely made it here in that thing," she said astounded.

"She's seen worse," he replied. Work had been done on the ship. Scorch marks and shredded metal remained mostly over the rear of the *Herald*, but the deeper holes were sealed. Veins of rust that coated the hull had been cleared away, faint glowing yellow lines now that traced over their paths.

"We more warmly refer to her as the *Handshake*," he said, gesturing to the dreadnaught. Then he jerked his thumb back to the arthropod ship behind them, "and her as the *Farewell*. Together, these ships are unstoppable."

"But we don't get both," she guessed.

"No," he confirmed looking mournfully over the length of the dreadnaught. "The *Resolvement* will take our tribe back to the First World for the cycle."

By the time they lifted off, Jadamara had done a thorough, yet brief, counting. Only fourteen other members of the crew that arrived on the moon had decided to return to Ehtlentin. Among them were Creline and his Painted Boys, Ava, Isla, Garvis, and a handful of Sincret's loyalists. Cass's devotees, and a dozen other skeptics, elected to stay behind and find their way off the moon on their own terms. Neither group trusted the Mongrelai, and those who followed them aboard the *Herald* looked wearily at the crystal warriors who had taken their rotting brothers and sisters. Jadamara counted eight of the imposing soldiers on board, and three in each feeder, making just fourteen of them as well.

Odds do not look good.

The leader assured her that their journey back to Ehtlentin would be quicker than their arrival at the moon. The ship lifted off and she clasped the orphans' hands on either side of her, who did the same, until the fifteen of them interlinked in a circle. The hum of the anchor reel propagated through their bones as it launched the tether that would bring them home.

They arrived at a mountain that looked more like a volcano than their city. Rivers of melted writ-stone, now cooled, had flooded down the slope of the mountain, into the ocean surrounding it. Half-melted Psyperial towers protruded from the rock, their twisted forms appearing like scorched trees along the mountainside. A sickly green color stained the shallows around the docks, along with debris from Alliance, Ohwen, and Psyperial ship alike.

The massive disc-like cloudship that once eclipsed their escape lay in the ocean – a ruin – as dead as the city it had come to save.

Jadamara blinked to make sure it wasn't her eyes playing a trick on her. She put her face back to the periscope and again found the vessel half sunk in a watery grave. Alarms buzzed and the Mongrelai went to work at the ancient machines on the bridge.

"Jadamara," called the leader. It surprised her to hear him say her name, she did not know his. She approached the chair as she had done with Sincret. Just then, another beeping rang from behind them.

"Oh, oh, oh!" exclaimed Isla excitedly. A device blinked red in her hands. "Wait! We have to wait!" She scrambled to them. "My friend gave me this to contact her! If it is ringing, it has to be her!"

Or a trap, Jadamara thought wearily. Isla read the message to herself first then showed her, who handed it to the leader.

"Coordinates," he stated. "Every second we waste is a second Damaeon moves out of reach."

"Please," Isla begged. "There are survivors!"

"They aren't the only ones." He pointed towards the viewscreen. A boxy Alliance carrier hovered in the distance. Beside it loomed another cloudship, shrouded in the same white fog that had drifted around its predecessor. "The Alliance and the Ohwen. They want to parley."

Jadamara's thoughts raced, "Then let's meet at Isla's coordinates."

The message was sent, received, and confirmed. Jadamara approached the viewscreen.

"What is that ship?" she pointed towards the cloudship.

"That is an Ohwen capital ship. Their people keep to themselves in deep space, I imagine one hasn't been on this planet since we were here last, when we fought them. Their shield technology has improved since then," he speculated. He released the controls as the ship navigated on its own. He sighed and Jadamara could sense his disappointment. "We never got a chance to harvest that tech."

"Never say never," piped a yellow Mongrelai in the control pit.

"The last time I saw this city, the Ohwen drove us out and

we left Damaeon behind. The last time I saw the Ohwen, I surrendered to their Queen," he said.

"The Psyperials seem to be having better luck," she noted.

"Ha, the Psyperials are famously unlucky. It has made them famously resourceful."

She did not appreciate his admiration of her enemy, but had more questions. "If you fought in the Great War, how have you lived this long?"

"I died many years ago when I became Mongrelai," he said plainly. "If you choose to become one of us, you will learn how to fight death as well. That is all I will say for now." The mystique answer only satisfied the superficial layer of her curiosity.

"So why start a war with us? Why risk fighting us if the Enemy are so dangerous?" she asked.

"You are referring to the harvest. The harvest is necessary to maintain a technological edge over the Enemy, and more recently the Virion. We adapt the equipment we collect from your realms to resist Virion influence. All your contrivances, all your networks; they are just doorways for the Virion. If you don't adapt, they will turn your technology against you and spread like disease, just as they did to the Undying."

She accepted the explanation, and the familiar, yet ancient, technology aboard the *Herald* confirmed his story. "With a name like the Undying, you'd think they wouldn't have a lot of trouble surviving."

"The only time their people age is when they have children. Their longevity allowed them to build an empire that stretched farther than any of the other realms. They created worlds where history never passed from memory. They grew a culture that valued life and peace. When the Virion slaughtered them, it was..." He did not find the right word, "...hard. Like watching a boot smash a flower."

A society pretty much as backwards from ours as it gets, she reflected.

"The gateway between the First Realm and the Undying Realm was one of the three that closed 800 years ago. To reach them, we had to pass through the gateway from the First Realm to the Cold Realm, and through a parallel gateway from the Cold Realm to the Undying. Once the Virion fortified that parallel gateway, entering the Undying realm became impossible. Instead, we decided to fortify our own gateway. We have held it ever since." Again, Jadamara regretted wanting to know more.

The coordinates led to a spot on what they once considered the second level. Igneous writ-stone swathed the area, but three figures stood out amongst it. The *Herald* slowed and hovered well away from the meeting location. The Alliance and Ohwen held at the same distance.

"C'mon, we are going down in a feeder," said the leader.

Jadamara enjoyed the view from the cockpit more than her previous experience in the entryway. Two Mongrelai came with them, as well as Isla and Creline. The feeder lifted away from the dock, and the six descended towards the surface. The vessel touched down next to the three people she now made out as Ehtlentins.

Isla ran ahead. Jadamara sensed a moment of tension before the woman with black and purple hair recognized the young girl sprinting at her. They wrapped each other in their arms and giggled ebulliently. The smile remained on her face as she saw Jadamara and Creline, then disappeared as the Mongrelai stepped from the feeder. She clutched Isla tight against her.

The sound of another vessel approaching turned their heads. The Ohwen ship touched down with much less gusto than their own craft had. The first down the ramp was a tall hulking man flanked by an equally impressive woman. Their height dwarfed the other Alliance officer who followed them.

Those two are Ronto. The Ronto people lived within the Alliance, and once formed the backbone of their military. The Great War left them all but extinct, they had never recovered their numbers since.

A triplet of stark contrast followed behind the Alliance officers. A beautiful woman in a white gown and shawl walked down the ramp in front of two gold amored guards. The deep brown of her eyes matched that of her hair, which had been braided into a crown upon her head. Her pale skin glowed in the hot Ehtlentin sun, but no sweat glistened off her arms or stained her clothes. Jadamara decided this woman would be her new definition of grace.

The purple haired Ehtlentin girl holding Isla did not dress so modestly. Her brown top covered only what was absolutely necessary, and even then, blended with her skin to give the illusion she was wearing no clothes at all. The skirt around her curved waist looked more like a net and did not do much to disguise the fact that she only had a thong on underneath it. Jewelry jingled quietly around her wrists and ankles. Amethyst engravings matched the purple of her hair, eyes, and painted nails. She would be Jadamara's new definition of sexy.

The purple haired girl spoke first, to everyone's surprise.

"Thank you for all meeting here. I'm Quantine, I represent the people of Deep Home," she said.

Jadamara recognized the name. Her father had been raised in the Deep Home orphanage. So had Sincret. "How many of you survived?" she asked.

"A little over 700, but we've run out of food," she replied.

"We can send provisions," said the Alliance leader. "I am Colonel Raz Taigo." His massive hand swallowed her's in a handshake. He nodded towards Jadamara and the Mongrelai next to her. An awkward silence settled.

"I am Glade Jadamara of the *Spear Throw.* This is…" She trailed off and looked up at her once-captor.

"I am Alphago of the Mongrelai." His answer jarred the Ehtlentins and Alliance officers, but the Ohwen woman remained as still as a porcelain doll.

"Did you blow the shield generators in this city?" asked the Ohwen woman without introduction.

"No," Alphago replied.

"That was us," interjected Jadamara. "Or rather, one of our own. We didn't know his plan." She felt like it was a cop-out and turned to Quantine and the other two survivors.

"We are so sorry," whispered Creline, freeing Jadamara from the obligatory apology.

"Was it Sincret?" Quantine asked. Creline nodded in affirmation. "Where is he?"

"A Psyperial kidnapped him…" he answered. He stopped there and looked expectantly at Jadamara.

"…And she came here," she finished for him.

"Your query arrived in one of our stealth ships an hour ago," said the Ohwen. "She flew into the labyrinth and anchor jumped to the root where the Psyperials are entrenched."

"We should have a black box if we are going to discuss this," Jadamara warned.

The woman pulled out a flat white device from the silver belt around her waist. "We are speaking in private. And if we all start fighting, we are all doomed anyways."

Jadamara took her word for it, though she felt reluctant to trust anyone as well dressed as she was. She skipped the background, they didn't have time. "We are on our way to get Sincret back. The Mongrelai need him." She felt Quantine's eyes on her. A knowing smile appeared on her face.

"If he makes it out of their pyramid structure, he will answer to us," said the Ohwen woman.

"And who are you?" asked Quantine.

"I am Emire, First Princess of the Ohwen. We came to liberate your city," she said matter-of-factly.

"Liberations historically do not work out in this city," replied Quantine.

"Not when the city doesn't know what's best for it; not when the city we're trying to save explodes," she retorted.

The Mongrelai pointed towards the half-sunk cloudship in the distance. "The explosion did not do that though. Their Shadowed warriors are impressive, aren't they?"

Colonel Taigo laughed. "They are, but not unstoppable." He pulled out a dark purple crystal, much like the red one Jadamara had seen in the hand of the Shadowed who killed Eva. "These are the weapons we found on them. They activate when we run a writ-current through them. They behave differently depending on their structure, a lot like our ingevein crystals." He became suspicious, "How do you know of them? What do you know of them?"

"You don't want to ask," Jadamara interrupted, "and we don't have time. What about your people?" she asked Quantine.

"We only just finished clearing the rubble trapping us. We had to rappel out through the waterway just to get here. We are completely buried and most haven't seen the sun in days. The passage out is too dangerous for the young and elderly to make but there is a waterway shuttles can fly through."

"You have elderly?" Jadamara asked. Old age was synonymous with wealth, and she thought the wealthy would have been holed up in a bunker well away from the lower levels.

"We have Uncut, Once-Cuts, and Twice-Cuts living together, as well as quite a few outsiders," Quantine responded.

Jadamara felt bad asking her next question. "Do you have warriors?"

"Only a couple dozen. Most of the Painted Boys changed their allegiance to the Psyperials when they eradicated the Twice-Cuts. Your group left with the Painted Boys who deserted with Cass. What about them?"

"We lost some to the rot, some to labyrinth beasts, and many to the Psyperials. Those that survived broke from our group after Cass died." Creline replied, choking on the last sentence. "Alphago assures us that we can get into their pyramid. Once we are there the fighting will be hard. We need all the help we can get."

The Colonel and Princess took a brief aside, then the Princess said, "We can shuttle your people out. Our capital ships will coordinate with Deep Home once you open a frequency." She held out a communication device for Quantine.

The Colonel spoke next. "We will help you find the war criminal, Sincret. I'm not going to order my men in for an extraction, but I will open it to volunteers. My daughter, Hera, will lead them," said the Colonel. His Ronto daughter nodded in agreement.

"Again, we don't have a lot of time to pass around a sign-up sheet, Colonel. If they see us coming, they will blast us out of the sky before we get close," Jadamara urged.

"They won't," said Alphago confidently.

"You can expect eight of our snubfighters and twenty soldiers on your ship in an hour. It looks like you have a dock," said the Princess as she evaluated the dreadnaught hovering in the distance.

"There is room for your ships. But the leaving will be much harder than arriving. We could use transports once we have the criminals," said Alphago. The two Ronto looked at each other.

The Princess answered. "We can spare two troop carriers, but they won't fit in your dreadnaught. Our stealth tech can hide them until you are ready to be extracted. But you will need to create a hole in their defenses for them to get in and out."

The chances seemed to stack against them as more holes riddled their plan. *That pyramid is enormous, we won't know where to begin*, Jadamara thought.

As if reading her mind, Quantine said, "We have schematics to their pyramid. They call it the *Omedegon*." She held up a book unlike Jadamara had ever seen. Three dimensional blueprints sprung from each page as she brushed her hand over it. "Detention levels," she commanded. Pages rushed by her hand until an image of the whole pyramid appeared, where red sections stood amongst the blue."

"Where did you get this?" said the Princess in awe and anger.

"My brother," Quantine said. "The Psyperials captured him from the Retine mines. He can help us once we are inside."

Us? Jadamara could not picture the scantily dressed woman going up against the armored Psyperials. She wanted to say something, but the determination in Quantine's eyes kept her silent. The Princess looked over the book enviously.

"Good. Great," said the Colonel. His praise eased the ten-

STAR STORY BOOK ONE: ANCHORED

sion, then he approached the Mongrelai and it rose exponentially again. He stood before the crystalline warrior, towering over Alphago yet giving him no less of a dangerous appearance. "This is the first time we've seen Mongrelai since the Great War, and we have not forgotten it. I would have blown you out of the sky had Princess Emire not asked otherwise. Betray us, and my daughter will bury you in that labyrinth."

An hour later, chaos ensued as the Ehtlentin, Alliance, and Ohwen forces squeezed into the hangars within the *Herald*. The Alliance snubfighters hung like bats from its ceiling near the railgun. The pilots remained inside their craft, feeling uneasy as they looked down at the floor meters below. Shuttles dropped off Alliance soldiers who walked below the hanging fighters and marveled at the rail gun which divided the hangar in two. Crews loaded munitions on board through the docking inlets on the sides of the ship. Quantine's Painted Boys arrived last in an Ohwen shuttle. It lowered into the dorsal hangar bay where Creline greeted them.

On the bridge, Alphago retrofitted an adaptor for Jadamara's ingevein. She entered the dreadnaught's ingevein network for the first time, and felt uneasy from the disorganization she found. There was no one voice channeling the information, but rather hundreds. Making sense of it felt like grabbing a handful of strings and tracing them back one at a time to their function, then doing so a hundred more times.

"Whew, that is too much," she said, exhausted.

"The redundant systems protect us from Virion hacking, at least until they run out. Our network is only accessible through hard-wiring for the same reason. One pilot can control this ship with the use of CDs, as Damaeon did, but had you run into a proper battle, you would have been destroyed."

Jadamara scoffed. *Proper battle my ass.*

"There was a time when this dreadnaught would have punched straight through that Ohwen cloudship." His statement felt uncharacteristically like bragging. "You may also notice the organization is not as calculated as the computers you are used to. We network the systems through a crystal called creeper coral." He pointed at the faintly glowing lines which spread outwards from the bridge, tracing along the thick steel wires. "A fair bit rusted away, but what is left will keep her together." He cleared his throat, becoming aware of his boisterous explanation. He couldn't help sounding condescending with his next comment. "System conditions is the simplest to grasp. When something blows up, you will know. I will be concentrated on piloting but you can share the information with me. More importantly, share it with the others working damage control."

She delved back into the incoherent world. Like Sincret had done with his brief period flying the ship, she largely ignored most of the data. She found access to internal and external cameras, and watched the soldiers gathering around the Colonel's daughter in the hangar. Hera briefed them on their relatively simple plan.

"The pyramid has a network of tunnels that allow their ships to move through it. We will punch a hole into the network through this point." A corner of the pyramid lit up. "This section of the ship is essentially a giant laboratory. It detaches from the main body, and will be our point of entry. Currently, it is connected to the main body. Once we punch through the hull, we will hold the landing zone while the Ohwen, Painted Boys, and our shuttles head towards their objectives. On their way out, they will initiate lockdowns to seal all but these three passages, which will make our job a bit easier."

Three soldiers raised their hands and the rest mumbled to themselves.

"Hey! Follow orders, don't ask questions. You'll be thankful to not know the details if one of those shadowy bastards get you. Speaking of which, if you encounter one alone, you already fucked up and will probably die. Stay together in the phalanx and pound 'em with rounds."

The twenty hooted, "Ooah!" then separated. Jadamara searched the other feeds.

The Ohwen had congregated in the cantina room where

they had access to the three hangars at the rear of the ship. The Princess Emire did not come with the band of twenty soldiers, but her younger sister did. The woman wore an all-white jumpsuit which stood out against the blues and blacks of the soldiers around her. Her name was Second Princess Bela, Jadamara only met her briefly. She looked identical to her older sister, but during their conversation proved far less pretentious. Garters around her arms and thighs housed dozens of silver throwing knives. The thick platinum belt around her waist holstered a pistol, two sais, and five pockets which promised more deadly tools. She sat cross legged on the abandoned bar with her eyes closed. Most of the other Ohwen had the *Omedegon's* schematics open in front of them, especially the heavily armored commandos who would be heading into the heart of the pyramid.

Jadamara felt the motion of systems around her and pulled away from the *Herald's* network again.

"We are heading to the Rim," Alphago announced over the intercom. "ETA two minutes before jump."

An overwhelming dread rattled Jadamara. It felt as if she suddenly woke up and realized she was in a war vessel heading into the heart of a battle.

This is not me. This is not me. I don't fight in wars. I can't do any of this. She had never been one for self-pity, but could not help thinking how unfair life had been the last three weeks. *The first inter-universal war and I am right in the thick of it. Lost my ship, lost my crew, I am losing my mind and I might lose my life.*

They jumped and emerged at the first turn in the root of Ehtlentin's labyrinth. The Rim lay behind them, no more than a speck of light amongst the swallowing darkness. Ahead of them, at the bend where the tunnel curved, a dozen Alliance and Ohwen craft circled over a swirl of thick artificial clouds. Their lights strafed over white plumes of writ-cloud contained within in a globe around the advance base.

Somewhere in there are the transports that will extract us if we can't leave on the Herald, she knew.

As if reading her mind, Alphago got up and sat across from

her "The Ohwen are the true power in your realm. Their Frozen Queen, these Princesses; one or all of them are Anchored, and they may have guessed the same for Sincret. We shouldn't count on them. Nor the Alliance, nor the survivors from Ehtlentin."

What about you? she wondered. "This morning you told me we all need to unite."

"And you told me that would never happen. I believe you. Our partnership with the Ohwen and Alliance will only last for as long as we are useful to them. I don't know what their plan is, but judging by the munitions the Ohwen snuck aboard, it does not seem amicable."

The next jump would take them to Retine, where the *Omedegon* had fortified itself. The anchor reel recharged and Jadamara clutched the straps around her tightly. She forced her breathing to slow and pushed out with her gut. The breathing exercise gave her the sensation of laughter, which leapt from her mouth.

"This is so fucked up," she said to herself. Creline let out a sound that was half-bark, half-laugh. He smiled at her, obviously relieved someone else was thinking the same thing. Lights on the bridge shifted yellow to red, and she delved into the *Herald's* ingevein network.

The anchor reel clanked as they arrived at their destination. A hail of Psyperial bolts hit them in seconds. The shields sprung to life. She sensed the redundant vector shields working together to punch through each blast as they came. The globe shields had been localized in front as well, soaking up the occasional bolt that slipped through the barrage. The thunderous boom of the rail gun below them echoed through the ship, and she heard the Mongrelai cheering. After a second's delay, another eruption from the rail gun shook them. The first round exploded against a Psyperial vector shield that leapt from the defensive turret drilled into a massive stalagmite. However, the shell burst into a fiery plasma that poured over its globular shields. The second round blasted through the flaming shields and into the turret, destroying it along with the better part of the massive stalagmite it was built upon.

They fired the two ammo rounds in concordance to destroy the next three defensive installments. When they approached the fourth, Psyperial snubfighters flooded in from all sides and sprayed their hull with bolts. Explosions rippled against layers of globular shields. Guns on the sides and rear of the *Herald* sent hundreds of flak bolts outwards to disrupt their missiles before they reached the vector shields. She sensed the two Mongrelai feeders detach from the flank docks. They revolved around their vessel, discouraging the Psyperials from making strafing runs in formation.

Several larger frigates that once devastated the Ehtlentin cruisers upon the mountainside, lifted from the cavern walls and encircled them. The closer they drew to the *Omedegon*, the tighter the net became. The frigates closed in, their long-range cannons fired at the rear of their *Herald*. She felt the gravity shift to and fro as the Mongrelai outmaneuvered the artillery before it reached them.

There's no way the transports will make it through this, even with the hole we are punching through, she thought doubtfully. The last base was not one facility but a line of artillery spread far and wide apart.

We won't be able to take out more than half of them at this rate. She thought despairingly. Then hopefully, *We are still in pretty good shape.*

"Long range munitions," she heard Alphago order. The rail gun raised and fired a munition that arced the great distance to the pyramid, and detonated against the side of it. They fired two more rounds and the pyramid slowly started to rotate.

"How are we getting through their shields?" she asked incredulously.

"We can melt their shields like we did with those turrets, and we can peel them apart to slip a round through. You are seeing the latter," he answered. The pyramid slowly turned the damaged hull away from them. As it did, their landing target came into view. "Begin hammer protocol." The ship sped up, but she felt Alphago holding back. "Almost there."

They bypassed the final defenses lining their path and were shaken by impacts in the process. The corner of the pyramid, which would be their landing zone, rotated into view. The *Herald* picked up speed and angled downwards. When it leveled out, their entry point lay directly ahead of them. "Hold on!" he shouted. Five rail-gun rounds fired in rapid succession and drowned out even Alphago's virtual voice she heard through her ingevein. She closed her eyes and felt the *Herald* lodge into the chasm it created with a thunderous boom.

Metal screeched against the dreadnaught's hull as it burrowed deep into the *Omedegon*. The rail gun fired three more times, the sound reverberated back into their ship. Jadamara felt her ears ring and her head grow light.

The metallic screech persisted until their ship finally settled upon the bent metal innards of the pyramid.

We are inside, she thought excitedly. Getting in had taken a toll. The side cannon had torn off during their entry. There were several cracks in the hull near core systems that would need patching before they left.

"Hangar doors opening," he said over the comm.

"Roger that," replied the Hera.

The hum of engines from the levels below came to life. Soon after, the sound of energy bolts melting metal rose and became fainter as the Alliance fighters cleared away the landing zone, then continued forward to the tunnel network. She tapped in to the cameras to watch their progress. The six snubfighters hovered just in front of the *Herald*, a barrage of bolts ripping away walls, machine, and any Psyperial unlucky enough to be in their path.

Inside the hangar, Alliance and Ohwen soldiers boarded the shuttles that would deposit them close to the choke points they would defend. She saw Hera take one last weary look around the hangar before she disappeared. *Time to board our own shuttle.*

She, Quantine, Creline, the Mongrelai, and a team of

Painted Boys jogged to the Mongrelai shuttle. They walked along the rafters between the rail gun and hangar wall, where the Alliance snubfighters had hung moments earlier. The shuttle appeared to be a whole different make than any of the other Mongrelai ships she had seen. She wondered from where they had collected this particular craft. Quantine sat next to Jadamara once on board. Despite the tasteful light weave armor she had adorned for the battle, she still looked like a delicate flower next to the Painted Boys around her.

She even smells like one.

She noticed Jadamara staring at her. "Looking good goes a long way with these Psyperials," she said, then turned to an armor clad Creline. "You would be wise to do the same, half their soldiers are women and just as fickle."

"Yeah, I think I'll stick with what I know," he replied.

"What about you, handsome?" she asked towards Garvis. The young man seemed stuck halfway between awe and humiliation.

"Leave him alone," said Jadamara. "He's fought them before. We'll see how much good looks count when we are fighting through gas-filled corridors."

"They can see through the gas," she said confidently. "And that's what the big guys are for. Oh, and by the way, I have fought them too, and from what I've seen you won't get far running from a Shadowed if you're wearing full armor."

"I don't plan on running from them," replied Jadamara. "In fact, if you see one with a mask that looks like a face on fire, let me know." She wanted vengeance, Ava had too. The young girl had begged Jadamara to take her along. She turned her away though, she couldn't afford to lose another friend. The memory of their life before Ehtlentin slipped away with each death of the people who remembered it. She finally agreed to stay back and help the refugees, but made Jadamara promise her to avenge Eva. It was an easy promise.

Since the day they fought the Shadowed in the labyrinth, she had run scenarios over and over in her head. *How else can I fight with my ingevein? What else can they do with their crystals?* She had not maintained her ingevein though, and could feel its energy source draining. Her blaster had proved useless, her knife would be a last defense. *Let's hope the Mongrelai have more experience.*

The shuttle cleared the hangar entry. A melted mess of metal surrounded them on all sides. The three Alliance shuttles moved down the tunnel created by the rail gun, and expanded by the snubfighters.

Hera's voice buzzed over the shuttle's speakers. "We've reached the tunnel, but our bolts aren't getting through. Stand clear for missiles." A bright light burst ahead of them. Debris came crashing down on top of them but the line held steady.

"They're here!" an Alliance pilot screamed as Psyperial snubfighters appeared on the other side of their exit.

"Punch it!" she heard another voice say.

A flurry of lights whipped back and forth ahead. Explosions lit the tunnel, preceded by the screams of panicked pilots.

"They've got us lined up!" yelled an Alliance pilot.

"Clear a path," ordered Alphago.

The Alliance ships parted and he punched the acceleration. Their shuttle jetted overhead the others and into the spray of green bolts that thudded against their shields. They crashed through the opening, and into the Psyperial vessel shooting through it. The two crafts scraped against each other, then deflected away. Bolts from the other Psyperial snubfighters followed them as they turned to head down the tunnel. Three peeled off to follow; however, as soon as the first of their bolts landed against their shuttle, a trail of blue fire erupted from behind it. The charged plasma hung in the air and coated the squad of ships. Two managed to land their flaming craft, but the leader took the brunt of the fire and spun wildly until it crashed against the tunnel floor as a smoldering fireball. The passengers hooted.

"It's called cold fire. You can thank the Virion," said Alphago to Jadamara, noting her astonishment.

"Don't we need them?" asked Creline, referring to the Alliance snubfighters still battling their way out of the entry point.

"They will catch up," replied Alphago.

"We are close to my brother," said Quantine. A rectangular inlet appeared along the tunnel wall. She pointed, "There."

The shuttle slowed. "Go," commanded Alphago to his warriors.

Two Mongrelai walked to the door. They stripped off layers of heavy cloth covering their crystalline shells. Every layer that dropped revealed more of the beautiful armor. The sight of it made Jadamara feel as though she needed to look away. Their perfect glowing forms came to view. Only after all the layers fell did she realize that one of them had a womanly figure. Just as soon as they finished, they opened the shuttle door and a gust of wind filled the vessel. She watched through squinted eyes as the pair touched the ingevein-like consoles embedded in the crystal along their forearms, then disappeared out the opening. The wind stopped as the door closed behind them. She unbuckled and climbed into the empty seat next to Alphago.

The two soldiers flew outwards ahead of them, carried by shrieking glowing crystals around their wrists ankles and back. Two turrets sprayed trails of bolts towards the Mongrelai who weaved to evade the incoming blasts.

It's like they're dancing, she noted in awe. They flipped and rolled their way towards the turrets. Jadamara lost sight of them, but two explosions signaled their mission succeeded. They reappeared on the platform and split up to search the area. *Doesn't look like anyone is home.* The coalition had hoped for as much; the success of their lightning strike mission centered around keeping ahead of the undermanned Psyperial defense.

They touched down and the Painted Boys quickly fanned out to create a perimeter. Several halls lay ahead of them, Quantine pointed them down the middle one. Creline counted off ten of them to follow. Alphago and the female Mongrelai took the lead, and the other Mongrelai followed behind them. Jadamara, Creline, and Quantine walked at the center of the pack.

"Let's pick it up," said Alphago. The group began jogging.

A notification from Jadamara's ingevein nagged at her. She acknowledged it and her heart leapt at the information it supplied her,

JV? she realized.

His ingevein signature emanated from farther down the hallway. She contained herself and turned to Creline who bobbed up and down beside her. "JV is here," she said.

It took a second for her words to register. When they did he looked surprised as well. He didn't say anything, which is what she hoped for. *We have our own secret now.*

They slowed as the hallway ended. They walked out into a tall room filled with machines Jadamara could not begin to make sense of. The walls were black, as well as the desks, and tiled floors. Magnificent glass tanks containing green liquid hung from the ceiling many meters above, with tubes draining the solution downwards into apparatuses below. Shelves lined the walls and stacked upon one another reaching upwards. An eclectic mix of machine parts occupied most of the space. The careless arrangement reminded Jadamara of the junk shops in Omphala. She inspected the shelf closest to her and jumped when she saw the eyes of a humanoid contrivance staring back at her. The group jumped in response, Jadamara blushed when they saw the source of her alarm, though no one said a word.

They walked further into the lab and she sensed JVs signature becoming stronger. The smell of filthy animals grew stronger as well. Soon, organic matter replaced the machines lining the work benches. Creatures, both familiar and foreign, hung in jars of the same green fluid. Beneath airtight seals, corpses of native creatures lay splayed open half-dissected. Soon, even their morbid forms were traded for darker replacements. They passed three Ehtlentin bodies in a line; all with gold streaks in their hair, and gold irises to match. The sight brought mumbles to the surface of the refugees' lips.

Alphago held up his hand. "Quiet," he said sharply. A soft clicking sound ahead became audible. The group crouched behind a line of crates and Alphago peered around the corner. Jadamara found a crack to look through. A small black contrivance stitched away at an Ehtlentin boy laying upon a glowing table. The Painted Boys looked at each other. Quantine gestured for them to calm down.

"Which way?" Alphago asked Quantine. She pointed towards the direction they had been heading. Jadamara wondered how far the chamber stretched, till she noticed the soft glimmer of reflecting light and realized they had reached a corner. "Then we go around," said Alphago. "Quickly."

They skirted around the equipment until they reached the wall.

"I don't think we will need to go out of our way to find JV," she whispered to Creline. Quantine turned around and looked at them suspiciously. *Can I tell her?* she wondered. A series of hallways dove into the wall, Quantine selected one. Hundreds of metal doors lined both sides of the long, wide corridor. Creline ordered half the boys to stay at the doorway. Quantine led them down the hall until they stopped outside a door half the distance down.

The door JV happens to be on the other side of. Exuberant joy rose in her, followed by immediate fear. They could barely manage JV on the *Spear Throw*. She didn't say goodbye to him earlier because seeing him broke her heart. She knew what to expect from her mother, she knew telling him she needed to leave him had the potential turn into catastrophe. That didn't seem to matter anymore. She wanted to save him, no matter what state he was in. And if she couldn't, she would end his suffering before the Psyperials could do any more harm.

"Stand back," said Alphago. A Mongrelai heaved a piece of machinery off his back and slammed it against the door. The Mongrelai pounded hard on the door as warning, then began melting it away with the device. Globs of glowing metal fell to the floor and slid off his crystal boots. Most of it seemed to flood into the cell though, and Jadamara yelped as she imagined the flow creeping towards JV's paralyzed body. With a loud clang, the Mongrelai ripped away what remained of the door and released it from the tool she used to bore through it.

"No," Jadamara whispered

A young man with purple hair and one purple eye sat in the cell where, she had hoped against reason, to have found JV. Tattoos covered his body from empty eye socket to toe. The markings glowed faintly in the darkness, betraying his labyrinthian origins. Beneath the Retine paint, a rainbow of hues could be seen, tracing the path of his teslac

He reached for the red shirt next to him, but instead of pale flesh, a black metal appendage grasped the garb's folds. Tangled within the Psyperial machine matrix, she could make out the distinct pattern of lights from JV's ingevein.

"Brother," breathed Quantine, who rushed by Jadamara and wrapped the boy in a hug. "What have they done to you?" she asked, touching the faint a rainbow of glowing lines beneath his shirt, distinct from his blue glowing tattoos. She turned his metal arm over in hers.

"Nothing I can't come back from. Thank you," he replied in a raspy voice. The quality of it sounded familiar, she heard it in the voices of several orphans who had served prison sentences in the Retine mines.

He has crystal lung, a missing arm, a missing eye. He is from Retine. She did pity the boy. He looked so young wrapped in his sister's arms. Yet, his visage fostered an instant hatred in Jadamara. Born from the fact that the only conventional way of extracting an ingevein, was upon its host's death.

"This is my brother, Lavelokine," Quantine said to the group.

He broke away from her. "They will know you're here, so let's go," he urged.

She heard Garvis over the comm, "Hey guys. The Alliance escorts never caught up, but the Psyperials have. They're heading for you too." She heard the ringing of gunfire through the static.

"I told you, you won't get far in the tunnels," complained the boy to Quantine.

STAR STORY BOOK ONE: ANCHORED

"Can you lock down the dividers like you said?" Alphago asked.

The boy looked unfazed by the appearance of the Mongrelai.

"I have my finger on the button." He pulled out a book from under his bed and flipped to a hologram that had been translated in Ehtlentin. "It will be a lot harder for you to get to the prison block once I push it."

"We aren't going to the prison block," said the Mongrelai. The boy looked at his sister, who looked at the Mongrelai.

"Damaeon is in the heart of the pyramid." His own holographic projection of the pyramid rose from his wrist, a tracing blinked in a room at its center. Two yellow lights danced on the outside of the pyramid as well indicating the location of the feeder vessels defending the rear of the *Herald*. "We'll lock it down now, and hitch a ride with my team."

Jadamara, Creline, Quantine and her brother looked uncomfortably at each other. "It will help the people defending the *Herald*. But it will also put a wall between us and our Alliance fighters," Jadamara said.

"Who haven't showed up," Creline finished.

"Do it," Alphago commanded. Quantine nodded. The hologram lit up as the boy touched it, then blinked out of existence when he closed the book.

Alphago parted them as he doubled back through the corridor. The rest followed, trying to keep pace. Scaled armor rattled around her and exhausted breaths of Painted Boys dampened her ear. Beyond them, she heard the faint groaning of machinery; the scrape of heavy metal doors closing and churning of cranks drawing layers of the pyramid apart. Down the hallway, foreign voices echoed off the chamber walls.

Alphago and the two other Mongrelai broke into a sprint and charged down the hall. It took the fastest of the Painted Boys twice as long to reach the entrance. By the time they did, two of the Mongrelai were already hovering near the center of the chamber, reigning down bolts upon unseen enemies. Alphago had risen two dozen meters above the hallway they exited. An orange light beamed from his visor and scanned over the wall.

"Stay here!" ordered Creline to the nervous group. "Circle up." They began condensing back towards the hall when Jadamara felt an eerie presence among them. The shadow of a crate stretched outwards and separated completely into its own shrouded form. A fiery orange whip crackled to life from the darkness of its spinning cloak, illuminating the flame-shaped mask of its wielder, and biting through the arm of her first prey. The Painted Boy screamed and all turned their weapons towards the Shadowed warrior. Jadamara raised her blaster as well, but felt a mild disorientation, then a complete loss of balance, overtake her. Their first barrage missed the Shadowed, or disappeared into the folds of its cloak, but soon none of them had the strength to hold their weapons. Her pistol felt heavy in her hand, she let it drop and fell to her knees too. She focused into her ingevein to try to make sense of the weakness overcoming her, but the act of doing so seemed to cure the nausea altogether.

Everything feels okay through the ingevein, because everything is okay with me, she realized. She stayed hunched over but looked around until she found the second Shadowed with a mask resembling a weathered, elderly man. His hands extended forward as if waiting to clasp a child's hands, except the children in front of him lay writhing on the ground.

You first. She brought her pistol close and balanced it on her knee. The bolt launched when it reached maximum charge and landed in the one place Jadamara hoped it would not be swallowed up. The orange blast exploded against the Shadowed's mask. It sent him off his feet into an unmoving heap on the ground. She heard the gasping breaths of the others recovering around her. She searched for the fiery Shadowed and found the creature weaving up the wall to Alphago, it's flaming whip trailing behind. She locked eyes with the Shadowed as they had days ago in the labyrinth. It looked away as it slung its writ-whip towards Alphago and wrapped it around his leg. The Shadowed pulled hard, swinging itself up while yanking him downwards. The creature arced and landed upon him. Crackling lighting racked his body when the Shadowed made contact and the two of them crashed to the ground.

The Painted Boys ran forward with their spears but backed off as the arcs of energy continued to leap out of the Mongrelai's armor. A bolt contacted a Painted Boy, sending him flying backwards with a melted hole in his chest plate. With the same movement, the Shadowed launched a splash of lightning towards a group of three huddled together. It wrapped around them and lit the cloth it contacted of fire. With another push of her hand, the three launched backwards and crashed loudly against the wall.

Before the Shadowed could bring her hand back, Alphago snatched her by the wrist. His other hand shot up and clamped around her throat. He rose, bringing her struggling body up with him, then hurled the black mass away. The throw sent the Shadowed through a nearby table and the equipment on top of it. A mix of metal, glass, and liquids crashed down along the trajectory. It slammed against a crate a few meters past the table with a sickening thud.

At the same time, globs of melted metal began trickling down the wall as Alphago's charges burned a hole to whatever room lay on the other side. Jadamara turned her head back to the Shadowed coughing on the ground. Alphago approached in his frustratingly slow manner. Jadamara did the same, though far more timidly. She felt Quantine's body heat next to her. Her typical devious smile had been wiped from her face. Her readied blaster shook along with the tremor of her hand holding it.

But she still looks determined. She nodded at the girl and the both continued towards the creature. It stripped off its mask, revealing a feminine tattooed face underneath. The woman's eyes burned aggressively, and darted between the enemies advancing towards her. She let loose a fearsome battle cry and a torrent of flame that washed over everything in front of her. The wave of fire reached Jadamara and Quantine just as her ingevein's shield sprung to deflect it. The blast diverted around, but it's heat baked the air within their shell. A shield twice the size and luminance sprung from Alphago's arm as well. The flames burst against it, but did not slow his steady progress towards the Shadowed. On their other side, she saw Creline covering himself behind a crate. The flames ceased and the creature raised its hand towards Jadamara. She felt a familiar tug on her torso send her through the air as an invisible force contacted her. This time, she landed against Lavelokine and sent them both tumbling over.

A glowing rope extended from Alphago's wrist and wrapped around the Shadowed's arm, but a crackling flame dagger appeared in her hand and she sliced herself free. The rope retracted back into a device on Alphago's forearm. His other hand raised a blaster. The Shadowed flailed her arms wildly, sending crates, tables, chairs, and equipment flying towards him. He moved with incredible fluidity, dodging the first three objects as they reached him. He fired a bolt after he evaded the fourth, then another after the fifth, and two more after the sixth. Each bolt sizzled a new hole in the Shadowed's garb.

Her arms gave up the futile effort and fell in to clutch her smoking wounds. She retreated up and over the crate behind her with unnatural speed. Alphago launched the glowing rope after her, snaring her foot; he yanked, halting her progress. The rope snapped into a more rigid form, allowing him to swing her in a circle as if she were on the end of a pole instead. When he brought her to the ground, she smashed over several more tables and tumbled to a halt at Jadamara's feet. She drove her dagger towards the woman, but stopped just as the blade began sinking into her chest. The woman looked wide-eyed at her. She moved her blade to her throat instead and held it against her.

She's crying? she realized uncomfortably as she remembered her own helplessness at the hands of Eylea.

Another knife dug in next to Jadamara's. It belonged to Lavelokine, and he twisted it deeper until the woman coughed blood. He stabbed her twice more and she stopped moving. Jadamara could not move as well, until he pulled her up by the arm and shook her back to their situation. He returned to the Shadowed once more to collect a crystal from the woman's robes.

Alphago swung his rope through the melted hole, where it caught grip. He let it fall, then motioned for them to climb as he ascended into the air and towards his comrades still fighting at the center of the vast laboratory. Creline quickly rappelled up the wall and peaked his head through the opening a second later to motion that it was safe. Quantine and Jadamara went next, then the Painted Boys from lightest to heaviest.

Jadamara climbed carefully over the heated ring and into the service tunnel on the other side. She helped the Painted Boys up, keeping an eye on the battle within the lab as it drew closer. Lights erupted amongst the machinery as the three Mongrelai pulled back behind the cover of lab clutter. The three launched simultaneously into the air, but one quickly fell behind. The damaged crystals on his armor lifted him awkwardly away from the charging Psyperials. He lost the ability to outmaneuver their bolts with each one that landed, however he made it outside their range and they began missing.

The first two Mongrelai arrived as she pulled the last Painted Boy up. When she looked back at the third, she saw something she had not noticed before: a thin, upside down figure flush against a machine stalagmite hanging from the ceiling. Web-like glittering lines traced over her black jumpsuit. Her dark hair served to hide her in the shadows, but a pale face slowly appeared as she followed the wounded Mongrelai's progress below her. She lifted herself from the machine and drew the sparkling web from the upper half of her body, waited, then dropped the net into his path. It enveloped him before he realized what had happened and constricted to pull his limbs tight against his body. The crystals on his armor ceased howling, and his cocooned form fell to the floor.

"Val 'hala," said Alphago softly. A second later, the thump of a muffled explosion beat down the narrow hallway.

He's another ashen husk now, she thought, knowing the Mongrelai would rather die than be captured. *A quick way to go, a better way.*

She realized Alphago was pulling her weight and she picked up the pace. The line jogged down the narrow corridor until it divided in two. Jadamara pulled up the map, Alphago put a marker for the pickup location.

"Right," she said. Another wall lay between them and their destination, but she doubted it would stop them. Wind gusted through the service corridor as they drew closer to the pyramid's tunnel network. They reached a spot that looked as good as any to burn through, Alphago paused. Scorched welts riddled his smooth armor and lightning bolt lines weaved amongst the craters, coalescing at the points where the Shadowed siphoned energy from the crystals to create her electric storm.

"Do your thing," she said expectantly to Alphago. He stared at her a moment.

He took a bigger thrashing than I thought.

Instead of burning through the wall, he simply released the wall panel and moved it aside. A thick jungle of pipes and wires ran behind it. The obstacle course proved trouble for the heavier soldiers, but eventually they found their way through to the far wall panel, and waited for Alphago's order.

A deep Mongrelai voice buzzed on the comm, "Almost there. We have company, so be quick about it."

"We do too," said the Mongrelai woman guarding the corridor from which they entered. Quantine released the final wall panel. Air from behind them rushed into the enormous tunnel beyond. The force of it ripped the sheet of metal out of her hands, almost taking her with it.

"Load the feeder when it arrives," Alphago ordered, then reentered the jungle.

The two Mongrelai feeders weaved their way down the tunnel, spraying bolts backwards at the squadron of Psyperials pursuing them. The sound of their roaring engines grew louder, and Jadamara grew concerned as missed Psyperial bolts slammed against the tunnel walls near them. One of the Mongrelai broke from the other and looped around, taking the snub-fighters head on. They pulled up to avoid the spray of its blasters, but Mongrelai missiles followed two of the vessels to their fiery end.

A ramp extended out from the other feeder as it pulled up to the square opening. They had not needed to use the extension when they boarded the ship from the ground, it looked like it had not seen action for some time. *Falling to their death is probably not a concern when they can float.* The pressure from the writ-field holding the ship afloat beat against her. *Oscillating writ-field pressure, tornado winds, and a precariously perched ramp.* She heard gunfire from behind her and chose to take her chances.

They crawled on all fours across the ramp. The heavily armored Painted Boys found themselves at an advantage for once, and helped Quantine and Jadamara across. Lavelokine made it through last and they all peered backwards through the metal jungle. Alphago cut his way through the ensnaring wires and the engines below them roared to life.

The hulking Mongrelai made it halfway to them when an explosion erupted within the tangle of wires, covering him and everything within in fire. The heat bellowed outwards and deflected against the feeder's shields. They waited, aghast until they were certain nothing would move from within the wall space except for the inferno incinerating it. The ship rocked as bolts from the reformed Psyperial snubfighters homed in on them, signaling their deadline to move on. Another roar of the engines sent them down the tunnel towards, what Jadamara hoped, would not be more of the same.

CHAPTER 14
Sincret

The woman who called herself Eylea bound, blinded, and debilitated Sincret for the duration of the journey. The spider contrivance, clamped to the ceiling of the Ohwen ship she stole back, encased him in a writ-field that kept him between sleep and consciousness, as if he were too feverish to rest no matter how bad his body ached for it. The harder he tried to focus on writbending himself free, the worse his sickness became. He eventually gave up, and lay in silence for the long hours of their journey, until he became bored of complacency and groaned as loud as he could behind his gagged mouth.

The woman descended the ladder and crouched over him. "Surprise," she said as she stuck him with a needle.

He awoke again hours later, but this time feeling the best he had in months. *Impossibly good,* he thought as he opened his eyes. He lay clothed on a comfortable cot, two hands rested on the sides of his head and sent a tingling sensation through his body. Alarm rose as he realized he could not move. He thought back to his last memory of Eylea anesthetizing him, then more memories flooded in uncontrollably. They flashed before his eyes in rapid succession, each bringing up the emotions attached to them. *Joy, pain, loss, life, love. Too much. It's too much.* Then the flood abated as the man above him removed his hands.

The man, dressed in folds of dark cloth, stood next to him. *He feels familiar, this place is familiar.* The door on the far side of the room drew his attention. *This is the place where I died last*, he realized. He could not bring himself to focus on the man's face, he feared it would be the same one from his dreams. He remained paralyzed, but felt a slight give now against the resistance. The loosened restraint calmed him somewhat and he summoned the courage to look at his captor.

The face did not inspire feelings of fear or danger, but affection. The instinct surprised Sincret, it made him wonder if he had not yet slipped away from the man's influence over his mind. "Brother," he said automatically.

The man smiled and said, "It is good to see you again, Damaeon." He lifted his fingers as a gesture for him to relax. Sincret felt control return to his muscles and lifted his body to a sitting position. They appeared to be in a comfortable section of a much larger, colder chamber. A bright fire illuminated the space, creating long shadows that stretched to the door on the far side of the room.

"I've been here," he said.

"Many times, over many lives," the man replied.

"Aemon," Sincret guessed.

"Yes," he replied again, though with a smile. His shoulders relaxed and the awkwardness of the situation faded somewhat.

"I remember so much now, but it still seems so far away, I still can't make sense of it," cried Sincret.

"I can help you," Aemon said calmly. Sincret regarded the man hesitantly. "If only to show you how much you mean to me."

He didn't see the point in refusing the man. He had no secrets, only questions. *This is it, this is where it ends.* Yet, he had not enjoyed the answers so far, nor the cost they came at. *Unraveling this mystery will not free me,* he knew. *I am Sincret now, who will I become once it's over?*

"I would prefer to talk," he answered. Aemon nodded and lowered his hands.

"It's hard to explain where to begin. I suppose the start of our story. You and I came into this world together 800 years ago, and we have spent many lives with each other since. You may recall moments from your first life 800 years ago, but what you would remember is not pleasant. Our world had just cracked in half, and the disasters generated from its splitting wiped out almost everything on the planet. Our father, Hadeon, saved as many people as he could, and became the first Battlelord of Psyperia.

He raised us by himself, as our mother died during our birth. We lived for a hundred years and helped our father build a republic that served the people, survived the storms, and allowed us the anonymity necessary to be reborn into it. He kept the nature of our existence a secret from us, so we could learn the fear of death just as our compatriots. We died on separate ships in the same storm, and were reborn to separate mothers in different bodies.

Our father identified us when our writ-gifts manifested during our second lives. Like everyone who can writbend, we went to the Shadowed Temple to learn how to control it. He explained our heritage and the nature of our dreams, then passed on the objects he felt important to us from our first life. We trained under the same master as we had from our first life, donned different masks, and served the people. War broke out between our fledgling society and a satellite nation. You died seizing their capital, and were reborn again into your third life.

"The cycle repeated many more times; sometimes I found you, sometimes you found me. Our rebirths always occurred within the Psyperium, and always killed our parents. We look different each time we are reborn, but our original appearances can be evoked if our teslacs come under stress."

A contrivance, made of the same dark writ-alloy material as Eylea's spider, floated through the air with two drinks in tow. It seemed a lot jollier than the woman's machine though, and the drink it offered Sincret tasted earthy and floral.

Aemon sipped and continued. "It took time for Psyperia to form into the empire it is now, yet once it had stabilized, you began to feel deceived. Through all our rebirths, our father, our Shadowed instructor, and the man we call the Lazaeron the

Remaker, had never died. The structure of our society allowed their longevity to go unnoticed, but eventually you demanded an explanation for why we were bound to rebirth, and not them. They did not give you answers, and when you died for the fifth time, you were not reborn into Psyperia. The years wore on, and our father became distant, and concerned. He stepped down as Battlelord and others filled the position."

"For the first time, I lived in a world without you. Despite the undulating chaos that came with your ascendances, I always loved you. Without you, I felt empty in a way I never had, and the fight to keep our people alive seemed endless. I was assigned a position guarding a political idealist named Chlaruth Gins, and much to my surprise, fell in love with her."

"Soon after, you found your way back to us and were reborn into our society. When I finally acquired you as my apprentice, I discovered where you had gone in your absence. You had become Mongrelai." Aemon suddenly looked upset and diverged.

"I tolerated the mischief that abounded your childhoods, but destroying a city and all of my defenses by far is the worst thing you've ever done. I expect you're largely unrepentant. That will change with age, and wisdom." Sincret did not have a response. Aemon shook his head at the boy but could not contain the smile that crept its way in. He offered Sincret a seat but he waved his hand to refuse it.

Aemon curled his fingers and a chair skidded over the floor to a stop behind him. He removed drapes of his robes, tossing them onto the floating contrivance until the mass of black cloth floated away like a shadowy ghost. He brushed off the black uniform underneath and relaxed on the chair.

"I couldn't bodybend your mind to see your memories after the Mongrelai turned you; but you still remembered them, and those memories drove you mad. You spoke of universes beyond ours, but also about freedom and change; ideas which I had been wrestling with as well. Chlaruth became Battlelord, and I had my chance to stay by her side as her Shadowed Hand. We began speaking of creating a child, and even changing the laws so we could raise it ourselves. Our father had forbidden us from procreating, and had even sterilized us in past lives. I knew that if she had my child, she would die, yet I wanted, senseless and unceasingly, to have a one with her anyways. I sterilized myself to safeguard her life, but despite that, we conceived a boy."

He did not miss Sincret's eyes widening. Images of his past lives formed as Aemon told his story, but his recent memory of the armless Psyperial boy came to the forefront.

"You've met him on the Mongrelai moon," he stated. "He disobeyed me to take revenge on you; I disobeyed our father when I created him. Both choices had consequences, but I would make the same choice again. I did not want this fate for him, I wanted his first life to be in Psyperia with our people. It was selfish to bring him to this world, now I may have lost him."

If he knows that, he's already seen his son's shredded arm in my memories, he's already heard his son's screams. "I'm sorry," Sincret said.

Aemon's voice croaked, "I did not expect he would inherit some of your more precocious traits. But he also has a true heart, like yours. I did not know what to think when we discovered Chlaruth was pregnant with him, but when I confided in you that the baby would be mine, your reaction cleared my uncertainty. You were so happy. At that moment, I realized your lunacy was not delusion. However, I could not live in a world without her, so I searched for a way to save her."

"I knew if the secret to immortality existed, Lazaeron the Remaker would know it. As the months drew on, her strength slipped away, and I became more desperate. I struck a deal with his daughter Anansi the Spider." He blushed. "I agreed to make a child with her as well, and she promised Chlaruth would survive her childbirth. Then it all fell apart. When our father found out about Chlaruth's pregnancy, he destroyed shield barriers around our city and brought a literal storm down upon us. Shadowed came in the chaos and slaughtered their way to me. I could not escape them or the storm, so I fought my way through both, but I was too late."

"When I made it back to these chambers, I found her dead and you split in half at her feet." Sincret cringed and Aemon looked at him apologetically. "My son lived though. Had our father reached him any earlier, he would have murdered him in her womb. I feel the act would have ended him right there. You died defending her. Damaeon, you saved my son."

Sincret cried. *Can I believe I'm that good of a person? These feelings don't belong to me, though they are as real as my brother.* The journey which burned the path to his answers finally cooled, and he felt stable. He looked back and saw the faces of the people who had suffered for it, the people still suffering. *I am Damaeon, but I cannot walk away from this life as Sincret.* He wiped the tears. "I have others depending on me now," he said.

"They seem to be doing alright. They rammed your ship into the *Omedegon* and are fighting their way here," Aemon replied, "along with the Mongrelai, Ohwen, and Alliance."

"The Mongrelai want me," Sincret said with certainty.

"The Alliance and Ohwen want me," Aemon said empathetically, "and I need Glade Jadamara. She will be here soon."

"Um, what? You might need some help getting her cooperation. Let me talk to her," Sincret warned.

"I hope you will, once she is here," Aemon answered. Sincret sprung from the table and up the steps towards what he could only describe as a throne. He arrived at the peak. The dimly lit chamber beyond had a cold elegance about it. A single red carpet, like the one covering the sitting area, spanned the distance to a grand wood and metal doorway. Torches illuminated its path, but their light did not reach to the ceiling. Shadows shifted amongst the pillars and Sincret knew what moved in the darkness.

Aemon ascended to the top more slowly, then clutched the throne to support himself.

"Are you hurt?" Sincret asked.

"Nothing I won't recover from. I underestimated our Ohwen enemies and got a knife in the leg for it. I fear I've underestimated them again."

"Your enemies, not mine," he corrected. Aemon nodded in acknowledgment. "Jadamara is not your enemy, and all my people want to do is survive."

"That's all my people want as well. Believe me when I say the Ohwen don't want either of us to survive. The disease you call the rot is just a construct of their creation. It's a control, and from their castle in deep space they reap the rewards of your short life-spans. Your people huddle in cities, tethered to them for access to longer life for themselves and their children. Their revolutions deteriorate then pass from memory just as quickly. Even you took your master's life when you thought you were finally dying from the rot. You suspected he never cut you because he wanted to watch you die of it. He, like many with power, wanted you desperate."

That guy was so fucked up, Sincret reflected. He had become aware of his master's evil many years before. *He liked to see me suffer, even more so at the hands of others. He wanted me broken in my banishment, crawling back to the safety of his home.* Sincret had exploited the weakness, and after finding his place amongst the street urchins, freedom from his master just meant bearing through one staged, brutal beating the last day of each exile to satisfy the man's hunger for dominance.

He enjoyed seeing the rot seep into my bones, waiting for the moment I would breakdown and beg to be cut. He saw the same desperation from Uncut on the street. He saw their terror as cleaners shoveled lifeless loved ones onto carts. He saw their anger turn to violence, violence turn hedonism, then all desire give way to death. *They could not escape, I thought I would not either.* It took longer for his symptoms to manifest, but his master delighted in the show until Sincret discovered the gifts which came with his curse. He vividly remembered the moment his rage and focus aligned, the stream of their combination swirling through him as energy collected at his fingertips. Then he sent that energy into his master.

"Your master was Ohwen, so in a sense, they have already tried to kill you," Aemon finished.

STAR STORY BOOK ONE: ANCHORED

Sincret jumped. "What did you say?" His master never talked about his home, just that he did not come from Ehtlentin nor Omphala.

"Wasn't his mission to restore Ehtlentin to its former glory? Or at least that is what he told the council. You knew he didn't give a damn about windowless shuttles or outfitting their military."

"He only ever cared about the citywide shields," Sincret answered.

"Which could conveniently contain an enemy should one ever appear, perhaps from a gateway in the labyrinth. To know one is coming, you must have someone watching the gateway," Aemon suggested.

"Eylea's ship," Sincret said. *So maybe he has a point. If they cursed our teslacs, then they are puppet masters to everyone on this planet. We will cut their strings as we cut out their poison.*

"Eylea, yes. Her name is Kyphothree, for now. She tells me you were quite forward with your distrust. She made your confidence her weapon."

"She didn't play fair," he said.

"Well, neither do you," Aemon replied.

I will get even, eventually. "What comes next?" Sincret asked.

"Next, you and I need to travel to my son's gateway and pray it opens to us. The Alliance and Ohwen know we don't have the strength to repel them without reinforcements. Once the bombs their agents are planting explode, their fleet will attack. Hopefully, when they do, they will not find us trapped against a wall. But we can't leave yet, first I need Glade to arrive."

"We call her Jadamara," Sincret corrected.

"Tell me about her," Aemon requested.

Sincret told the story, and by the end of it, realized with certainty she had been pivotal to finding his answers. Aemon explained how she could help him find his.

CHAPTER 15
Glade Jadamara

The Psyperials hounded them after they boarded the feeder. Bolts rattled against their global shields while the engines roared under them. She saw five Mongrelai take flight from the feeder behind them. They floated like seeds on the wind and lassoed themselves to the pursuing Psyperial fighters as they passed. What they did next, Jadamara did not see, yet the pounding of bolts ceased for the time.

She sat in the cockpit. "There is a hatch ahead that can take us closer to the heart chamber." She marked the point on the schematics then looked back at what remained of their squad. "It will be a long climb, and we'll be in a hurry." The boys stripped off their armor. The female Mongrelai in topaz armor, who Jadamara discovered was named Saza of the First World, pulled out bundles of cloth from a compartment and tossed them at the Painted Boys. They dressed themselves in the light, yet durable, drapings. Even Quantine donned several pieces. Lavelokine handed out gas masks and the group waited nervously. The ship swerved and sent the unbuckled passengers piling on top of each other against the starboard wall. It came to a halt just as suddenly.

The hatch on top of the feeder fell open. *Of course, there's no ladder,* Jadamara thought.

Saza stood under the hatch. "Come on," she urged her." She took Jadamara by the waist and lifted her above the opening. She pulled herself up the rest of the way, and raised herself unsteadily towards the hatch. The wind howled against her, she froze rigid when she contacted the door latch. She could not find a way to open it.

Quickly. She heard another Psyperial fighter squad approaching. She looked back over her shoulder at three incoming beetle ships. Creline pulled himself up behind her. She pulled back her arm and her ingevein sprung a shield over it. The field around her wrist grew static and fiery. It crackled out of control, then she forced her fist into the latch. The burst of energy blasted a crater in the lock and the heavy door swung towards her. She threw herself back, narrowly missing it, but began sliding down the outside of the feeder. She scrambled for anything to grab onto, but found only its smooth hull, as slippery as the underwater fish for which they were named.

"No!" screamed Creline. He crouched as if to dive after her, but a metal hand snatched her wrist first. Lavelokine pulled her back up, then flung her towards Creline with cyborg force. She wasted no time climbing the ladder, Creline followed close behind. Lavelokine pulled Quantine upwards from the hatch, but looked distractedly at the Psyperial beetle craft.

"Come on," he yanked her up as the shields soaked up the first of the Psyperial bolts. The two forces came together in explosive energy. He sprung up to the ladder. The feeder swayed underneath them.

"No!" she heard Quantine scream. Jadamara searched frantically to see through Creline and Lavelokine, but found no window. "No!" she screamed again, though more distantly.

The scream "no!" conducted up their line, ending with Jadamara. The echoes died within the tunnel and they waited helplessly for the girl's fading scream to end. The sound exhausted with the tympanic bang of her body rattling the metal panels fifty meters below. The sound froze them.

"Keep climbing!" yelled Lavelokine unsteadily. Jadamara climbed as fast as she could to escape her horror, but she could not outrun it. Her boots slipped on the ladder and caused her knees and elbows to suffer for her clumsiness. Tears blurred what vision the darkness of the tunnel spared, when she wiped them away, the tips of her exposed fingers slipped on the bars again.

I can barely breath. I really liked her. It occurred to her that Quantine may have been the only relatable woman she had seen in the past month, but nonetheless she made a fast friend of her.

"We have to keep going," whispered Creline. She stirred out of her reverie and remembered why she paused in the first place.

"We are here," she said. They looked up and down skeptically at each other.

"What can the three of us do against an entire ship?" Lavelokine finally asked.

"As far as I see it, our only way out is to keep going in. If Alphago was right, the Alliance and Ohwen are heading to the heart chamber also, to capture Aemon. Maybe we can hitch a ride out with them."

"We can't count on that. More likely we get there and the Shadowed have killed them already. We are close to a hangar, if you can steal us a ship, I can fly it out of here," said Lavelokine. The suggestion hung awkwardly in the air.

"We are going to the heart chamber," said Creline, not with a tone of command, but one suggesting the boy was free to go his own way.

Lavelokine saluted sarcastically, "Sir, yes sir." Jadamara felt Creline wringing his hands around the ladder handle.

He may be pivotal to this operation, but he's still just a regular urchin, she thought.

The hatch door opened easily to them, and the three snuck out into a hallway. The metal walls had turned to dark stone, and torches hung from them in place of light fixtures. The flicker of their flames made wavering shadows from their bodies.

"Oh damn," she said as she looked down the dimly lit corridor. "These shadows aren't meant for us to hide in." Her pistol hummed to life as she pulled it out. Its red light illuminated their features, and soon Creline's glowing blue sword and Lavelokine's dagger added enough light to dissolve the darkness

She started to move, when Creline said to Lavelokine, "You know this place best, you should go first." The mood tensed as they waited for an anti-authoritarian statement from the boy.

Instead, he just said, "Yeah," and walked to the front of their line. Jadamara turned to Creline after he passed. He looked uncharacteristically alarmed, and his eyes darted between her and Lavelokine.

"Good idea," she said to him. Then to Lavelokine, "Thank you for your help. I'm sorry what it cost. Your sister was a unique person." Her attempt to connect made him choke on his breath.

"She may have lived," he replied. Then, almost as if he realized his naiveté he said, "Let's just make it to your friend." But Jadamara did not pay attention, and instead smacked her failing ingevein loudly against her hand. The lights on it flickered in and out, then shut off altogether.

"Double damn," she said. "Getting through that hatch took everything my ingevein had left."

"Your power light was wavering when I met you, you should have let me open it," Lavelokine said.

"You know how to use that thing?" she asked.

"No, actually." He inspected the glowing device embedded into his arm. "I don't think it works how it should. I think they just wanted to see if they could put it in me." She felt bad for the boy again. The Retine mines may have taken parts of his body, but what the Psyperials replaced them with had taken part of his humanity.

I would feel a lot worse if he weren't lying. She hoped he didn't suspect the same for her.

"I know who it came from, and I'm sorry for that," he whispered empathetically. He lowered himself and motioned for them to slow, then put on his gas mask. They did the same. The farther they went down the hall, the thicker the smog grew. Jadamara pulled down her goggles and removed her father's knife, it glowed only faintly through the mist. The weapon used to be a short sword, but lost most of its mass and charge through use.

However, the dense remnant crystal remained as sharp as it had from the day it was created, and much more durable. She was as ready to drive it into Lavelokine's back if Creline's reservation proved valid.

Who am I kidding? Could I kill this boy? Their mission had left a bloody trail, but her hands were relatively clean. *I probably killed that Shadowed,* she lied to herself – she had seen him breathing.

A hissing sound came from the ceiling and plumes of gas with it. She pulled her mask tight against her face. *I'm okay,* she thought in relief as she breathed the filtered air. Creline was not though. He choked next to her and fell to his knees retching in his mask. She reached for him but stopped when the edge of a blade pressed against her neck. Lavelokine's machine hand reached around and pinned her head against his shoulder.

"Drop your weapons, or you both die," he whispered in her ear and began pulling her down the hall. She hesitated, but tossed them forward. "Good," he started, until she pulled off her gas mask and tossed it at Creline as well. She reached to pull Lavelokine's arm away but only succeeded in driving it further into her flesh.

"Dumb," he said angrily. The fingers of his machine hand divided and folded, forming into a collar that constricted until its cold joints pinched the flesh of her neck. With his other hand, he drove his dagger halfway into the back of her thigh. The pain took the breath out of her and gas seeped into her nostrils. He yanked her backwards and dragged her behind him. She pried ineffectively at the collar, then at the ground, then paralysis took her and all she felt were her heels scraping over the stone floor.

She slowly regained consciousness once they cleared the fog and peeled her eyes open at the sound of a creaking door. She raised her head and followed the red carpet to the enormous arch they passed under. Thick doors swung closed and metal locks reverberated when it sealed the two pieces together. Blocks of dark writ-stone slid away from pillars around them and flew overhead, stacking themselves into a wall which eventually sealed the entirety of the doorway. Shadowed dropped from the ceiling down to the barricade, but Lavelokine slung her around before she could see them finish their fortification.

He put the knife to her throat again and walked them forward. Her legs quivered underneath her, she worried she might piss herself. Her arms clawed feebly to support herself, and she attempted to blow away the hair sticking to her cheek. She finally worked it aside when they came to a halt in front of a staircase. At the top, a pale golden throne loomed over them, and a man sat upon it. He wore the trappings of an officer but she had difficulty making out his face. She did recognize Sincret standing next to him.

"Lavelokine," Sincret said disapprovingly. The boy tensed under his peer's scolding and looked at the man in black instead.

"You named this woman desirable, and I have brought you her," he said ceremoniously.

"Well done," Aemon replied. A soft clap emanated from the shadow of a pillar. Kyphothree stepped forward, a sly smile on her face. Aemon pushed himself up. "Wait for me," he said, then disappeared down the other side of the staircase.

"Let her go," said Sincret.

"Why would I do that when I worked so hard to get her?" responded Lavelokine.

Sincret didn't see the point in answering. "Where is your sister?"

The boy didn't answer, so Jadamara did for him. "He murdered her." The words hit Sincret harder than she hoped.

"No, no, no," Sincret mumbled to himself.

"That's what we all said." Her ingevein woke from its power saving mode to alert her that her hack of Lavelokine's ingevein had completed. She pushed the tip of his dagger away. "Before that, he left a grenade beneath Alphago." She untucked herself from his grip, and limped forward. "And just a moment ago, he may have very well murdered Creline." She balanced the paralyzed boy as she moved away, withdrew his blaster from his belt and raised it to his head. *Now I'm going to do what I wanted to do the moment I saw JV's ingevein in your arm.*

As if reading her mind, Sincret said, "Me first."

The red crystal in Lavelokine's pocket crackled to life and its fiery blade bit his leg, then cut through it completely and continued its spinning journey towards Sincret. The force tipped his upper body just so that the bolt Jadamara fired between his eyes blasted through the side of his face instead. The two attacks sent him spiraling to the ground. He landed hard, unable to break his fall.

Kyphothree laughed hysterically and nudged herself from the pillar she rested against. Sincret whipped the stiff energy blade which bent as the wave made its way to the tip. It crackled loudly and extended another two feet in length, then fell sizzling to the ground in its new whip-like form. Jadamara pointed the pistol at Kyphothree then checked behind herself, expecting to see Shadowed upon her, but the black figures seemed preoccupied with a faint booming sound at the door.

Kyphothree drew two pistols from her belt and spun them skillfully around her fingers. Sincret flurried his whip upwards until it circumvallated over his head. Electricity crackled around him, and the roots of his hair turned white with the increasing energy. *Sleight of hand, she is confident we can't touch her*, Jadamara expected. She looked closer and found an iridescent shimmer where a shield surrounding her bent the light.

He doesn't see the shield, she thought. She followed a vein which came to life near the crescent of iridescence and she traced its path to the pillar behind Kyphothree. Sincret made his move, but Jadamara's bolt fired first. It sailed well over Kyphothree and into the invisible spider-like contrivance above her. The machine blasted apart, becoming visible once more, and the shield surrounding Kyphothree faded from view. The force of its own components detonating sent Kyphothree sprawling on the ground, fortunately missing the electric snap of Sincret's writ-whip.

Jadamara fired two more bolts at the woman but only succeeded in hitting the staircase. Sincret yanked the whip back and it circled around him again. It's tight red form blossomed into yellow flames which sprayed outwards from his hands in a low arc towards Kyphothree. She rolled away and tumbled down the stairs. Jadamara took aim again, but found herself dodging the wild spray of white concussive bolts shooting from Kyphothree's pistols. She fired two bolts back just as wildly, but when she pulled the trigger a third time, flames leapt from her overheated gun and licked her hand. She threw the weapon and clutched her burning fist. Kyphothree patted her own smoking clothes where Sincret's flames had taken life. Two large cracks of thunder on the stairwell drew all three of their attentions.

Sincret's writ-whip had reformed, and it snapped against Aemon's green counterpart which reached twice as far and burned twice as bright. He effortlessly batted away Sincret's attacks, and with his other hand sent Lavelokine's smoldering pistol flying towards him. The projectile smashed into Sincret's head, catching his hair on fire. Sincret's writ-whip extinguished and he used his hands to stifle the blue flames.

"Enough!" commanded Aemon. His voice boomed towards them so loud the air hummed well after the word passed.

They looked between each other. Sincret ran down the stairs towards Jadamara, and Aemon followed more slowly behind him. She allowed Sincret to take the weight off her wounded leg. The blood smeared over her jumpsuit made the wound look worse than it was. Only the tip of Lavelokine's blade had punctured through.

Aemon continued past them to the sliced boy breathing shallowly on the floor. The ingevein still vibrated within his metal arm, working to clear what remained of Jadamara's hack and lift his paralysis. Lavelokine touched his face delicately with his other hand. The tips of his fingers pulled away a mix of mangled flesh and blood. He stared at the charred vestiges of his face, now clinging to his fingers. Whether he could see it, Jadamara did not know. His mouth, remaining eye, left ear, and a few thousand hair follicles no longer existed, just a scorched hole at the end of the bolt's blazon trail. *He's lost more visible fea-*

tures than he's kept. The paint under his skin glowed unnaturally. The fluorescent dyes used to tattoo Retine Uncut remained just under their skin, as with the dye used in Ehtlentin. Yet the swirls of color dove below his skin deep into his arm and shoulder, coating his teslac network. The vibrant painted network created a diffuse glow below his muscles. *His teslac looks like Sincret's, but not exactly,* she thought. She suspected it had been another experiment the Psyperials had subjected him to. Aemon traced the patterns with his hand, and eventually ended at his stump.

He pulled the boy's pant leg up, Lavelokine groaned in discomfort. Below the cloth, another colorful network rose up the boy's leg. He spoke to himself in Psyperial, and moments later a floating contrivance appeared. It was made from the same unusual artifact material as the scattered pieces of Kyphothree's spider. The droll of an old router connecting to a network hummed from the machine, apparently communicating a message to Aemon who nodded and replied in Psyperial. A writ-field leapt from its single eye and lifted the boy off the ground.

"I am Aemon, I've heard a lot about you from Damaeon," he said to Jadamara in an Omphalan common, his accent similar to Eylea's. She stared past him to the floating black monolith that had returned with him.

My father's black box, she thought, surprised. "Why do you have that?" she backed away. It appeared in much better shape than when she last saw it. The lacerations her father's murderer tore into its metal casing looked shallower, and some had been patched completely. When her mother tried to have it repaired, it had been in such bad shape that the engineers in Omphala suggested selling it to a museum instead. She gave up on restoring the box but refused to sell it. She granted authority of it to Jadamara when she became her mother's first mate, and Jadamara granted control of it to Gren when he became hers. The box was never more than a bad memory though, so they put it in a storage where it remained until Gren used it to cover their retreat out of the labyrinth. It recognized her and lit up as she approached.

"I need you to access it for me," Aemon replied.

"What happens when I do?" she asked.

"We find out who murdered your father, and why," he answered.

That's not exactly what I was asking, but sounds good. "What happens afterwards?" she clarified.

He realized what she meant. "We did not come here to conquer, and my government will demand a reckoning for the devastation I've caused your people. If we get through this, I will do everything I can for you, give you anything: ships, the resources to build a new home, share our knowledge, arm you, defend you. The least we can offer is to clean the rot from your body, and give you the lifespan we took for granted until coming here. You have my word this will happen regardless of whether you access the box or not."

She did not miss the qualifying statement that prefaced his promises: *if we get through this.*

"Okay," she agreed.

She put her hand on the box. It recorded her genetic code, appearance, scent, gait, and expression. She spoke her access code in Ehtlentin: "Glade ja da mara," which translated into "Glade of the spear." Then in Coralan dialect, "Oileán dhá chathair," which translated into "daughter of two cities." The machine hummed, and gave her options to proceed. She could access its records, or arm it. *The push of a button and everyone here gets a taste.*

She chose the former option instead. Her heart jumped when the list opened to her. The last record appeared at the top, dated sixteen years ago. She selected the meeting record, and a holographic projection lept from the box. Two life-size men stood in front of them. Jadamara gulped at the sight of her father, the boys shifted uncomfortably at the sight of theirs.

The two men looked as opposite as the worlds they came from. Her father's red eyes scanned his counterpart with uninhibited curiosity. His red and black hair was woven into a single braid that reached halfway down his back. He wore a brown leathril vest with a gray weave underlay and brown weave pants. The man who stared back did so behind black wrappings which covered his face, save for an exposed streak which two blue eyes gazed through. The rest of the man's body was shrouded in black. Her father became nervous, as he should have; the black box would not normally allow anyone inside the negotiation who did not reveal their face.

"I am Scopolamine," said her father. The man did not reply but kept walking forward. Scopolamine's eyes darted between the man and the black box. "You are looking for a way out of the labyrinth." The man remained silent. "But you're not keen on passing through Ehtlentin. Hey, friend, hold on."

The man became a blur of cloth then appeared in front of Scopolamine and seized him by the head. A panel on the black box flipped upwards and a claw extended from it to separate them. Before it could, another image came into existence beside it – a spider-like artifact contrivance similar to Kyphothree's – which blasted the limb in two as it reached for the struggling pair. The claw dropped to the ground, and two more artifact contrivances appeared adhered to the black box. The three machines destroyed its defenses one at a time, until Scopolamine's only hope was his hands clawing at his murderer's wrappings.

He eventually managed a grip on his assaulter and ripped the bands of cloth downwards, revealing the man's nightmarish face. His lips, teeth, and better part of his jaw had been incinerated away. The wound looked fresh, and painful, but the man did not flinch when Scopolamine swatted at the vulnerable tissue. Instead he clutched him harder until Scopolamine screamed and his arms fell to his side. The man lifted her father's limp hand to the black box which lit, and immediately calmed. One of the artifacts crawled down to the interface screen.

"Scopolamine ja da mara," shouted Scopolamine against his will.

The man kept one hand on Scopolamine's head, with the other he searched the black box's cache of data for the information he needed to escape the labyrinth unnoticed. The maps downloaded to a disc which ejected from the black box into his hand. He spared one last look at Scopolamine before summoning a fiery blade and decapitating him.

Jadamara gasped as his holographic head tumbled towards her. Her mother did not allow her in the morgue to see her father before they cremated him, and never told her the details of his death. Jadamara wished she could unsee it.

The cloaked man summoned more writ-energy into his hands and began slashing at the black box. The holographic image of the black box ascended into the air, retreating while it wailed an alarm. The recording finished, the holograms disappeared, and the three descendants of the two men looked between each other.

"You guys really are assholes," Jadamara said, wiping tears from her eyes. *Cowards. I hate you after all.* "Our lives means nothing to you. Who was he?"

"You mean more to me than anything," yelped Sincret. She ignored him and waited for Aemon to break from his quiet contemplation.

"Our father, Hadeon" he finally answered. "He murdered many of our people then fled to your world. He needed a way out, so he contacted your father." He gestured to Sincret. "Your captainship of the *Spear Throw* seems to be more of a curse than blessing. For that, I am sorry."

"Ruthless," was all she could mutter.

His hovering artifact contrivance displayed the map piece containing the rare bit of knowledge her father died for: a passage a few meters wide, and many long, that led to deep ocean. The pressure both inside the air pocket, and within the massive body of water sitting on top of it was displayed around the illuminated depiction. *He wouldn't be getting through there easily.* She wanted to know more, but the map disappeared. A moment later, a stifled explosion rumbled from the other side of the great doorway. The artifact contrivance seemed to be communicating with Aemon again.

"Your friends made a prison break, it appears," he said.

"That was plan A, but we are at plan D or E at this point," she replied.

"One of your squad found our armory and is detonating crystals outside the door," he continued.

"Creline," she said to Sincret. His initial confusion turned into a grin. His eyes lit up, Jadamara felt relieved to see them alive again.

"You really should let me talk to him," he suggested to Aemon.

Aemon regarded Jadamara. "Agreed. But I have one more question before you do." He motioned for the Shadowed to remove the stone barrier, then called one towards him. A feminine figure in dark purple cloth answered his summons. A mask made from frosted writ-steel stared lifelessly under her hood. "Who are you?" he asked her.

The woman removed her mask. "Remember me?"

"Second Princess Bela," he said.

The warrior Princess, Jadamara realized. *I saw her moving those stones with the rest of the Shadowed, she knows how to control their magic.*

The Princess took off the layers of cloth down to her white jumpsuit. The lights on it glowed vibrantly in the dim room and cast rays of blue and gold around them as she removed the last layer.

She nodded towards Aemon's leg. "How is it looking?"

"It's fine," Aemon answered expressionless. "I'm wondering why you haven't tried putting another knife in me."

"That's not my mission," she answered.

"What exactly is your mission?" he asked.

The Princess clenched her teeth. "To steal data from your libraries, signal the attack on your ship, and negotiate your surrender."

"Well done, Princess. It appears you've gotten the better of me twice now," Aemon praised.

She stretched and exhaled in a manner of basking in her victory. "Don't be too hard on yourself. As far as writbending goes, you're not bad." She looked at the mask she still held in her hand. "This one, not so much," she said, then dropped it on the pile of purple cloth. Though they both spoke in Omphalic common, Jadamara did not understand the word writbending. She inferred it meant magic.

Aemon laughed at her pomposity, and flashed a knowing smile. "Not all of us received training from the Undying."

A slow smile formed on her face, as she picked up on his selection of words. "But we have," she connected.

"So, there is another gateway, and you have been through it," Aemon inferred.

"I have," she said, "and what I saw on the other side has placed me firmly in the business of closing them. That starts with you coming with me."

Another boom at the gate turned their attention to the doorway. Dust shook loose from cracks in the stone.

Aemon looked to Sincret and nodded towards the door. Sincret jogged down the expanse of the room, but as he reached the stone barrier, it blew inwards. Stones, Shadowed, and dust flew into the chamber. The cloth figures surrounding the doorway flipped midair and landed on their feet. As they did, they formed a semi-circle around the opening. A familiar roar echoed through the chamber.

"Who wants it first?" roared Gren. He pointed an enormous repeating blaster at the circle of Shadowed. It hummed as energy charged its bolter crystal in preparation to spray a barrage towards them. Creline, the Alliance Ronto Hera, a platoon of Painted Boys, and Alliance soldiers rushed past him and formed their own defensive circle against the unmoving Shadowed.

"Wait!" coughed Sincret through the dust. "Wait!"

All parties held still. Creline stepped forward and peered through the dust. "Sincret?" he asked.

"Yeah! Stand down!" Sincret ordered. A wind gushed through the chamber as Shadowed cleared the dust.

"Shit!" shouted Gren as his repeating blaster powered down. He caught sight of Jadamara and waved. "Hey, Captain!"

Creline glared at Kyphothree. "Eylea," he growled.

No crooked smile appeared on her face this time. "Creline," she responded.

Hera walked to his side, dwarfing the boy with her tall figure. Her Alliance battlesuit was covered in blood. "Bela," she said sharply.

"Hera," responded the Princess.

"Aemon?" asked a Shadowed in dark blue robes.

"Stand down," he answered.

"How's your mission?" asked the Princess to Hera.

"Going pretty well despite all the double-crossing: the Mongrelai sealing us out of the main tunnels, your people abandoning our defensive line, no Ehtlentin backup at the prison block. It makes me wonder if we are really friends."

No one replied.

In the silence the faint fizzle of cold-fire melting away the chamber walls could be heard above them. Aemon mumbled a curse under his breath and motioned for the Shadowed to form around him.

"The Mongrelai, huh?" Sincret asked Jadamara.

"Relax. You're the only person here no one wants to murder, me excluded," she said to him. "And even if they do kill you, it won't be the end of the world. As for us…"

Sincret took the hint. "Everyone needs to leave!" he shouted. The command evoked a racket of noise from the Painted Boys and questionable glances from the Alliance soldiers. "Aemon, where can they go? The Mongrelai just want me. They'll kill everyone in here to make that happen. I'm tired of running."

Jadamara wondered how far the Mongrelai would go to take him. *As far as they need to,* she knew. The sound of Aemon's heavy breathing drew her attention. He knelt on the floor, white hair replaced his dark locks, grey eyes stared emptily through the stone in front of him.

"It isn't just you they want," he said with effort. "Let's stand together brother." He pulled himself from the ground and

by the time he rose to his feet, everyone he suspected would dis-
obey the command fell unconscious to the floor. Jadamara hit
the ground first.

CHAPTER 16
Aemon the Proven

Aemon's Shadowed worked quickly to remove the Alliance and Ehtlentin from the chamber. A line of bodies floated over the staircase and towards his safe room, except for one: Second Ohwen Princess Bela, who panted heavily on the floor. Aemon felt her resist his grip on her teslac. *It listens to her; it won't speak to me. But there is something beyond that.* Her teslac felt unlike any he had ever explored. He would not have been surprised to feel the unique properties within it anchoring her to this existence, as he had felt within himself and his family. He would not have been surprised to discover she was not Anchored, just a sycophant of the Frozen Queen. *But she is somewhere in between.* His curiosity pulled him towards her like a magnet. As he approached, he moved deeper into her mind.

The Princess had proven a command of writbending outwards, but channeling her focus inwards to defend against his invasion was a talent even his most skilled Shadowed disciples struggled with. He felt this resilience to his influence only once before from Paudochton the Shield, his most capable body-bender.

She drew a sai from her belt, screamed and slashed blindly in front of her. He pulled away.

She gasped when the battle inside her diminished. *She will be incapacitated for some time*. He could not decide if it relieved or worried him. *Keeping her here is probably not a good idea.* But then he thought, *neither is letting her into the safe chambers with the others.* He stared up at the sounds of melting writ-steel above him. *Whether she is ready or not, the Mongrelai will be here soon.* A brush of writ-phenomenon washed past him: a message from his Shadowed.

"Your people are stowed away safely," he said to his brother.

Sincret spun the red crystal in his hand anxiously. The smooth stone felt natural in his palm, but the more he focused on the sensation, the more facets opened to him, and he found himself struggling to contain the energy which wanted to burst forth. Aemon knew the feeling all too well.

"Calm yourself. Writbending is as much about what you do not think, as it is what you do. That crystal is a totem; a piece of matter meant to define an energy that has always existed. Its pull does not have to change the way that energy feels inside you. It can be a tool, a rock, a treasure, nothing at all, or everything. Its dimensions can define your projections. You can kill with it, or be killed by it." Aemon held out his hand. Sincret gave him the crystal. It glowed in his open palm casting the space around them in red light. "Or you can share it. It can keep you warm, it can light your way." He gave it back, then with his empty hand brought forth a flame over his palm. "Whether you hold it or not, you can still choose how to bring forth your energy."

Sincret clasped it with renewed resolve, but frowned. "I've chosen to kill a lot of people. These Mongrelai murdered my friends. I won't stop at just defending myself, I will destroy them."

"Violence is often the first use of power, especially when violence has been done upon you." He rubbed his brother's shoulder. "I want to show you another way." He climbed the stairs to his throne and dotted his fingers over the console on its armrest. *We can't delay any longer. The Ohwen finished placing their bombs, and their coalition fleet has arrived,* he thought. His artifact contrivance told him as much. He did not predict the raid on the *Omedegon's* library, nor the presence of Mongrelai, but his contingency plan accounted for them nonetheless.

He punched in the commands to release the heart chamber from the *Omedegon*. He would detach the Remaker's lab as well, before sending what remained of the massive pyramid towards the coalition's advancing fleet. *Hangars are empty, families evacuated,* he assured himself. The Pyramid was built to endure the most violent storms, conquer empires, and colonize their cracked planet. Yet it had become a refuge for the explorers against enemies they had made and a sanctuary from the bizarreties of a world they knew little about. Despite the transformations of the crew, the damage, and the emptiness, it remained the symbol of their unity. Now it would give everything for them.

The gravity shifted as writ-generators adapted to the downwards velocity of the heart chamber. The roar of cold-fire melting writ-steel continued, until the chamber changed directions, and one of the feeders drilling through blew away. The other that remained fell away shortly after, but not before depositing its passengers into the hole it had burrowed from the tunnel network to the heart chamber. The Mongrelai continued burning through until they hit stone, then with a deafening boom they burst through the ceiling.

Stone, dust, and lava blew outwards. Two glowing figures swooped through, and a third crested the opening. Aemon stretched his hand forward and the exploded writ-material falling to the ground changed course. The shattered rocks and lava fell upwards, back into the hole where they smashed against the crystalline warriors. The two Mongrelai searching the empty room turned back. They weaved between columns until, by Aemon's will, the stones that composed them began slipping away and shooting towards the Mongrelai. Only one warrior reached the staircase.

The Mongrelai kept his distance and danced around the volley of blasts from Damaeon's pistol as well as the writ-stones Aemon sent towards him. Two glowing ropes extended from his wrists and wrapped themselves around two incoming stones, which he swung towards Damaeon. When the arc fell short of hitting him, the warrior swung the stones around again to hurl them towards the two brothers. One of Damaeon's bolts sparked against the Mongrelai's chest, but he was forced to leap out of the way before the stone crashed into the staircase behind him. The other stone left a second later after changing course to fling at Aemon. The stone landed low, or exactly where it should have, and blasted the stairwell upwards at him with astounding force.

The hail of stones stopped, and the Mongrelai advanced. His partner arrived at the perimeter of the dust and matched pace. The aerosolized debris shifted as an invisible sphere moved through it. It caught their attention, but too late. Aemon's artifact appeared and sent a single concentrated beam of energy into the second Mongrelai's neck. The other extended a staff and swatted it away. Lightning crackled as it landed against its metal shell.

Damaeon lit his red crystal and charged. Aemon summoned his own writ-whip and leapt from the staircase. His arc took him over the Mongrelai. He batted away his whirling staff, sending energy from the static weapons burning into the air around them. He landed and swept his writ-whip low, but the Mongrelai spun away towards Dameaon.

The other three Mongrelai finally pierced the hole and jetted towards them. Aemon swept his hand and sent the closest Mongrelai off balance, then turned to face the reinforcements. He brought back his writ-whip into his hand and morphed its form chaotic. The energy collected in his palm, then sprung from it as he released a spray of electricity. The blasts sent one Mongrelai dodging around a column, another chose to shield himself in the folds of his cloth trappings, while the last spiraled helplessly into the ground. She crashed hard but tumbled her way back to her feet. As she circled, Aemon summoned a fiery writ-knife into his hand and threw it at her, then launched himself at her as well. He had never moved so fast, and the exertion from testing his limits changed his form back into the semblance of what he looked like in his first life. The fiery writ-knife projectile melted partway into her armor then disappeared as he released control of the writ-phenomenon which created it. He charged into her and pierced her with another.

The second flaming dagger vanished as he ducked under her left hook. Two more daggers appeared in both his hands. He stabbed underneath her exposed underarm, but she grabbed him by collar nonetheless. She swung him over her head and into the ground, the impact took the air out of him. He clawed at her hands, but her fist outlasted his prying fingers.

Think.

He dissolved his shirt from its solid state into gaseous writ-particles, allowing him to slip out of it and free himself from her grip. He scrambled backwards, flinging the remains of his uniform to cover her helmet. However, her hand reached out blindly and dug into the skin around his collar bone, twisting into a second unbreakable grip. Much like with his uniform, he willed the writ-particles in his skin to vibrate, and release from the tissues they had been incorporated into. Aemon spun away from the Mongrelai, leaving her with only the bloody patch of skin in her grip.

He used the wash of pain from his exposed nerves to conjure a firestorm to cover his retreat, but it did nothing to stop the Mongrelai's advance. He continued to twirl away from her, sending splashes of flame against her shield. For the first time in a long time, Aemon knew he faced an opponent who could best him. Damaeon's own duel had taken him and the Mongrelai over the staircase and into the lounge beyond. The two floating Mongrelai split up. Aemon's new opponent launched a missile from his wrist. Aemon reached outwards and a lash of writ-phenomenon detonated the concussive projectile early. However, his defense did not save him from its debilitating effects. He dove away from the two and reached out to feel the teslac networks within them.

Nothing. The same emptiness blocked his path into their minds that he felt when he probed Damaeon's memory of his Mongrelai life. He searched for organs and vessels, but the crystalline armor deflected his mental probe as it did most of his writbending. *I do better when I'm close*, he realized. He writ-pulled the Mongrelai towards him and retreated into his own teslac network, body-bending his muscles to prepare for the engagement. However, a white blur intercepted the Mongrelai as it lurched forward. Princess Bela had awoken. Her knee landed against the Mongrelai's helmet, then she planted on his shoulder and flipped onto the second warrior behind him. Aemon threw a bolt of light towards the first Mongrelai before it could recover. The eruption blasted it down the room. His body rolled erratically as the chamber once again changed course downwards on its journey out of the *Omedegon*. The gravity shifted and Aemon felt his feet gain traction once more.

The Mongrelai and Princess exchanged blows beside him. Their blades, fists, and feet ricocheted off each other in a mad dance the Mongrelai seemed to be leading. The Princess's battle-suit gave her an advantage in speed but little protection against the barrage. She stayed close and pivoted around the hulking figure. Iridescent waves of summoned writ-shield washed over Aemon's forearms as he entered the duel. The Mongrelai saw him coming and twirled a blade to repel him. It landed harmlessly against the writ-shield encasing his left arm, and he swung at the Mongrelai with his right. She pulled her head back and his fist missed her. Then, just as quickly, she sent her helmet back towards him. The impact pierced the skin on his forehead and blood trickled down his face. Her foot slammed into his diaphragm, sending the air out of him and his body ten meters backwards.

The Princess went on the offensive as well but the Mongrelai batted her attacks away as effectively as she had when she was her only opponent. The Mongrelai turned her helmet towards to the Princess. Her deep purple visor stared for just a moment before a glow of light from the borders of the semi-transparent crystal flowed inwards. When the light touched in the center, it flashed outwards with blinding intensity. The blinding bolt sent the Princess flipping backwards, frantically dodging the unseen strikes she expected but never came. Instead, the Mongrelai's visor lit once more but instead of a flash, a concussive beam of white light shot from it. The bolt sunk into the Princess and dispersed across her whole body. She crumpled to the floor.

Bolts, whips, blades, rockets, flames, shields: I have an attack, she has an answer. Aemon thought highly of his own skills. He often inventoried his repertoire of abilities as he fell asleep. Within the library of powers he had discovered lay answers to defeating every enemy before. Besides his Undying master, no one in Psyperia had the skill to challenge him. No one on this world did either. *I have met my match,* he thought discouragingly. *But there are other ways to end a battle.*

Gravity adjusted a final time as the cuboid structure that once rested in the core of the great pyramid settled onto the labyrinth floor. The wind howled through the punctured opening into the chamber, bringing the sounds of the distant battle outside with it. On the staircase above, Damaeon's body toppled over the golden throne. A Mongrelai rose from the other side of the staircase and aimed a wrist towards his limp body. Aemon's artifact appeared next to the floating warrior, this time using its condensed beam of energy to melt a crystal around the Mongrelai's ankle. The loss of buoyancy distracted the Mongrelai. The contrivance swooped down, encasing Damaeon in a shield and lifting him upwards.

To me now, he told the artifact through his writ-voice only it could detect. He pulled a handful of crystals from a belt pocket and tossed them towards his own approaching opponent. The stones crackled to life as his writ-current ran through them, sending electricity scattering into the air. The Mongrelai charged through the static field unhindered. The ground below her shifted as Aemon removed the stones under her feet and sent them towards the Mongrelai he had blasted down the corridor moments earlier. He did not wait to see if they landed and instead pulled another gem from his pocket and threw it between himself and the charging warrior. The pebble exploded into writ-dust which flooded the area in a thick fog. Mongrelai bolts lit the dust as they streaked by Aemon's hidden body. When she reached the spot where he had been standing he was already ten meters above her, soaring to the contrivance swooping towards him with his brother in tow.

He grasped an opening in the artifact's spherical plating with one hand, and with the other he summoned a blast of air below them to speed their ascension. *To the opening,* he commanded his artifact. The three Mongrelai still capable of flight lifted into the air after them. The unconscious Princess lay unmoving on the floor beyond. Aemon hoped he would see her stir, but forced his attention back towards the armored assailants closing in. They reached the opening the Mongrelai had burned through the ceiling. Within the hole, Aemon sensed the broken writ-stone he previously poured into the passage. This time, he gripped the debris and ripped it outwards back into the chamber. Writ-stone, writ-steel and faintly glowing magma jetted from the hole. He held the materials still as the three of them passed into the tunnel. Once inside he writ-bent the floating field of rubble into an impassable tornado behind them.

He closed his eyes and concentrated on maintaining the whirlwind. He felt the Mongrelai blast the debris apart, but as they did, he collected the scraps and reintegrated the disintegrated rocks into the circulating storm. Though, the farther they progressed down the tunnel, and the more debris the Mongrelai blasted away, the more his control waned. He felt his heels clip against metal protruding into the narrow tunnel, until one piece caught his boot and ripped away his hold on his artifact, as well as his grip on the debris field. He fell awkwardly into the insides of what used to be a wall, and the swirling debris field covering their retreat fell away.

He turned towards the exit behind him. His artifact and his brother had momentarily abandoned him. His artifact levitated Damaeon through the opening and into the dark labyrinth, then doubled back to retrieve Aemon. The Mongrelai burst through the opening, dodging their way through twisted metal and wires as if they made the strenuous flight a hundred times before. Their dancing figures became distorted as a bright writ-shield sprung from the armor of the leader.

There go most of my options, Aemon thought as the glowing barrier expanded to create an iridescent wall between him and the Mongrelai. The shield touched the tunnel walls, glowing brightly as it passed over the various shapes the twisted metal created. The detail was not negligible to Aemon. Creating a writ-shield to block energy could be done relatively easily, but creating a writ-shield to block physical matter required quite a bit more power. He rose to his feet with feigned difficulty, even though he clutched a very real ache in his spine to mask his hand retrieving the knife from the back of his belt.

He erected himself completely and let the blade fly. He focused on the feeling of it leaving his hand, writ-bent it to stay on target, then changed its trajectory just before it passed through the Mongrelai writ-shield. He expected the knife alone would not catch the Mongrelai off guard, but as he hoped, the sudden change of direction surprised her. She barrel rolled into its point instead of away from it, crashing into the other two Mongrelai. Aemon turned to climb up the rest of the tunnel when he felt himself lifted from the ground by his artifact's writ-field. The contrivance pulled him upwards through the tunnel as it had his brother, three white bolts chased after them. Each detonated against the writ-field encasing his body, the final blast landed as they cleared the opening and cracked the writ-field apart. The disruption left Aemon hanging in midair for a moment before gravity brought him arcing back to the ground. He slammed into the outer steel hull of the heart chamber.

The two brothers stared up at the massive iridescent gateway shimmering in the distance, and the trail of floating Psyperial structures passing through it. The gateway which connected the two realms, unlocked by the combined presence of Aemon and his brother, had finally opened. His fleet, which stood sentinel on the Psyperial side of the gateway had arrived, and the battle would finish.

Aemon intended to keep the rest of the Psyperial government on the other side of the gateway for as long as possible. He had hoped he would have accomplished more in this world by the time he let them through. *They will no doubt attempt to reign me in once this is all over*, he knew. However, his methods had produced results: he had shown the Psyperial's strength, he had found his brother, and he knew where to begin looking for his father. *But it is not over yet.*

He watched the newly arrived reinforcements chase the abandoned *Omedegon* towards where the Alliance, Ohwen, and Psyperial forces battled in the distance. Explosions from missiles and bolts lit the field around the pyramid as it forced its way forward. Within the confines of the labyrinth, the ships hammered each other at point blank range. The flow of new arrivals pushed the coalition forces back at the rate the flaming pyramid advanced. It rotated as it charged, bringing undamaged hull to bear against the coalition's steady battery. Flames previously covered by its figure revolved into the brothers' view and revealed walls of fire climbing up its slant.

The sight reminded Aemon of the firestorm which flooded Ehtlentin days earlier. *All Psyperia will see this*, he knew. *It wouldn't be my last resort if it wasn't the costliest. Though, it could have been avoided had Getaeight unlocked the gateway earlier.* Nonetheless, he expected the maneuver would save more than it doomed.

He had given the evacuation order when the heart chamber dropped from the pyramid; he hoped it had given the rest of the crew enough time to escape as well. During its charge, scores of Psyperial safe rooms and ships departed from the flaming structure. The various vessels either landed upon the cavern floor, or regrouped with the remainder of the fleet, except one: a single snubfighter which weaved its way through the battle and skimmed the labyrinth floor towards the heart chamber. Two identical snubfighters followed it, spraying green bolts to divert, if not destroy, the rogue ship.

Aemon did not see how the situation resolved. Instead, an enormous blast erupted from the bottom of the *Omedegon* as the

Ohwen bombs detonated around its engines and drew his attention. The pyramid's course tipped downwards, until it smashed into the cavern floor with a roaring crash and another burst of light. Writ-shields surrounding the unstable phenomenon-generators lost power and flaming green discharge from the uncontained energy erupted from inside the structure. Lightning storms crackled within the superheated smoke, forcing both the coalition and Psyperial fleets to distance themselves from the volatile remains.

Expected, he thought. His Shadowed reported as much from the Ohwen boarders they interrogated amidst the battle. *The Omedegon was doomed.*

Another thunderous boom echoed, this time emanating from the Remaker's pyramid, which had also detached from the *Omedegon* and landed several dozen kilometers away. The Mongrelai's dreadnaught, which remained embedded in the hull, fired its cannon and roared its engines to back itself out of the metal cask. A spray of yellow bolts shot from the rear of the dreadnaught where the last remaining Mongrelai feeder had attached to the hull. It used its shield and blasters to stave off the Psyperial fighters which had taken note of the activity.

That is unexpected. How is it still functioning? He wondered. *The ship looked like it was falling apart when it first attacked us. They will never escape, let alone anchor jump in one piece. The point of retreating out here was to show them this is over.* Aemon again caught sight of the rogue fighter coming closer. It managed to shake its pursuers within the chaos surrounding the dreadnaught then dove to the ground and kept with its course towards the heart chamber.

Also, unexpected. Aemon hoped that bringing their own battle outside would discourage the Mongrelai; make them see escape would be impossible. Now the plan seemed counterproductive. *Our reinforcements are too far away though, and theirs are much closer.* His brother realized this at the same time and jumped to his feet. He approached the hole he knew the Mongrelai would ascend from. Soon they did.

The three Mongrelai pierced the opening in succession. The leader trained her weapons on the brothers, while the other two raised shields to defend from Aemon's artifact. Aemon prepared to writ-bend a shield around himself when the leader lowered her weapons and the three of crystalline figures landed in front of them.

The leader investigated the blackened holes in the spaces between her armor, working her way towards the knife lodged in her helmet. At first, the two metals screeched against each other as she pulled it out, but the sound quieted as blood on its tip lubricated the remainder of its exit. She stared at the blade. *Keep it within twenty meters of me and I can sink it back into you,* Aemon thought.

She reached the same conclusion, though it didn't seem to bother her. She looked at the approaching fighter, tossed the knife back to him then removed her helmet.

He had never seen a Mongrelai, let alone fought one before today. He was just a boy when they last appeared near Psyperia 400 years ago. They eradicated three satellite cities in two weeks and by the time the counterattack arrived, horror stories and ruins were all that remained of their incursion. The only images they had of the invaders were stories described by the handful of survivors. Aemon did not know what to expect, but the beauty of the woman surpassed whatever expectation he had formed.

She appeared every bit a normal human, save for two slit pupils which studied him. Red stains soaked half of the weave underneath her armor, but she did not seem bothered by the injuries. A yellow crystal vein glowed under the skin below her left eye and disappeared beneath curly hazel hair. Blood trickled from the gash on her cheek where his knife penetrated her helmet. The laceration only increased her fierceness. He tucked his knife back into his belt, as much as to collect his thoughts as to distract from his lack of social grace. He became aware of the wind around them, freezing his sweat and turning his overheated body hypothermic.

"I am Saza of the First World," she said.

"I am Aemon the Proven." He decided to cut right to it before the incoming fighters instigated another fight. "Why are you here?"

"Same reason as everyone else; you two," she answered.

He took time to choose his words carefully. "You're welcome to us. But as the Ohwen and Alliance have found out, you're not leaving with us."

She scanned him, attempting to see through his stone expression. Her nostrils flared, collecting the pheromones that could betray his fear and attraction. She found nothing except the faint passing of wind as he writ-bent the molecules leaving his body away from them; a strategy which had become second nature to him during tense conversations.

"The Ohwen want you captured, the Alliance want you dead," she replied, "we may just settle for a conversation."

"You have a funny way of starting a dialogue," Damaeon interjected.

As if on cue, the rogue Psyperial fighter cleared the top of the cube and swooped down upon them. The triangular vessel angled towards their party and began landing. Before it set down, a battle-damaged pilot jumped from the cockpit. The engines from the snubfighter continued to wail in preparedness, but its blazing engines did not stifle the booming of the dreadnaught, still freeing itself from the Remaker's pyramid.

"Alphago," said Damaeon. The Mongrelai landed between the brothers and his own soldiers. He shared the same slit pupils as Saza, but none of her natural beauty. His scarred face looked overly weathered given his boyish features. He had disposed of his crystalline armor, and only the burnt tatters of a weave covered him now.

"Damaeon, and you must be Aemon," he said, appraising the brothers. "The two sons of the Citizen."

Aemon remained silent, which suited Alphago, who stared a moment before turning to Saza and asking, "Hvordan kunne jeg vaere sa dum?" He turned back to Aemon, pointed towards his white hair, then met his grey eyes again. "You created the child that formed this gateway? The boy designated as Getaeight?"

"Yes," Aemon replied.

"He survived his transformation to Mongrelai, and is being transported to the First Realm. If you come with me now, I will reunite you." Alphago offered.

"What would await us in the First Realm?" Aemon asked.

"Imprisonment," Alphago stated.

"Then perhaps we are better apart, if his identity is unknown. To know he is alive, is enough."

"I am bound by duty to report his heritage to the other tribes," replied Alphago.

"If you send a transmission, the Ohwen will intercept it. If you try to leave, my navy will gun you down." Aemon gestured to his fleet traveling down the tunnel. The vanguard of his reinforcements would be over them in minutes. However, Alphago's reinforcements arrived first. Blossoming swirls of wind blew over them as the *Herald* cleared the height of the heart chamber. Its propulsors struggled to keep it afloat in the air, and it swayed side to side, threatening to roll bottom-up.

"I would blast you and Damaeon to shreds, here and now, if I thought it would solve anything," Alphago shouted.

"If you need assurance that I won't have any more children – that *we* won't have any more children – then we can make that promise," Aemon offered, nodding to his brother, who nodded back in agreement.

"That would be a start, though you should have known better already," responded Alphago. "Where has your father been in all this? Why did he not close your son's gateway, as he did with yours?"

"Our father tried to prevent my son's birth. He fled to this realm after he failed. I had hoped we would find him here," answered Aemon.

"And have you?"

"We have a lead."

"Then you have enough to spare you lives," Alphago

said. Saza placed her hand on his shoulder and seemed to be communicating through their comlinks. A moment later, the dreadnaught turned away and landed beside the heart chamber. It hummed as layers of grounded writ-shield encased it. The screech of Psyperial snubfighters pierced the air as the first squadron reached the heart chamber. The ships made several passes, no doubt evaluating the situation, and ascertaining the reason for Aemon's comm silence.

"For tens of thousands of years, we've kept your realms separate and safe. It's a thankless endeavor and your people perceive our methods as barbaric - but only because they live in ignorance of what lurks beyond your realms. It is long overdue for them to find out," Alphago said.

The truth of the multiverse is the secret that drove Damaeon to insanity when he returned from his Mongrelai life, Aemon knew. *This Mongrelai has seen things that scared him too - likely the same enemy our father found on the other side of the gateways formed from our births. The gateways he split our planet in half to close.*

"The Enemy and the Virion," Damaeon said. "No one will believe us without proof."

"You are the proof. That is the proof," replied Alphago, gesturing to the gateway.

"So, tell everyone we are Anchored? And what, assuming they believe us, hope that they care more about alleged enemies in other universes than the fact we've been deceiving them for generations? It would be chaos!" exclaimed Damaeon.

"More chaotic than it is now?" asked Alphago.

"It has to be done," interjected Aemon, before his brother could respond. "We owe an explanation to our people, and to the people of this realm, for our actions. Otherwise, it may be war without end."

Damaeon grumbled in reluctant agreement.

"There is another gateway, though. The Ohwen Princess Bela has been through it. She says her mother intends to close it," Aemon quoted.

Alphago seemed startled. "Is this princess around for me

to speak with?" he asked. Aemon motioned to the hole burned into the heart chamber. "Do you mind if we stay for a bit?"

Aemon wrapped his arms around himself. Specks of dried blood fell away as he rubbed his arms, he winced when his hands passed over the gooey wounds. He looked in the distance at the *Omedegon*, which remained crumpled on the cavern floor whilst damage control vessels futilely sprayed extinguishing solution onto its flaming corpse. The squadron of Psyperial snubfighters circled overhead loudly and the comlink in his boot vibrated against his calf with a hundred urgent messages. All the elements worked together to annoy Aemon, who realized he didn't want to deal with any of them.

"Let's have a drink," he said.

CHAPTER 17
Glade Jadamara

In this City: Glade Jadamara remembers her mother

The red jacket hangs adrift
No heat to warm it
No body to hold it
Colors fading
And being forgotten

Jadamara, her crew, the Mongrelai and the coalition forces awoke gathered in the heart chamber where their various stories formed into one cohesive revelation: the future would be dangerous, just as the present was. Outside, a ceasefire had been negotiated. Within the destroyed heart chamber, before the bloodied Psyperial Battlelord, the group created plans. Jadamara could not tell what to make of the man now that she had time to consider his character. His words were as calculated as his tone was flat. His sexlessness neither attracted or repelled her. He did not have a memorable face, though she knew she would never forget it.

Perhaps that's just because half of it is covered in blood, she thought.

Indeed, half of his body was soaked in his and the Mongrelais' blood. The room they resided in matched his battle torn appearance. Rubble, strewn around the once pristine audience chamber, made it seem more of a battle arena, and the man sitting on the throne above them, the champion. His loyal retinue stood beside him: the silent, eerie, masked woman who had tended to them when they woke, his orb-like artifact contrivance, Kyphothree, two armored storm-marines, and three cloaked Shadowed.

His audience had many questions, but they listened in silence to the man who, for all intents and purposes, had defeated them. He explained the origin of their universes, his and his brother's anchorage to existence, their reincarnation, the birth of his son and the gateway to their world, the truth that the rot was created by the Ohwen, the necessity for their occupation of Ehtlentin, his people's intention to remain in their world, and his hope that they could do so peacefully. He passed the floor to Alphago next, who spoke of the wars looming over them, and the need to unite lest the Virion and the Enemy find a foothold within their realms.

Gren needed clarification. "So, five universes: The First Realm, Psyperia, the Undying Realm, our realm and the Cold Realm. One of them, the Virion, are looking to conquer the rest. Meanwhile, there are demons lurking in First Realm still looking to conquer it, so the Mongrelai conquer us to take our technology to fight both," he said to Alphago.

"Yes," he responded.

"Sure. And the Psyperials came conquering, because you couldn't keep it in your pants," he said to Aemon.

"If you saw our world, you would want a new one as well," he responded.

"Right, because your dad cracked your planet in half trying to clean up his mistake. Or, mistakes," he clarified, motioning to both Sincret and Aemon. "Though, I'm glad to hear that even after 300,000 years, your dad still has an active sex life – gives me hope."

"He spent most of those years hidden; frozen in cryo-stasis just as Bela's mother, the Frozen Queen. He told me that our mother changed his mind; he decided to join society, he decided to have children. I used to believe that, but now I wonder if his goal wasn't just to open the gateways. As I said, he visited the

Undying Realm for certain, and brought back my teacher to train generations of Shadowed, but now I'm certain the other gateway led to the Cold Realm. I think the Virion are the reason he closed them."

"So how do we close them?" asked Jadamara.

"I do not know," he replied. "That is why we need to find my father. He is the only person to have ever done so. We also need to know where your gateway is, Bela."

All eyes turned to the Ohwen Princess who stood apart from the group, outcast by the truth that when spoken out loud made her people seem the worst of their enemies. She did not comment on Aemon's conclusion that the rot was artificially created. *Perhaps she did not know.* Jadamara wanted to give the woman the benefit of the doubt, but for everyone that shared their stories, she remained silent. In the hour they had been talking, the only statement she made was her intent to kill herself if Aemon entered her mind again.

"It is not my gateway," she said. "I am Anchored, and re-incarnated, but my mother found a way to keep gateways from forming when she created me and my sister." She paused, clearly debating how much she wished to share. "Another gateway formed though, thirteen years ago, after our mother gave birth naturally to our sister Erika. I was taken through it to train with the Undying writ-benders when I was young. But I could not tell you where it is, even if I knew. My mother has plans for it."

Gren stared venomously at Bela. "Right, we've heard about your mother's plans. As far as I'm concerned, she killed my mother, and my father, and my sister." Bela remained expressionless as Gren advanced. "No reply? You're not going to try explaining how my little sister not making the cut was some sort of miracle for our society?" he asked angrily.

"Cool it," Jadamara said, "these guys' father literally killed my dad, but we're done fighting." Jadamara's words shook Bela from her thoughts. She looked like she wanted to ask questions but returned to her reticence.

"Speaking of criminals," Gren looked at Sincret next, "I

can't imagine you're particularly welcome in the Alliance after you obliterated one of their cities."

"I can't imagine I'm welcome anywhere on this planet," he agreed. "So, we're finding another. We are returning to the Mongrelai's moon base to plan for the next cycle, once the *Herald* is repaired." His response evoked murmurs from the Painted Boys and Ehtlentin refugees. Gren, though still larger than the hulking Alphago, stared at him wearily.

"You'll want to lock that ship up, tight, when you're not using it," he warned him.

"Damaeon pulled the *Herald* from the orbit of a collapsing star when he lived as a Mongrelai, he pulled it from the molten Flows of the labyrinth in this life. He won't need to steal it because it already belongs to him," replied Alphago

"You've got to be shitting me," said Gren in disbelief.

"You're still welcome aboard it," Sincret offered. "Everyone is."

"Not so fast," interjected Jadamara. "You're still my first mate Gren, you're coming with me and we are finding the man who killed my father." Gren seemed relieved to have his purpose stated so clearly. She turned to Aemon. "That is, if you intend to keep your promise."

He nodded. "It makes sense that you should be the one to track him, you'll be able to pursue him easier than anyone from our realm. Kyphothree will go with you though, that is a condition."

We'll need a big ship, she thought. Kyphothree eyed up Gren. *Better make it two separate ships.*

"We can work together," she agreed.

A month later, Glade Jadamara found herself looking at the most incompetent dock technician she had seen. Sincret insisted he check her ship one last time before she departed from Retine city where the Psyperials had established their new capital, but seemed more focused on delaying her departure than expediting it. She longed to escape the eerie glow of the city to which they had been confined, but now she too felt the desire to linger just a moment longer.

"Well, there are no thieves on board," he announced with certainty.

"That's too bad, we can always use a thief. Are you sure you wouldn't rather come with us?" she asked.

He smiled and considered the offer again. "Do you have room for 400 more?"

"I think it would be a bit cramped," she replied.

They laughed. Neither had expected so many Ehtlentins to follow him into space, let alone on a ship also inhabited by Mongrelai. The warriors had proven to be more than accommodating to the new situation, and more personable than they expected. Some of the youngest volunteers even aspired to take the turning and become Mongrelai one day. Another hundred Psyperial crewmembers would depart with them as well and Sincret intended to fill the ship with more representatives from the nations they would visit. The Mongrelai had come to calling the plan the peaceful harvest.

The *Herald* sat on an elevated platform beside her much smaller craft; a vessel which had been plundered from the Rim and gifted to her by Aemon. The *Spear Throw II*, which she had named to honor the Jadamaras before her, was the opposite of its predecessor: nimble maneuvering through its double hexagon in shape, protected with white armor, and equipped with three massive engines for speed and interplanetary anchor jumping. A turret on the top of the vessel offered protection from threats above, while twin blaster cannons on the bottom could be trained on prey below.

The elegant interior felt both comfortable and efficient, with room for three crew members, though only Gren and Jadamara would live inside the ship. They found a contrivance while searching it, and despite their best efforts, it insisted it remain with the ship and its new crew. Jadamara did not mind, and it proved helpful as she familiarized herself with the vessel over the last several days.

Kyphothree and the Psyperials had already begun searching for the artifact spacecraft Aemon and Sincret's father had stolen. Aemon warned the search party that the artifact was as likely to kill them when it saw them, as it was to try and escape. However, Jadamara already determined she would visit the remains of the *Spear Throw* first. She needed to pay homage to the dead, which she now knew included JV.

Her worst fears had been realized, he had succumbed to the second rot. Worse though, were the nightmares she had of the man called Lazaeron the Remaker, extracting his ingevein in the last moments of his life - the device which he integrated into the traitor, Lavelokine. That, combined with the fact that Lavelokine had survived, and that both he and the Remaker returned to Psyperia, had soured her confidence in Aemon. The Battlelord seemed to have his hands tied though, and his government swept him away before she had an opportunity to tell him so.

Once outside the labyrinth, she would have her own political storm to navigate. Days earlier she received a message from Ava's father, promising retribution for the death of his daughter, Eva. The business tycoon, infamous for his company's contracts with militaries and criminals alike, had been the voice of opposition against the Psyperial settlement since they arrived. His daughter's murder threw gas on a fire that was already raging. The man had called for the complete eradication of the Psyperial occupants, and those who consorted with them. If it wasn't for Colonel Raz Taigo, who had officially been named Admiral of the Alliance Fleet, there would still be a blockade at the mouth of the labyrinth.

Some within Raz's ranks believed the order to dissolve the fleet was biased, and that the Psyperial's returning the captives, which included his daughter Hera, had swayed him. However, everyone who saw the battle a month earlier knew the Alliance had neither the strength nor the resilience to hold the blockade alone, especially as Psyperial forces continued to amass within Retine City. The Ohwen dropped off Ava and Isla in Omphala, along with many of the Ehtlentins who survived within Deep

Hold, then they anchor jumped back to their home.

As the Ohwen ships left the planet, so too did the biologic control they had over it. First Princess Emire did not stay to answer Aemon's accusations regarding the rot at the formal Alliance hearing. Second Princess Bela also fled, but to Psyperia to serve as an ambassador of sorts. Even still, few in the Alliance hierarchy believed Aemon, though he made sure the world heard who was responsible for the disease, and who could cure it. He sent emissaries and medics forth to share their newly developed cure for the rot; they spread his influence while offering freedom from the Ohwen's.

The Ehtlentins also had a voice now. Culus' book In this City had been recovered from Jadamara's cabin and sent to Omphalan news centers. Several members of Sincret's followers felt compelled to add their stories to the book, Jadamara included. In the wake of testimony about the corruption in the city, the Ehtlentin people became a celebrity population as well as an endangered one. A mix of fear and awe washed over the Omphalan citizens as refugees who had been captive aboard the *Omedegon* arrived at their city. They came with the opalescent hair and eyes of their heritage, but also the rainbow glow of the Psyperial cure coursing through the teslac networks. Their alien appearance unnerved others, and division between the two peoples spread where many hoped for unity.

Jadamara took the cure as well but had Culus perform the operation himself. Then, she requested a second procedure which she asked to keep off the record. Both would save her life in time, both left their mark.

"You'll be alright," said Sincret. She took a deep breath.

"Will you?" she asked.

He shrugged. "Just a couple months ago you wanted to kill me. If I could make a friend out of you, persuading others that I'm not so bad should be a breeze." He pulled out a silver ring from his pocket and handed it to her. A light glowed underneath the band. When she put it on, the ring glowed brighter, then the light extinguished. A sensation coursed up her arm, as if a second ingevein had been integrated into her body.

"A tracking device?" she asked. "How romantic."

"In a way, yes. You will find it does much more than that though." He showed her a matching ring on his own finger. "These are artifacts I unlocked lifetimes ago, that one is bonded to you now so only you can use it. You'll find it uncannily helpful once you unravel its secrets."

The ring seemed to probe her as much as she probed it. Even as he spoke, it commanded her attention. Finally, the sensation settled, yet she remained acutely aware of its presence. "Thanks," she said uncertainly. They embraced, and held each other for a long while. "Take care of yourself Sincret, keep in touch when you have time."

"Same for you," he said. They finally released each other, Jadamara left a kiss on his cheek as they parted. She took one last look at the boy she had come so far with. From their meeting in Ehtlentin to their journey through the Flows, their escape into the stars and the return to the ruins, they had faced trials both around and within themselves that neither could have expected, or faced alone.

She loved him, and he loved her. She had the fortune, and the curse, of knowing it was fact: the consequence of their coupling on the Mongrelai moon proved it. Now, the tears she cried were not just for him.

She walked to her ship and did not look back. Gren gave her a concerned glance but she met him with determined eyes.

My story will continue.

EPILOGUE
Thaeon Scarred Arm

Book of the First People: Rantings of the Forgotten Fifth

There once were four leaders of the First People
Caught amid a war
They gathered for deduction to avoid the destruction
Knocking at their door
The Warrior fought, the Scientist thought, and
the Prince fraught night and day
Yet it was a remarkable Citizen, a man of the
people, who sought the cleverest way
He prayed to an Angel, he showed her his heart
And she in return gave him hers
She opened a gateway to another dimension
Where matter and dark matter blur
Before the four fled to find new worlds
She gave them each a gift
They thought of the lifetimes they'd spend Anchored
And each came up with a wish
The warrior wanted to wield a grand weapon
that would one day win the war
The scientist had need of knowledge to create a disease
which could not be cured
The prince begged his people be made immortal
to stem the loneliness he must endure
The citizen asked for just the chance to see the Angel once more

Alive, Getaeight thought, *and not alone.* Before he opened his eyes, he could smell the odors of the two girls watching him. He knew they sat an equidistant way across from him. One, clean and young; the other, filthy and tasting of burnt rotten flesh. He pushed himself up, but a shooting pain in his right arm brought him back down. He held the limb over himself, the pain ceased as he acknowledged it. Muscle had rewoven themselves around charred bones and fresh layers of flesh had grown to keep up with it. A zig-zagging line at his elbow demarcated where the regeneration had begun. The new tissue extended to the distal knuckles of his fingers which he wiggled unbelievingly.

He searched the room and his brain assembled a hundred thousand memories from his life to intuit the origin of the first girl facing him. He guessed her age at thirteen years, with brown hair and deep brown eyes. She was neither Ehtlentin, Omphalan, Mongrelai, or any other people he had met. *Why do I feel so certain of that?* His mind rushed, but not so much as the world seemed to slow. His other senses began catching up. *We are on a ship. We are traveling by anchor tether. I am Mongrelai.*

So too was the second girl staring at him. *Ehtlentin as well, and she hates me.* Dirt, burns and blood covered her body and face, but he recognized her. *She was an accomplice of the boy we were set after; her name is Cass.* Her profile flashed before his eyes as clear as if he were holding it. *Ex-military, she murdered her commander during the Pazish rebellion. Her platoon busted her out of prison.* She made no attempt to show anything but contempt for him, yet when their slit eyes met, she wavered. He reevaluated his own expression, placed a wall between his feelings and the muscles displaying them.

"Are you okay?" asked the young girl in Omphalan common. The question startled him, mostly because he understood it without his translator.

He formed the words he had heard spoken during negotiations with the Alliance in Corala. "Yes," he answered as he pushed himself up. "What happened?" he asked.

"They turned you, you were dead until a few hours ago," she said. She let the words sink in, then asked, "What's it like?"

Horrible, he thought, but he did not know how to reply. "You mean to find out?" he asked instead.

She nodded without further response, though Getaeight surmised there was more to her intentions than she let on. The sound of footsteps ended their conversation. An unarmored Mongrelai appeared in the doorway.

"Welcome," he said to Getaeight. He acknowledged the other two with a nod. "In my life before this, my people called me Talor Krir. Talor Krir died in the ruins of his vessel though, and I rose as Mongrelai. I chose a new name for myself, Ashtar, the planet of my rebirth. Now my people are the Mongrelai, and they have given me a second name: Steel-Raised. You have been reborn today, what name do you choose?" he asked Getaeight. A single name came to mind, one he had considered before but not expected to be called for another decade.

"Thaeon," he answered.

"Thaeon Scarred Arm," Ashtar completed. "And you?" he asked the Ehtlentin girl.

"Cassine," she answered without looking up.

"Cassine Corpse Climber," he announced. He turned to the last girl. "Your time will come to take a new name, young one. And you will be far better prepared than these two. What do we call you for now?"

"Erika," replied the girl. *Ashtar discomforts her,* thought Thaeon.

"Erika of the Ohwen," he finished. "Your room is prepared, Ezkero will show you the way." Another Mongrelai appeared and led her out.

Once they had gone, Ashtar Steel-Raised sat across from the two new Mongrelai. "I have a great truth to share with you. It is a story about the day our ancestors changed their universe, and by the time I finish telling it, we will have arrived at the world it started. My world. The First World."

OMPHALA
A 52-card game for the people

Based on <u>Star Story Book One: Anchored</u>

Setup:
1) Decide who will go first.
2) Remove Jokers from deck.
3) Deal 7 cards, look at them.
4) All players place two cards from their hand face down [FD] in front of themselves to create their Front Row.
5) All players place their remaining 5 cards face up [FU] to create their Back Row. (Final setup depicted below)

Front Row →   [FD] [FD]
Back Row → [FU] [FU] [FU] [FU] [FU]
(player)

Play:
1) On their turn, a player may perform 2 actions using cards from their Back Row (Front Row cards are your victory points and cannot be used). A player can also use an action to draw a card from the deck to place in their Back Row.
2) Each suit performs a different action:

♣ [Club] **Attack Front Row card** (defending card goes to graveyard if attacker has equal or greater power. Attacking card goes to graveyard if defender has greater power).

♠ [Spade] **Attack Front Row card** (defending card goes to graveyard if attacker has equal or greater power. Attacking card goes to graveyard if defender has greater power) OR **Steals Back Row card** (steals opponent's card if equal or greater).

♦ [Diamond] **Shield Front Row card** (turns face down, adds to the power of the card it's placed on).

♥ [Heart] **Enhance Back Row card** (stays face up, adds to the power of the card it's placed on).

EXAMPLE: On my turn, I enhance my King ♣ in my Back Row with a 5 ♥ in my Back Row (one action), which turns my King ♣ into an 18 ♣ (13 + 5). Then I attack a facedown card in someone's Front Row with my 18 ♣ (second action).

EXAMPLE: I use my Queen ♠ to steal a Jack ♦ from another player and add it to my Back Row (one action), then I use the Jack ♦ to shield one of my Front Row cards (second action).

3) If you successfully attack/steal a card during your turn, the card that you attacked with (and any ♥ enhancing it) is immediately flipped over and added to your Front Row (like saying that card(s) completed its mission and is now retired).
4) Draw two cards from the deck to end your turn.
5) The player to the left goes next.

End of Game:
1) The game ends when there are no more moves possible for any player to make.
2) Count how many cards remain in each players' Front Row (including shielded / enhanced cards). The person with the most cards wins.
3) If there is a tie, the person with the highest total power (actual point value of cards) wins.

Other Rules:
1) Only one ♥ or ♦ can be placed on a card. You cannot place a ♥ on a ♦.
2) Shielded / enhanced cards are considered a single card (until the end game when they will count as 2 victory points). Both

cards will be destroyed if successfully attacked, both cards can be stolen if paired in your Back Row. You cannot reverse a pairing.

3) When adding victorious cards to your Front Row, always place them to the right of the most recent card you placed in your Front Row.

4) Only 7 cards are allowed in the Back Row (paired cards are treated as single cards). You may discard cards when drawing new cards with actions.

5) If a player has 7 red suit cards in their Back Row (and no black suit cards), they may shuffle their Back Row into the deck and draw 5 new cards. This can happen the moment a player receives their 7th red suit card. Redrawing does not count as an action.

Two-Player Changes:

1) Players draw 1 card before their turn and 1 card after their turn. The player who starts the game does not draw a card before their first turn.

Omphala Deck:

♦ DIAMONDS ♦
Ace = Glade Jadamara
King = Gren
Queen = The Frozen Queen
Jack = Getaeight
10 = City Wide Shield
9 = Labyrinth Hideout
8 = Anchor Break Field
7 = Striated Walls
6 = Black Box
5 = Hidden Reinforcements
4 = Contrivance Cannon Fodder
3 = Civilian Militia
2 = Unity Propaganda

♥ HEARTS ♥
Ace = Quantine
King = The Undying King
Queen = The Shrouded Lady
Jack = Lazaeron the Remaker

10 = Artifact Ring
9 = Writ-whip
8 = Ingevein Device
7 = Alliance Escort
6 = Uncut Disciples
5 = Obsidiron Bodyguard
4 = Rotting Mentor
3 = Ehtlentin Blade
2 = Post Traumatic Growth

♣ CLUBS ♣

Ace = Virion General
King = Raz Taigo
Queen = Aemon the Proven
Jack = Hera Taigo
10 = Virion Invasion Fleet
9 = The Herald
8 = Ohwen Cloudship
7 = Artifact Vessel
6 = Alliance Strike Flotilla
5 = Undying Writbender
4 = Psyperial Snubfighters
3 = Mulgtai Allies
2 = Ragtag Misfits

♠ SPADES ♠

Ace = Hadeon the Betrayer
King = Sincret the Dreamer
Queen = Anansi the Spider
Jack = Kyphothree
10 = Shadowed Warriors
9 = Ohwen Princesses
8 = Scorched Earth
7 = Artifact Contrivance
6 = Virion Infiltrator
5 = Painted Boys
4 = Coralan Info Broker
3 = Undying Scout
2 = Ehtlentin Pickpocket

Made in the USA
Monee, IL
09 July 2023